I0663628

The Windsor Love Connection

Will she give love a second chance?

The Windsor Riverside Romances
Book 2

Lizzie Chantree

Lemon Meringue PUBLISHING

Formatted with Vellum

About this edition

The Windsor Love Connection is written and edited in British English rather than American English. This includes spelling, grammar and punctuation.

Chapter One

Daisy puffed out her cheeks and then swore as she stepped on a plug lying innocently on the floor. She hopped around holding her foot and gave the plug an evil stare as if it was the cause of her predicament. She was trying to forget about her broken relationship, the distressing way she'd found out that her errant husband had died, and the hushed voices of her neighbours. The tiny apartment she lived in, on a pretty street in the south-western city of Carcassonne in France, seemed oppressive all of a sudden. She'd spent years creating a safe haven there for herself and her four-year-old daughter, Brontë, but looking around now she realised that she'd been kidding herself that she'd made the right choices. She shivered and wished she'd remembered to put on an extra pair of socks.

Daisy felt her bottom lip wobble, but then her doorbell chimed. She angrily brushed any stray tears aside and when she opened the door her lips curled into a genuine smile.

Nico, a dreamboat and part-time model, lived a few doors down. She guessed that he flirted with her because they were the youngest tenants in their block of flats by at least twenty years. There was no way she'd ever take him up on his offers of a sleepover, because love hurt. She'd learned that the hard way – twice! She'd be thirty next year and she knew he didn't want love, just some fun. His friendship meant too much for her to risk it, however tempting his knowing smile and sparkling blue eyes were.

'You're here!' he said happily, leaning forward and kissing her on both cheeks. Daisy closed her eyes for a second and inhaled his spicy aftershave, wondering what it would be like to open the door to a handsome lover like Nico and not worry about the consequences. 'Are you busy?' he asked, his sexy French lilt making Daisy forget her problems for a moment and step back to let him inside. Brontë was playing happily in her room, so Daisy shook her head and led him into the tiny kitchenette, clicking the switch on the wall as there was hardly any natural light in the building, even though the sandy coloured walls were beautiful and made of local stone.

'No. I was just thinking about Harrison and wondering what the hell to do with my life,' she sighed, taking two mugs out of the cupboard, wishing she'd bought some bottles of beer. His forehead creased and he pulled her into a hug, which she sank into. He sat her in one of the few chairs in the apartment while he made them both a cup of tea. She looked around and wondered if it was weird that she had more flowering plants in the house than she had chairs. Most of the other colourful things in her apartment were about Brontë and her happiness. It wasn't exactly as if Daisy had many visitors, so what was the point of spending money on furniture, she reasoned. The plants kept her company.

Nico handed her the steaming mug of tea and perched

his pert bottom on her tiny work desk, placed under the living room window, which was half obscured by condensation. The window faced a wall, so wasn't exactly inspiring to work from, but at least she tried.

'You still thinking about starting a gardening business?' he asked with interest, moving a few of the mood boards and design ideas she'd printed using the old printer that Harrison had left behind when he'd moved out.

'I don't know...' she dithered. 'I've got to do something,' she said, jumping up as she'd also left her paltry bank statement on the desk and Nico could probably read that too from his position. She quickly scooped up the papers and shoved them in a floral storage box on one of the shelves she'd built next to the desk. 'I just don't think I'm ready. I need to sort out a school for Brontë soon and most of this...' she pointed to the mood board, 'is just daydreaming.'

'Your ideas are spot on, though,' Nico insisted. 'What about when you helped the neighbours on this floor grow indoor gardens and herbs and spices? We don't miss not having outdoor spaces so much now. Your designs were genius!' he applauded, making her blush.

'That was just practice,' she brushed off. 'Plus you all paid for your own plants and planters. And I would never have made the designs if you hadn't badgered me for months,' she added.

Nico chuckled. 'We all wanted to live in your apartment,' he waggled his eyebrows suggestively at her and finally she laughed. 'It's a mini oasis in here, even though it's tiny.'

Daisy flushed at the praise. For now, creating more indoor gardens was out of reach – as were her dreams of designing outdoor spaces. She was just about managing to function and keep a roof over her daughter's head, and there was nothing left over for a gardening business. She didn't have anyone to help her with Brontë and she couldn't ask Nico. He was always flying across the globe on modelling assignments and wanted to spend the next year abroad – another reason why romantic entanglements were off the menu.

'Come travelling with me,' he asked, not for the first time.

'Brontë needs stability,' she said, shaking her head at his mad ideas. Had things been so simple when she was his age? She thought back, then winced. She'd been twenty-four when she'd had Brontë. She'd got pregnant, married in haste, and then been persuaded that a new life abroad was the answer to her broken heart. She still found it difficult to think of her best friend Arthur. When their relationship had changed, so had he. Meeting Harrison soon after had been a disaster. Except for her precious daughter, of course. It hadn't taken Harrison long to tire of his little family and move on. She felt bile hit the back of her throat and quickly sipped her tea.

She'd love to go back home to her beloved Windsor and her family in the U.K., but her credit card bill told her that would never happen. Anyway, she'd let her parents down and left her friends, including Arthur, behind. She felt her lip wobble again. She watched Nico pick up a framed photo of her and Brontë and wondered what he thought of the fact that there were no pictures of her with friends. What friends? She barely had time to wash, let alone find friends, and she certainly couldn't afford to splash out on the trendy frothy coffee and cakes that social outings seemed to involve these days. Plus, while Brontë spoke French fluently and adored chatting away to Nico and their other neighbours,

Daisy's own language skills were embarrassingly lacking, although she could get by when she needed to.

Harrison had only spoken French to Brontë, which meant she'd grown up bilingual. It also meant that Daisy had been shut out of those moments. She'd struggled to grasp the nuances of what they were saying, until Nico had begun to gently help her understand the beauty of the language. Harrison's strict regimes hadn't been fun for anyone, but at least her precious daughter would have a wider world and more opportunities now. It was one thing Harrison had given his daughter before he'd moved out last year, if nothing else.

'Nico,' Daisy said as she reached for her phone. 'I know you hate having your photo taken...' she teased, 'But can I take a picture of us together? I've just realised I don't have many of friends.'

Nico fanned his face with his hand and laughed, giving her one of his standard model pouts. 'Are you going to post it on social media and finally inform the world I'm your lover?' he teased. 'I've been telling you how good we could be together for months!' He took the phone out of her hand and leant in to kiss her on the cheek, whilst expertly snapping a few photos on her phone. She felt her skin grow warm as he brushed her blonde hair out of her face and then pressed his lips to hers softly, making her insides squirm. He stepped back and took her hand.

'I'm really sorry about Harrison,' he said, his tone becoming serious. 'Even though we all hated him,' he added.

She flinched. She knew her neighbours hadn't liked her ex's brusque manner, not that he had been at home much.

'It's ok,' she shrugged, even though her shoulders

suddenly felt heavy. 'We'd been separated for almost a year. It was just a shock to find out how he died.'

Nico's face hardened and he went to look out of the window, despite the uninspiring view, while she thought back to her disaster of a marriage.

Opening the door to a police officer and being informed her husband had died had sucked the breath out of her. She'd had to hold onto the door for support. The fact that he'd been staying with a woman and a child had been a knife to her heart. He barely saw his own daughter. It made Daisy's head pound and her eyes smart with tears. This in turn made her blood boil, as she angrily dashed them away. She'd spent enough negative energy on that man to last a lifetime. Brontë didn't really know her dad, so when Daisy had gently explained that Daddy was now an angel, Brontë had just gone quiet for a few hours and then carried on playing with her toys. She didn't ask questions and after a few days actually appeared happier. Now she shook her head when Daisy asked gently if she'd like to talk about Harrison.

Harrison had told her he was moving out and had left devastation behind. Discovering he had died in a simple accident – slipping on a child's toy and hitting his head on the kitchen counter of all things – had been like a punch to the solar plexus and she'd doubled over, winded. 'He'd been living with one of his indiscretions when the accident happened,' she explained to Nico.

'Though visits to his own child had dwindled to noth-ing,' he replied angrily, just as Brontë realised he was there and rushed into the room, to be swung up into his arms as they began to chatter excitedly about her day in French. Daisy could literally feel the fires of hell radiating from every pore of her body as she pictured her husband crouching down to offer a kind word to another child, those precious hours and days when Brontë should have been his sole focus. She recalled her husband being charm personified on occasion and she'd been suckered in along with everyone else, so the joke was on her.

'You need to get outside more and stop staring at nothing but these four walls, however beautiful you have made the room,' said Nico as he propped Brontë on his hip. 'Let's go out for hot chocolate!' he said loudly and Brontë whooped with joy, making Daisy wince because a hot chocolate with whipped cream and marshmallows wasn't cheap, from the fancy corner shop Nico liked to frequent. She knew he would offer to pay, but her pride wouldn't allow that. Harrison had kept the purse strings tight. Now she did some online design work for a small gardening company to keep them afloat. She had never told Harrison about that because he would have scorned her for even trying. The company often used her designs, even though she didn't get credit for them and they sometimes forgot to pay her invoice for ages, but the photos they posted on their website of the finished gardens looked beautiful.

One day she might have her own business and customers, but for now her most pressing worry was how to pay for her daughter's *choco chaud.*

Chapter Two

The phone rang, making Daisy jump. She looked at it in suspicion. Few people ever called her – only her parents, Ted and Gloria, who flew all round the globe for work and Maya, a friend from home. She usually put her parents off visiting her place, when they came over to see their daughter and grandchild. She'd always meet them at the hotel they were staying at instead. She also pretended that her flat was bigger than it was and that she was happy there. Her mum and dad were both busy with work, though recently her mother had begun clucking around her and suggesting she might like to move home. Daisy suspected it was because she was thinking of retiring early and Daisy and Brontë would be her next project.

Daisy couldn't imagine her mum ever really leaving the corporate marketing department she ran for a popular brand of running shoes – not that she'd ever run anywhere in her life! Gloria was more at home with a paperback thriller and a glass of Pinot Noir, than a ten-mile run and a pair of leggings. She was incredible at her job, though.

Daisy only wished she had half as much drive as her parents. Her dad was a senior executive for a publishing firm and their house had overflowing bookcases, as he always brought new editions and early releases home. As a child, Daisy had stored a selection with pretty covers under her bed to read late at night with a torch, but her parents hadn't stuck their heads around the door to check on her very often, anyway. She guessed she'd been a pretty well-behaved kid. Ted and Gloria had travelled a lot when Daisy was growing up, and the majority of her care had been taken over by her grandparents, Joe and Olive. This was probably why she gravitated towards Maya and her rambunctious family, who also lived along the River Thames and spent lots of time with their own grandparents too, she surmised.

Her family probably assumed she was falling apart now Harrison had died – which she was, but in a way that boat had sailed years ago. The love she'd felt for her husband had faded quite quickly, with his brash treatment of her feelings, but she'd always held a tiny glimmer of hope that he'd change. She sometimes felt that Brontë was the only reason she didn't just curl in a ball and cry most days. Guilt followed her around like a sinister shadow because she was relieved not to have to deal with her husband anymore, or endure the knowing stares and sympathy from her neighbours. He'd often fallen noisily through the door after yet another late night 'working'. Living in a small community meant people round here looked out for each other, which could be wonderful. The flip side was everyone knowing your business, which was mortifying.

'Hi Daisy,' said the breezy voice on the phone. It was Maya. Daisy wished she could sound that carefree. Maya often regaled Daisy with news about their hometown,

Windsor. Maya had refused to let their friendship slide, however awful Harrison was to her. Daisy knew she should have learned from that. She'd been a terrible friend.

'Hi Maya,' she answered, 'How are you?' She remembered those simpler times when she'd lived by the river and spent her days with her best friends, Maya, Maya's sister Romy, and Arthur, often mooching about on her grandad Joe's steamboat, *Bertha*, and getting in his way. They'd all been more of a hindrance than a help to him, she recalled with a half-smile.

'I'm great,' answered Maya. 'How are you, more to the point?'

Daisy frowned. The answer to this simple question was so complicated for her. She could picture Maya's sparkling brown eyes flashing, her dark hair swishing around her shoulders as she twirled around. Becoming a world-renowned jewellery designer hadn't changed Maya. Daisy had enjoyed seeing her friend's company, No.1 Ethereal Lane, skyrocket to success over the past year. She drew inspiration from the plants along the river, but just recently had been bringing more of her Mexican heritage into her designs, which Daisy loved.

'I know I pretty much cut myself off from you all when I married Harrison,' Daisy admitted now. Maya's brother, Arthur, had been the hardest to leave behind, but she didn't mention that. 'I'm sorry,' she said. 'Harrison made me believe that Brontë and I were his world, and that leaving the past in England would give our family a fresh start.'

'Leaving Arthur behind, you mean...' Maya said bluntly. Daisy flinched. She was pretty sure that her husband had hated her close bond and relationship history with Arthur, even though it was old news. There had been tears and recriminations from Arthur that had hurt like hell. He had been her best friend before everything went wrong. After that, contact between them had dwindled to nothing, which she knew her husband had preferred. Naturally – but definitely mistakenly – Harrison had been her priority back then.

Harrison gradually isolated the people in his life, she'd noticed, so they relied solely on him. Daisy was furious with herself when she looked back, because she had been a pretty feisty, strong, independent woman when they'd met. Now she was a shell of her former self. The problem was that she'd also been hiding heartbreak and was defiant about moving on. Her parents had been abroad again at the time, and she hadn't been able to talk to Maya either, because she was Arthur's sibling. Harrison had arrived in her life at a time of rebellion, but how she wished she'd listened to her other friends and family. Hindsight was a great thing, but the problem was that you could only use it after you'd royally messed things up. She felt didn't deserve good friends like Maya and her sister, Romy. She'd let them down.

Daisy pictured Arthur's handsome face and the way he'd looked at her when they were together, then the image distorted and he was angry, shouting at her that she'd made the wrong choice.

'I want to talk to you about something,' said Maya suddenly. Daisy's stomach clenched, fearing bad news. 'There's a new development just by *Bertha*'s dock. My friend has invested heavily, but he's in a bit deep and needs to cut costs. I'm hoping you can help?'

'Me?' Daisy wracked her brain about how she could possibly help anyone, but she'd do anything for Maya, so she listened anyway.

'Yes, you! You're the only person who I can think of that can help him.'

Daisy's jaw dropped open, but a tiny spark had ignited. Maybe she could start to repay all her friend's kindness over the years.

'What can I do?'

'You can come home.'

'What? I can't do that. It's impossible.' Daisy paused for a moment. Maya was the only person she had told about her awful finances, in a bleak moment a few months previously. Maya had immediately offered to help, but Daisy would never accept that.

Maya carried on speaking. 'My friend Kris has used up his entire budget on the building. It's stunning – natural wood and glass – but he needs someone to design the outside space, and fast. The contract is worth a lot, and you wouldn't have to do the grunt work.'

'But...'

'Daisy, you've done it loads of times for your remote clients,' Maya reasoned. 'Kris has a show flat on each floor and I've persuaded him to let you rent one – fully furnished. All you have to do is be available to accompany a few potential clients around the other flats, from the perspective of someone who already lives there. He had that idea, not me,' she added hastily before Daisy could object. 'It's actually a genius thought. I'd buy a flat if the person who showed me round actually lived in the block, and wasn't just trying to fob me off with jargon.'

'Maya, you know I can't afford a fancy flat, or the trip home.'

'Kris will fly you and Brontë home, once the plans are agreed, and you will oversee the work in an advisory role – which means he needs you onsite. You'll get free accommodation for six months as payment and then after that you have the option to rent, or buy, the place. The building is currently empty anyway, so you'll be the first tenant. That also helps sell properties. You'd be doing him a massive favour. Me too.'

'You can't be serious?' Daisy was agog. There was no way she could design a project that big.

'Deadly,' answered Maya. 'He needs help pretty quickly, so you'll have to decide soon. He doesn't need frivolous stuff, just functional.'

'I'm not qualified,' said Daisy. This was a massive opportunity, but it felt like it was literally crushing her bones just talking about it.

'Daisy,' Maya warned. 'You've designed countless outside spaces for that stupid client who doesn't pay you half the time. You aced all your college design exams,' she barely paused for breath. Daisy tried to object but Maya stood firm. 'You designed indoor spaces for a whole floor of apartments in France, which I know you will have photographed... and what's more, I need you. My friend really is in dire need of a solution, and this would help us both massively.'

Daisy knew Maya was squeezing the emotion out of the situation to push an advantage, but a glimmer of hope filled her mind. Maya had never asked her for anything before. Could she be brave enough to go home? Probably not, she surmised.

'Think about it,' said Maya. 'Just don't take too long.'

Daisy had a thought. 'My mum has already enrolled Brontë in the village school back home,' she said slowly. 'She sorted it out, apparently, because of the Harrison situation. Can you believe it?'

'What?' Maya sounded aghast. 'Your mum is a bit of a

whirlwind, though. She probably decided and had it organised by the end of the same day.' Daisy could picture Maya reaching for a chilled glass of Sauvignon Blanc. Daisy sipped the glass of water she'd poured herself earlier, but pulled a face because it was lukewarm.

'She's been trying to get me to come home since she found out about the accident, and thought this might persuade me. How dare she?' raged Daisy.

'Maybe she thought it would be one less stress for you. She doesn't know how dire your finances are and that you couldn't go home if you wanted to,' added Maya helpfully – and then went quiet. 'You wouldn't let your parents help you when they tried before, either. Sorry... I didn't mean to be so blunt,' she added. 'Mind you, if you accept this offer, you could get back here. Plus you'd be helping your very best friend and my deliciously handsome and very single friend, Kris,' she laughed and Daisy could picture her waggling her eyebrows at the phone suggestively.

Daisy sighed. 'I don't know,' she said. 'My brain is scrambled about Harrison. I'll think about what you've said, though. I have to put Brontë first, and she hasn't got any family here now, except me,' she said sadly, without adding *and I'm not much use.*

'That's all I ask!' said Maya happily, then she went quiet for a moment and Daisy knew what was coming. 'Are you sure you don't want me to tell Arthur about Harrison?' They'd spoken about that a few days previously and Daisy's stance on it hadn't changed.

'No,' she said. 'I'll tell him in my own time. There's no reason for us to bump into each other, because he's always travelling. It gives me time to work out what I'm going to do if I come home. I have considered it lately,' she admitted, as Maya gave a little whoop of joy. 'But packing up everything

14

here would feel overwhelming, to be honest.' Daisy could hear the cogs of Maya's brain working, thinking out a way to protest.

'Um... okay, but...' Maya started.

'You don't need to worry about it,' interrupted Daisy. 'I can cope and Arthur probably doesn't even remember who I am, with the amount of women he dates, so it's not something he needs to know.' She paused and realised what she'd said and to whom. 'Sorry Maya, I know he's your brother.'

'It's okay,' Maya said quietly, but Daisy knew it wasn't. Maya had always been fiercely protective of her younger brother, though he had towered over them even as a teenager at six foot three inches.

Hearing on the town grapevine that her husband wasn't monogamous had been excruciating for Daisy. She'd tried to feel immune to the pitying stares of her neighbours, but it stung each time. She had been overwhelmed by a sense of relief when Harrison had finally left her. She hadn't felt that way at all when she'd found out that Arthur was dating a mutual friend, all those years ago. Her heart had shattered. She'd been young and naïve back then, she supposed. He certainly wouldn't have that effect on her now. He was a womaniser just like Harrison, and the thought made her shiver in disgust.

A partner with a child had been a new direction for her errant husband, though. He had never had time for children and the noise they made when they'd gone out and about, before having Brontë. Daisy shouldn't have assumed he'd be any different with his own child. He'd never listened to her suggestions about a brother or sister for their daughter, and Daisy hated the fact that she was secretly glad of that now. There was no way she could cope with two children on her own.

Daisy might not have loved Harrison anymore, but she'd certainly never wished him harm – a lot of pain in the nether regions maybe, but that was all. He'd been the father of her precious child, so whatever she thought of him personally (which was at an all-time low), she'd wanted him safe for the sake of their daughter. She'd even dreamed that he'd turn up at her front door one day and have finally grown up and realised how precious their child was. That was never going to happen now, though.

'It's been enlightening, lately,' said Daisy.

'In what way?' asked Maya.

Daisy felt tears scratch at the back of her eyes and sniffed, letting herself wallow for a moment. She'd been giving herself a stern talking-to about being such a wimp, but she still felt reluctant to make changes. At least as it was, she had Nico and her tiny apartment.

'I'm just tired,' mumbled Daisy, before admitting, 'Harrison mocked my curves, my clothes, my mothering skills and my little home when he was last here.' She heard Maya's gasp of disgust and wished she'd had the courage to tell her earlier.

'That was so awful of him...' said Maya with a growl. 'I wish I'd known. I'd have come round and given him a piece of my mind.'

'We'd been separated for a while, but it still hurts.'

'I know,' sympathised Maya. 'Come home soon,' she urged. 'You could be back with your family and friends for Christmas for the first time in years... and you might even finally meet your Prince Charming.'

The thought of that made Daisy's blood run cold. Christmas day had often been fraught for her, worrying whether Harrison would even remember he had a child, as he often hadn't. Daisy had always made the best of the day and saved hard all year to buy, or make, her daughter a few treats. The meagre allowance Harrison had given Daisy meant she'd had to work hard to survive, with online study at night while her baby slept and networking within the community to find online work to keep them afloat. She'd fallen into bed in an exhausted heap each night, romance the furthest thing from her mind.

'So,' Maya said, refusing to change the subject. 'I know it must have been a hard knock to find out about Harrison, but you can't judge every new man you meet by the way he used to behave. Not all men are like that,' she chided gently. Maya had recently moved in with Noah, a gorgeous movie star, so Daisy smiled and her mind drifted to Nico. Maybe she should give this romance thing a try – or even just let loose, and have a bit of fun with her very hot neighbour?

'Maybe I should give someone a chance,' Daisy mused thoughtfully. Then she looked at her tiny desk, with its neatly stacked paperwork and the mood boards behind it, and scrapped that daft idea. She went over to the window, the phone still pressed to her ear. She moved a couple of sea lavender plants, running her fingers along the tiny purple flowered clusters that left a soft herbal scent with marine undertones in the air.

'Call me in the next few days and let me know your decision,' urged Maya. 'Opportunities to change your life don't come along that often. I know it's scary and you have Brontë to consider, but surely being back in the heart of your family in Windsor will help you heal, after Harrison?'

Daisy bit her lip. The problem was that being back with her family was the thing that scared her most of all! She hated being a wuss, but they'd all find out how terrible her choices had been if she went home. At least hiding here, she could pretend.

'Come home,' Maya said again. Daisy tried not to remember the feel of the cobbled side streets under her feet, or to imagine walking up the main road from the promenade towards the pretty shops. They were mainly from the Victorian era and some had beautiful bow windows. The shops lined the street all the way up to the castle that watched over the river and was surrounded by lush trees.

'Let me think about it,' was all Daisy could offer. Perhaps the fact that Arthur barely ever came home now and many of her old friends had moved away meant she could tentatively step back into her old world, and work out what the hell she was doing with her life. The job offer would give her and her daughter a home for a while, and being back by the river might help her work out where it had all gone wrong.

Chapter Three

Daisy was too scared to move in case she woke him up! She hoped this hadn't been another bad decision, but the finality of her husband not being in her life anymore had hit her hard over the previous week. Pathetic loneliness had engulfed her, and she'd bought and drunk a whole bottle of cheap rosé wine. She wasn't sure what had happened next was ideal either, but it had certainly taken her mind off her impending decision for a few glorious hours. It was still ridiculously early and the sun was just breaking through the clouds outside and warming the air. She'd left her bedroom window open to let the evening breeze filter through, but she hadn't envisioned waking up beside Nico... again!

Finally finding the energy to reciprocate Nico's affections, only a few weeks after Harrison had died, was awful timing. At first, she'd felt bolstered by the new choices in her life, but now she'd made it harder to leave! Nico turned over in his sleep and his arm snaked around her waist over the covers, making her freeze. Then she gently lifted his arm and moved to the edge of the bed. She grabbed her discarded nightclothes and pulled her T-shirt and shorts on, worrying that Brontë might see Nico here. She couldn't exactly shove him out of bed and back into his own flat, but that was what she felt like doing because she'd finally made some decisions.

Panicking about the weighty prospect of a new job and the move home, and wandering aimlessly around in a half-daze most of the time wasn't helping. She'd spent hours and hours trying to plan the new garden design until her eyelids felt like they might fall off, she'd tiredly rubbed them so much. Nico's persistence had paid off when he'd arrived with a takeaway for them all and then snuggled up to her while they watched a movie after Brontë had gone to bed. Her resolve not to make her life even messier had wavered when he'd brushed her hair out of her eyes and kissed her. She'd promptly turned into a primal animal! The total lack of affection from anyone, including her husband, for so long made her into someone she didn't recognise.

'You don't always have to manage everything on your own, you are allowed some fun,' Nico had told her gently, while placing butterfly kisses up her arm and on that sensitive place on the side of her neck. It had triggered something in her. She still didn't understand what it was, but it scared the hell out of her. They'd spent a few incredible hot and sweaty nights together, the memory of which still made her blush.

In the cold light of day, he was only twenty-five to her almost-thirty, and he wanted to spend the next few years travelling. She admired that about him, but it wasn't what she needed long term. It had been fun, though. He had dragged her out of the lonely slump she'd found herself in. Realising that someone as gorgeous as Nico found her attractive made her finally understand that she needed to start living her own life and stop hiding from her problems. It must have been the pheromones or something that Nico gave off, but they'd got on so well, with or without the sexual acrobatics, and had agreed to remain flirty friends after the first night. Then they had fallen into bed again!

Nico was good for her. Perhaps she should give things a proper try, even if he went travelling. But being with someone had made her realise even more that she missed home.

She rubbed her sore eyes again and thought back to the moment when she'd taken delivery of Harrison's work effects. She shuddered, her arms wrapping around her body for comfort. She had been handed a large box of paperwork and personal items from his desk at the company where he'd worked as a salesman. It was still sitting on her chest of drawers. Daisy regarded it thoughtfully as Nico woke up beside her and yawned. The covers fell down, exposing his firm chest, and Daisy smiled and leaned in to kiss him good morning.

'What's in the box?' he asked, tilting his head towards it. The only other thing in the room was a tall freestanding mirror that Daisy had found in an antique market, and the wrought iron bed. She'd softened the room with fabrics in different textures and hues of orange and red. The little windows had shutters and a window box that was over-flowing with plump red geraniums and star jasmine, which filled the room with a floral scent.

'It's Harrison's personal effects. He wasn't honest with me,' she said sadly. 'He lied that he was selling dilapidated apartments, whereas in fact he dealt in luxury property.' She gratifyingly heard Nico growl in disgust and carried on. 'I was never invited to his office, so it was mortifying for his colleague to be sitting in my tiny lounge. She was looking around the place tearfully, speaking about how terribly he would be missed. He was their top performing agent and had super rich clients who loved him, apparently.'

'*Scélérat*,' seethed Nico, and Daisy agreed her husband had been a scoundrel. 'Why lie?' he asked, taking her hand and stroking the back of it, which made her smile.

'He lied about everything else, I suppose,' shrugged Daisy. 'Maybe he thought I would ask him for more money if I knew how well he was doing? I barely survived on what he gave us.'

'Oh Daisy,' sighed Maya. 'You should have told me. I could have helped.'

'I didn't want you to worry,' she said simply. 'I've always managed on my own.'

Daisy had wondered if the woman who dropped the work items round had been another notch on her husband's bed post, by the way she didn't seem to want to leave and held onto the box on her lap for the whole time it took her to drink a cup of tea, as if she was holding onto Harrison for as long as she could. Daisy had asked the woman if she had children, and then held her breath while waiting for the answer. The interloper had shaken her head whilst staring at a photo of Brontë on the dresser. With a deep frown, she'd said she hadn't known Harrison had a child. Daisy's insides had crunched up in anger and her teeth ground together, but at least she could exhale. This wasn't the woman whose house her husband had died in.

Daisy had painted the lounge walls of the flat a warm cornflower blue and had an abundance of window boxes overflowing with deep pink hellebores and white snowdrops next to herb boxes of rosemary, thyme, sage and oregano, which scented the air. Although the space was tiny and the functional furniture was all reclaimed, she'd created her own little oasis for herself and her daughter. She always felt like the flat gave her a hug of welcome when she walked through the door.

She'd breathed a sigh of relief when she'd finally consoled the woman enough for her to put on her coat and leave, and then she'd sat, numb, with the box of documents and paraphernalia on her own lap. At first, she hadn't wanted to open it and had moved it to the little galley kitchen counter, but she'd kept staring at it and Brontë had asked what was inside. In the end she'd waited for her daughter to fall sleep, her fair hair sweeping across her sweet face. Then she had brushed Brontë's hair aside, kissed her on the cheek and taken the box into her bedroom, so she didn't have to keep staring at it. She hadn't lifted the lid yet because she didn't know what to expect inside. Had she ever really known her own husband? She wasn't sure.

'Have you looked inside it yet?' asked Nico.

'No. I was trying to pluck up courage when you woke up. But I'm worried about Brontë seeing you here. We decided to stay as friends?'

Nico pulled her in for a sizzling kiss on the lips and a hug that she sank into. 'I'll go before she wakes up, I promise,' he reassured her. 'Plus, it was your idea to be just friends, *ma chérie*,' he joked, tapping her bottom and sliding his hand lower, making her smile. 'Then you had your wicked way with me again.'

'I'm sorry.' She hung her head, but didn't feel that sorry.

'It's the right decision for now,' he said gently. 'But who knows what the future may bring?'

'You're ok with that?'

'I am,' he said honestly. She could see he was, even though she'd kind have liked him to fight for her, at least a little bit. 'You mentioned you might be going back to England, and I'm going travelling.'

'The timing is off,' she nodded, sadly.

'It is, but I'm always here for you, no matter what. Okay?'

She smiled and reached out for another hug. She didn't feel the frisson of heat that went with the last one and in a way, she hoped that made the path back to friendship a bit easier. She'd never had a fling before, but now she knew what she'd missed out on!

'Do it now,' urged Nico, looking at the box. 'While I'm here so that you aren't alone,' he added.

Daisy opened the lid gingerly, peered into the box and then she jumped back as if she'd been slapped. There were photos of Harrison with various women at parties and events. Picking them up and looking at a few before placing them to one side, her insides were churning. It was hard enough thinking that your husband was a cheat without having the proof before your eyes. He'd always explained that he had to work away, and said for years that she was paranoid and the only woman for him. Although she wasn't stupid, she'd held onto a tiny bit of hope that it was true until the day he'd left. She reached further into the box and found two photo frames. Tears seeped out of her eyes because one was of the two of them just after they'd first met, faces turned towards the camera. The other was of Brontë when she was a toddler.

She brought things out and quietly showed Nico what was in the box, so that Brontë wouldn't wake up and hear them.

'Surely if he had photos of you both, his colleagues would have seen them?' asked Nico.

Daisy ran her fingers around both photos, and found

thick layers of dust. 'It looks like they've been shoved at the back of a desk drawer,' she said in disgust. Looking at her own younger face to see signs of happiness and joy, or even love, all Daisy noticed was a slight pensiveness around her eyes and what looked like a forced smile. Then, taking some papers from the box, she covered her mouth with her hand to stop herself screaming.

'What's wrong?' asked Nico in alarm, swinging his legs out of the bed and pulling on his clothes. He came to sit on the end of the bed near her, their legs not touching.

Daisy looked at the first letter. 'Harrison's last will and testament is being read tomorrow by his solicitor. I already know I'm the sole beneficiary. We made it when we got married. I've never even thought about it since then.' Then she looked at the rest of the paperwork. 'But these are his bank statements.'

'What's in them?' asked Nico, then he quickly back-tracked. 'You don't have to tell me if you don't want to,' he assured.

'I can't believe it!' said Daisy, sitting back in shock as her face drained of colour. 'He was wealthy! The absolute bastard,' she seethed, trying not to scream in frustration. 'I had to slog my guts out to pay the rent for this tiny flat and feed our daughter because he said he barely made any commission, but he was more than comfortable!'

'What?' gasped Nico as she handed the papers to him and his eyes quickly scanned the text. 'You're kidding me!' He dropped the letter in his lap as if it had scalded him.

'Plus he had a swanky flat, by the looks of the rent he paid each month,' she said, tears springing to her eyes again. She angrily dashed them away as dizziness overcame her. She put a hand on the bed to steady herself. 'He told me it was pretty much a hovel.'

Harrison had opened a joint account for her day-to-day expenses, but the other account he used was in his name only. Daisy got up and went to the kitchen, the paperwork in her hand. Nico followed her and turned on the kettle for something to do. They both ignored it when it boiled and switched itself off. Her hands felt numb as she scanned the figures. Tears crept silently down her cheeks when she read how he'd lived. The big, fat, paycheques, the hotel rooms and fancy dinners. There were no purchases for his wife and daughter, just the monthly transfer to Daisy's account, for less than he regularly splashed out on gifts for other women it seemed. Her vision blurred as she stared at the final balance, tears dropping onto the paper. She sniffed and wiped her eyes, annoyed at herself for feeling anything.

She switched on the little table lamp she'd found in a thrift shop and re-read the statement for a third time. She was rich! Not retirement rich, but wealthy enough to be able to move home to live near her parents and grandparents, or buy that flat Maya had mentioned. Plans began to formulate in her mind. Nico jolted her back to reality by making her a steaming mug of strong coffee, which she sipped tentatively, blowing on the surface and then putting it down.

'There's a newbuild, directly behind where my grandad docks his steamboat *Bertha,*' she told Nico. 'The flats will be snapped up soon but they have incredible views over the water and are only a short walk from town and the local schools.' Maya had added that temptation in their chat the previous day, knowing Daisy currently only had a view of brick walls, and realising too how much she missed her grandparents Joe and Olive. She even missed her mum and dad, however annoying they were – it had felt like she'd had to book family time in their business calendars to be able to see them when she was growing up. She liked her neighbours here, and her status with Nico had definitely changed, however much they both protested it hadn't, but she was feeling more and more isolated as Brontë got nearer to school age.

Daisy would miss Nico, but she didn't think she'd be heartbroken. They were friends with benefits now, but she was right not to get too attached since he was going travelling soon. Otherwise it could have been another disaster waiting to happen, she decided.

'That does sound amazing,' Nico conceded, although he looked a little bit sad as she turned to face him. 'It might take a while for you to be able to access his money, though,' he said, suddenly serious.

'The developer I'd be working for has offered me the journey home and a flat for six months as payment. He might extend the contract if he finds more work for me on a different project. Maya told me last night when she called me. I have some tiny savings from my online work that I haven't touched, in case of emergencies. It should keep us going if we're careful. I don't ever want to have to rely on Harrison again.'

'You couldn't rely on him before,' said Nico, with scorn in his voice. 'Whatever you get from him you deserve, Daisy,' he warned because he knew she wouldn't accept help, even if the money was rightly hers.

'Come and visit us sometime,' she said, changing the subject – and realising that she'd just made the decision to move home permanently. Nico's eyes sparkled at that, and he agreed he would before he said he needed to get home and ready for work. She kissed him briefly as he left, but they both knew that their moment of passion had passed and if they wanted to remain friends then they would have to find a new kind of normal. She hated the thought of leaving her one anchor here, but she needed to go home.

Could she really be brave enough to upend her whole life? Before, the thought of Harrison's wrath had prevented her thinking seriously about it, but now, what did she have to stay for? Daisy pictured living in a bright and airy flat with a view over water, instead of the crumbling walls here. Maya had said that the flats even had outdoor balconies. She could take Brontë to visit family, enjoy a river cruise on *Bertha* and maybe build bridges with her friends again, if they'd agree to start rebuilding too. She'd read a quote once about bridges needing to be built from both sides, but she knew that she'd toppled most of the connections herself. As she sat there and the room grew cold, she decided that she would take her daughter home, and she would be brave enough to say sorry to those she'd left behind.

Chapter Four

Daisy almost jiggled with glee as she peered out of the huge sliding windows of her whitewashed flat and out towards the river and her grandad's steamboat river cruiser, *Bertha*. The promenade edged one side of the pretty town, lined with stone and brick-built shops with an eclectic mix of window displays and hanging baskets. She tried to forget about her messy relationship history and enjoy the excited gossip of the parents at the school her mum had enrolled Brontë in. The huge adjustment of letting her mum help her still didn't sit quite right with Daisy, but her grandmother, Olive, had talked her round. Daisy grudgingly admitted that she might have been a bit harsh on her parents and it might be okay to let them into her life a little more. They'd always been married to their jobs, but it worked for them and Daisy was proud of their achievements, even if she didn't always show it. Perhaps now she was home, she could build those bridges too?

Brontë had been home-schooled until she was able to join the infants' class, and they'd spent Brontë's first

Christmas in the U.K. surrounded by the warmth of family. It had been a revelation and the shame of having put this off, because of her pride and her dire finances before Harrison's death, hit Daisy hard. She'd spent the last few months in France working every hour she could on the project for Maya's friend Kris, and now she was back home overseeing the project, which scared the hell out of her every day! She hadn't had a moment to think about her choices as she'd been so busy with the move, with work and with an excitable child. She'd had to rely on her parents a tiny bit which made her sad at how angry she'd felt at being palmed off on her own grandparents. Daisy knew Olive and Joe adored spending time with her and her life had been filled with love.

The move back meant they had a home here for now and she didn't have to make any other major life decisions for at least a few more months. Daisy's time in France had been pretty solitary, but suddenly here she was, back in Windsor and having to navigate big groups of men and women who all seemed to have known each other for years. There was no going back to her old home and, although she loved the openness here, she missed her little apartment in Carcassonne. She used to tuck herself away there where no one really knew her, or cared, except for Nico and she'd lost him too. She'd had a few friendly neighbours, but now Daisy could see that she hadn't given them a chance to get to know her better. She'd rarely stopped for a chat because she felt awkward about the language barrier and she'd always closed her apartment door behind her with a regretful sigh. Maybe she could make friends with the other tenants or owners in the development she lived in? The thought made her smile.

Brontë seemed to have adjusted well to moving back to

her mother's hometown without her dad, but reservations niggled at Daisy constantly about uprooting her child from the only life she'd ever known. It had been routine-led and they'd spent practically every moment together. Now suddenly there were well-meaning family members around the corner and across the road and lots of locals who remembered Daisy from childhood.

She put out a hand to steady herself at the thought of the daunting task of making friends, and heard a crash and some cursing in the newly refurbished flat next to the one she'd just moved into, which made her smile. At least she wasn't the only one having a bad start to the day.

Daisy's grandparents had always been best friends with Maya's grandparents, Owen and Ettie. This meant Daisy had grown up alongside Maya and her siblings, Arthur and Romy. They'd all played in the huge garden behind Maya's grandparents' house with its rambling lawn and herbaceous borders. The Victorian glasshouses were full of exotic blooms and an enormous willow tree stood by the river's edge, dipping its boughs into the river which ran alongside the garden. Unfortunately, Daisy had lost touch with Romy and Arthur when she'd moved abroad with her shiny new husband. Harrison hadn't liked her to spend too much time with anyone but him, even though he was often working or out with 'clients'. Thank goodness for Brontë and the eternal sunshine she brought because Daisy would have fallen apart without her. Over time, Daisy had felt too embarrassed to contact most of her old friends and let them know her marriage had failed – that she was a failure – because withstanding the 'I told you so' factor, and the fact that they'd all been right, was more than she could bear.

Maya had already offered Daisy advice about branding her little gardening business and she'd come up with a pretty design and the name Daisy May Bloom, because the pure white perennial plant was hardy and attracted bees and butterflies to gardens. It seemed fitting.

Brontë had already settled into school here, so Daisy was suddenly left with empty hours on her hands for the first time in years. Instead of glorying in her windfall from Harrison, and the time she now had to pamper herself, she confined her spending to necessities for their flat. She'd donated most of her things from France to the friends and families of the few neighbours she knew, and had bid them and Nico a tearful farewell, promising to come back and visit, and to call from time to time to let them know how she and Brontë were.

'You'll stay in contact?' Nico had made her promise, his strong arms wrapped around her, her cheek resting on his chest.

'Of course! You mean a lot to us,' Daisy had reassured him. 'I'll text you as soon as we settle in.'

In the first week of Brontë's new primary school she'd kept herself busy, so that she wouldn't sit opposite the playground and stare at the school gates all day. It had also taken some adjustment to register Brontë with just one parent. Even though she'd brought her daughter up on her own, Harrison had at least been an emergency contact. When she walked around now, she worried that everyone was looking at her and whispering about how her husband had been found dead on another woman's kitchen floor. In reality, no one could really know, and why the hell would they care? Harrison's secret life had made her paranoid, but at least in death he could finally provide for his child, and wasn't financing other women. Daisy hadn't spent his nest egg because she was so used to being independent. She would have to decide what to do with it when their free tenancy ran out on the flat.

By her second week back in the U.K. she felt at home in her flat, and she was even at the 'sticking two fingers up at Harrison' stage. She bought an abundance of plants for the generous balcony outside, including a leafy kentia palm with fresh dark green leaves that fanned out and removed toxins from the air. She'd also bought two wall-mounted outdoor heaters, as it wasn't quite spring yet and there was often a slight chill, but the balcony was too beautiful not to use every day. The next door flat's balcony abutted hers, and she hadn't decided yet if she should add some trellis and climbing plants like ivy or clematis to give them both more privacy.

She loved sitting out there at her new metal bistro table and chairs, and she'd even purchased a fancy coffee machine so she could watch the world go by on the river with a cappuccino each morning. Boats bobbed up and down on the water, and ducks and swans swam past in the dappled sunlight, enjoying the morning breeze. There were mature trees beyond the flat and the gardens were shaping up nicely already. Behind the back wall was a stretch of concrete and the ticket office for her grandad's boat, *Bertha*. She could watch him walk to work and Brontë often came out and gave him a wave before they set off for school in the morning. It was in stark contrast to her life in France, and she felt like a tiny bud on a tree that was unfurling and opening itself up to sunlight and possibilities. She heard another bang and some swearing from next door and frowned, glad that she'd already dropped Brontë at school. If her new neighbour kept using language like that when her daughter was around she'd have to have a gentle word.

When she looked up from her morning coffee and saw

Arthur carrying a chair onto the much longer balcony of the four-bedroom flat next door, she almost fell off her chair, spilling hot coffee on her hand which made her yelp. He looked up in surprise and his mouth formed an O before he promptly snapped it shut in surprise. 'Daisy?' he asked in confusion, coming to the barrier between their flats and holding onto the railings as if he needed the support. 'What the hell are you doing here?' his eyes darted around the balcony. He clearly couldn't quite compute what he was seeing. 'I thought you were in France?'

'I was. I came back,' she said quietly, her heart racing at the sight of her childhood friend. She saw a few lines on his forehead and his hair was slightly shorter, but otherwise he looked the same. She'd always felt she could get lost in his dark brown eyes, but now they were focused sharply on her and she squirmed in discomfort. She remembered how close she'd been with Arthur and his sisters at one time. They'd spent much of their time after school with their feet dangling in the river from the jetty at the back of his grand-parents' garden, shaded by the huge willow tree. Then she pictured their bodies entangled in her bed sheets after her twenty-first birthday party and her whole body flushed. Arthur was the one who got away. They'd pretty much spent every waking moment together for months after that and then... nothing. He'd withdrawn and she hadn't under-stood why. A few weeks later he was dating someone she knew, and she'd retaliated by doing the same, which hadn't ended well. She shuddered at the thought, because those feeling had been tightly locked away for years.

'Is Harrison here?'

Daisy gulped and tried not to meet Arthur's eyes. He had been the most important person in her young life at one point – until Harrison had arrived and swept her off her feet with his big brown eyes and dark blonde hair... not unlike Arthur's.

'He passed away.'

'What? When, how? I'm sorry,' Arthur looked horrified. 'I'm just in shock. Why didn't Maya tell me?'

'Not many people know I'm home and I asked Maya not to tell anyone because it was still so raw. Are you helping someone settle in?' She eyed the big rattan outdoor chair he'd just shifted into place, in front of the view of the water and cruisers.

'Me. I'm moving here,' he replied, rubbing his forehead, seeming perplexed that she was actually standing in front of him. 'Maya told me about the flats and it seemed too good an opportunity to miss. I've been thinking of settling back here for a while.' He moved the chair slightly and then turned back to her. 'I think Maya and Noah know the developer and they earmarked a flat for me. It's all about who you know,' he grinned and she saw a spark of the old Arthur she had known and loved... Daisy's mouth went dry and she sipped her cooling coffee for something to do. She couldn't believe this. Arthur had just moved in... next door! 'Are you visiting a friend?' he asked. 'I didn't know the other flats had been sold yet.'

'I live here with my daughter Brontë,' Daisy replied, and Arthur's mouth hung open again. 'Um... Maya suggested it,' she added with a frown. 'She said this place had just been built, when she heard I might move back home.'

'She said the same thing to me,' said Arthur, still staring at her as if he'd seen a ghost. 'I know you don't speak to Romy or me much these days, but Maya has kept me updated on how you are. Why wouldn't she tell me this?' He scowled. She noted how wonderful it was to see him, even though he was cross. 'We were all so close once,' he added. 'Are you okay? How is your daughter?'

Daisy hung her head and felt her cheeks burn in humiliation. She'd known she'd feel this way when faced with any of her old circle of friends and family, but it really stung when Arthur said it.

'We're fine now. Maybe Maya felt awkward telling you I was coming back, after I'd asked her not to mention what happened to Harrison.' offered Daisy. 'I've spoken to her about him. I know I wasn't a very good friend to you all. Perhaps she felt it was my story to tell.' She looked up at his handsome face as he tousled his short, dark blond hair. She remembered how it felt to run her own hands through it and she licked her lips in memory of his mouth on hers.

'Do you need help bringing anything up?' she asked as he stood there, seeming perplexed. 'It looks like we are going to be neighbours, which is the weirdest thing I've said for a while,' she laughed with a wobbly voice.

Arthur smiled and she felt an arrow shoot through her heart. Why this man had always meant so much to her, she didn't know, but for a while they'd been inseparable. They'd often held hands while they had lain in the little boat moored at the end of his grandparents' jetty, and stared at the sky while they daydreamed about their futures and watched the dragonflies darting about. His had been full of the exciting technology he would invent and hers were all about becoming a world-famous designer, of what she'd had no idea.

Maya and Romy would eventually wander down the garden and join them, often bringing snacks or the home-made biscuits that their grandmother Ettie made. They were all shapes and sizes and you never knew what they would be made of. Sometimes there would be big juicy berries from the fruit and vegetable patch in the mix and sometimes a weird selection of nuts or pieces of ginger. They were slathered in chocolate, though, so the children ate them anyway. Arthur had always had a huge appetite, but he managed to keep slim and toned because he enjoyed running. The problem was that shortly after they'd become friends Daisy had fallen in love with him, and the moment they'd slept together and he'd found out what her true feelings were, he'd run as fast as he could – into someone else's arms.

Chapter Five

Daisy tried not to panic. She certainly hadn't expected to land another job as soon as she'd moved back home. Her grandad Joe ran his steamboat cruises at the dock, alongside two fancy cruise liners owned by the Bowen brothers, Alex and Luca, who looked like movie stars. To one side of the dock was the bustling Riverside café that Daisy had already visited once or twice and further along Maya's best friend, Leah, ran a flower shop with a huge double window to the front. The Parisian blue woodwork and eye-catching flowering baskets full of trailing ivy, delicate snowdrops, early daffodils and deep purple crocus seemed to draw tourists from far and wide. The other side of the dock now housed Daisy and Arthur's block of flats that had been built to complement the town. The modern, streamlined exterior was built with natural wood and metals, which would age beautifully, softening with time.

Determined not to waste a moment now that Brontë was at school for part of the day, Daisy had been growing restless. Maya had clearly sensed this and dragged her out for more tea and cake at the Riverside, which she could now afford. The owner, a vibrant blonde lady called Penelope, had unceremoniously sat down with Daisy and Maya and introduced herself.

Daisy had been rolling her eyes in ecstasy after taking a bite from a delicate filo pastry that had layers of thick buttery vanilla cream and tangy raspberry jam. The jam was now oozing onto her fingers and she tried to lick them clean and quickly brush the crumbs off her mouth. Penny grinned and patted her shoulder in understanding. 'Good, isn't it?' she asked.

'Sublime!' replied Daisy when she'd finished, feeling a bit awkward at being caught stuffing her face.

'We've hired an amazing patisserie chef who has just moved here from Cornwall. My cakes were bought in before,' Penny admitted sheepishly, looking around as if afraid to admit it. 'I am a dab hand with sandwiches and lunches but I can't bake for toffee,' she laughed, her gaze darting across the shop to make sure her customers were all happy.

'Actually, Maya, I'm amazed you manage to get in here without being asked for your autograph,' Penny added with a teasing smile, but she had a good point. Maya's jewellery design business had been splashed all over the news, which Daisy knew had been difficult for her to navigate. She now lived with movie star Noah Benedict, who owned a huge mansion down the river, so it wasn't all bad... Daisy rather wished someone would come and sweep her off her feet, but then shook her head, as another man in her life was the last thing she needed. It had been comforting having Nico a few doors down at their French apartments, but now she had Arthur next door, which was the reverse of comforting!

Maya rolled her eyes at the teasing. She was a gorgeous,

bashful mix of her Mexican and British heritage and people often turned to stare because of her beauty as much as her new-found fame. Arthur had the same long sooty lashes and inquisitive dark eyes that captured your attention the minute they were focused on you.

'To be honest,' said Maya playfully, 'I was shocked myself about all that, but people pretty much leave me alone now since the original fuss has calmed down. It's a completely different story if I'm out with Noah, though,' she mock-swooned, her eyes glittering with love, which pulled at Daisy's heartstrings. Had she ever been that lovestruck about Harrison? She didn't think so.

'I adore the story of how you and Noah met,' sighed Daisy dreamily. 'Brontë can't wait to see him so that she can tell her friends she's met a real-life movie star!'

They all smiled and Maya took Daisy's hand and squeezed it. 'He literally poured my coffee all over me!' she laughed. 'We must organise a get-together soon. But listen, what can we do for you, Penny?' asked Maya, dark hair swishing around her shoulders, her brown eyes inquisitive. 'It's not like you to sit down when the place is so busy.'

Daisy glanced around the popular café and could see a queue forming at the till, the customers all taking off their coats and eyeing up the last slice of red velvet cake with buttercream icing.

'It was Daisy I actually wanted to see,' said Penny, her long blonde braids swishing around her shoulders as she turned to face Daisy.

Daisy sat up a bit straighter and brushed some crumbs off her jean-clad legs, her face flushed. It was her normal response, and ingrained. Usually when people wanted to speak to her, it was to tell her what they'd heard about her errant husband. She hated the fact that he could still hurt her, even though he was probably rolling around in hell and chasing a hot demon.

'Maya mentioned that you're a garden designer?' Penny looked to Daisy for agreement and, when she just sat there like an animal in headlights, Penny glanced at Maya instead, who nodded vigorously. 'I'm extending the café into the big conservatory at the back. It's huge and at the moment it's a waste of potential. There's also a garden area behind it that's a bit of a wilderness. I want to have tables and chairs out there for people to sit and relax, even though the view to the river is at the front.'

Daisy could already see Maya's brain ticking with ideas, but her own was frozen in fear. She'd only ever done garden designs, not the actual structural work – although she'd been dreaming of a job like this for years. Seeing the grounds around her new flat take shape at such a pace was enjoyable, but the design was pretty simple with its established trees, walkways and seating, due to Kris's limited budget. She'd love to try something more creative. 'Um... well...' she stuttered before Maya took over.

'Daisy will send you over a quote and a copy of her portfolio by next week. I've seen her designs and they're beautiful,' Maya gushed, giving Daisy a quick warning stare telling her to go along with things and not ruin the opportunity. 'The garden behind Kris's development already looks so much better after Daisy redesigned it.'

'They haven't finished it yet!' squeaked Daisy.

'But it's already a huge improvement visually and it doesn't take too much of your time to oversee it, does it? You live in the building,' laughed Maya.

Daisy gulped. Her throat suddenly felt parched. She did have a portfolio full of garden and interior plant-scape designs, small finished projects and aspirational designs.

Kris's development was a bonus because the space was huge, but she didn't have photos of the site yet, other than the ones she'd snapped on her phone. She'd shown Maya her ideas on the second night she was in town. They'd shared a bottle of Pinot Noir and caught up on each other's news, which had missed a great big Arthur-shaped piece of information. Before Daisy could speak, Penny had clapped her hands together in glee and stood up, kissing them both on the cheek and rushing to help an elderly customer who was balancing a tray of tea and cakes and a walking stick.

'I've never worked on a retail project before!' hissed Daisy, aghast. 'What if it's too much for me?' she asked, her voice shaking. She nibbled the edge of the flaky pastry and then wriggled her bottom in her seat, taking a huge bite and chomping furiously, flakes showering her plain, long-sleeved white T-shirt. Maya nudged her shoulder and almost made her spit out her mouthful of cake.

'Sorry,' Maya said, not sounding at all sorry. 'It's sacrilege to leave any of that cake, but this is more important. Penny is twice as busy now that the new bakes are so popular. She has the space, so it makes sense to utilise it. How exciting!' Maya clapped her hands in glee. 'Let's go and take a look, then you can decide whether to freak out or not,' she joked, and Daisy rolled her eyes, but then felt her pulse calming. 'All we do know is that at this time of year it will be muddy.'

'Paving slabs,' Daisy suggested immediately, and Maya's eyes sparkled with delight. 'They will be easy to clean and are durable.'

Maybe she could do this? At least it wouldn't take her far away from Brontë's school, Daisy thought to herself. She could be at work before nine every day if she needed to be. It would also give her a breathing space and fill her bank balance up a little, which had been freaking her out lately. She hadn't wanted to use much of Harrison's money. Maybe she could provide a healthy income for Brontë on her own? Her blood started fizzing, but with excitement this time, and Maya saw the change and got up, grabbing her hand to lead her outside to see the space before she changed her mind and ran for the hills.

'You've got this!' crowed Maya and, although Daisy wasn't sure she particularly 'got' what the hell she was letting herself in for, she had to at least try.

Chapter Six

Daisy heard Arthur close the door to his flat and go outside to bring in more boxes.... was he humming along to *Single Ladies* by Beyoncé? Daisy smirked because he was definitely off-key. Was he doing the whole move by himself, she wondered? It was probably a bit more exciting for him to be moving in than her. They both had very swanky flats with great views over the river, but Arthur's space was twice the size and he probably owned his home. Daisy's stay was temporary. She now knew what his flat was like, because she'd helped him drag a few boxes through his new front door the night before, then hastily left him to it when he'd offered her a very tempting glass of Sauvignon Blanc. Brontë was at her first sleepover at Daisy's parents' house and she was stressing about whether or not she'd get a phone call to collect her daughter. There was also the fact that she'd now have to visit her parents regularly if they wanted to see their grandchild in between work trips. Things did seem to be easier with her them recently. They suddenly didn't want to travel as much, now Brontë was near. Daisy hadn't been enough for them, apparently, but a grandchild was another matter, she fumed.

Daisy and Brontë had walked home with Brontë's little friend Florence and her mum, Anne. Bronte had invited them both in for an ice cream. They hadn't stayed long, but Daisy had never had more than one small child in her home before and the thought of more sent frissons of fear up her spine. Queasiness made her rock back slightly on her feet for a moment. Would she have to invite the other mums around too? Getting used to a new home was one thing, but the social norms that went with children making friends and going to school together were a whole new ball game.

Daisy poured herself a hefty glass of Pinot Noir as soon as she'd realised that Brontë was happy, thanks to a reassuring text from her mum. She felt as if she should be doing something productive with her free time, even though her bones ached with exhaustion from all the recent upheaval in her life. She had put on a wash and emptied the fancy dishwasher that was already in situ when they'd moved in, but in the end, tiredness won and she put her feet up and watched a romantic comedy and scoffed a huge bowl of popcorn slathered in butter and toffee sauce.

After the news about Harrison, Daisy had panicked about how to cope with a five-year-old on her own, but Maya had helpfully pointed out that she'd raised Brontë largely by herself up to that point. Yet she still fretted. What if Brontë had questions about her dad when she was older? The thought terrified her. Was she supposed to tell her daughter that her dad had died on his girlfriend's kitchen floor? She shuddered. She couldn't do that, so she would be forced into a web of lies when that was the last thing she wanted. Her daughter's mental health was paramount, so she'd have to make a decision about what to say when the time was right. Bloody Harrison was still causing havoc even now. She guessed he always would, as their connection through their child was eternal.

There was no way she'd bash his memory for fun, so she'd have to think very carefully, or perhaps take advice from Brontë's school about how to proceed if the topic ever cropped up. Daisy hated the thought of watching the pity appear on their faces when she explained what had happened, as all they knew so far was that she was a recent widow. On second thoughts, she sighed irritably, she'd cross that bridge when she came to it and get independent expert advice. Harrison's box of paperwork and 'keepsakes' had certainly pushed Daisy's confidence to an all-time low.

She wondered if Maya had sneakily had a hand in bringing Arthur back into her life, but shook that ridiculous thought away. What would her friend have to gain by that? Maya and Romy were among the few who knew how besotted she'd been with Arthur back then, and how he'd broken her heart. She knew Maya and Romy hadn't approved of Harrison, and Arthur had made it crystal clear that he hadn't. Over the years she'd wondered if that was why she'd jumped straight into a full-blown relationship – to prove to Arthur that someone wanted to commit to her even if he didn't.

She sighed and rubbed her tired eyes. She occasionally had the scary thought that Harrison might have tampered with their birth control to ensure a pregnancy, but she brushed that possibility away because it didn't matter now and accidents did happen, clearly. She had Brontë, the love of her life, and she'd always be grateful for their daughter. She'd come home to provide for her, heal her own emotional wounds and be near her family. She certainly wasn't looking for a reconciliation with that playboy, Arthur.

Maya had slipped into conversation that her brother was single, but it sounded like he hadn't changed. Apparently, he still dated voraciously and then left his girlfriends behind while he travelled all over the world for work. He probably had a different woman in every country, she scoffed. Players liked to play. The last thing she'd expected was that the guy she'd taken years to get over would move into the flat next door to the one she'd just rented! Damn and blast it, she swore under her breath and took another glug of wine, trying to concentrate on the couple in a passionate clinch on the television screen. They had been arguing a moment before, but definitely seemed to be over it now, and Daisy wished that her own problems with the very dashing Arthur Lopez were as easily brushed past.

Although Daisy and Arthur had spoken via occasional texts at first, she'd heard from various sources over the years that Arthur was a complete Lothario with a revolving door of female friends. Daisy shuddered. The thought turned her stomach, but she hadn't been able to control how much she still blushed when he was near, which infuriated her. His golden good looks seemed to make women drool. Those piercing brown eyes had made her trip over her feet as a teenager, so she was determined she wouldn't be that stupid now she was a grown woman. She certainly didn't want her daughter to hang around with a man who treated women with disrespect. Daisy sighed and straightened her shoulders, then stuck her tongue out childishly at the wall to Arthur's flat as she headed off to bed.

The alarm shrilled on her phone bright and early the next morning. She groaned and turned it off before swinging her feet down onto the cool floor. She rubbed sleep from her eyes and stretched her arms out. So much for a good rest. She'd tossed and turned all night, picturing

Arthur naked and tangled in his own (probably silk) sheets, next door.

The room was quiet without Brontë rushing around and singing or nattering as she got ready for school and ate her breakfast. Daisy's mum was walking Brontë to her class this morning. It was a popular school, but Daisy sometimes felt like she was the one starting out, with cliquey groups of inquisitive parents looking her way every time she stood to one side of the playground and twiddled her thumbs, while wishing her daughter would hurry up and join her.

'What are you up to today? You working?' asked Arthur as he came and stood on the balcony next door. He nodded towards the stack of papers and open computer on her bistro table set. Daisy sighed. She'd just sat down with her first steaming cup of coffee of the day and needed to get on with working out a quote for Penny. It was already giving her a headache and she pinched the bridge of her nose with her fingers.

Arthur was dishevelled, his blond hair all mussed up and sexy – like he'd just jumped out of bed – and Daisy felt her hackles rise. It was still before nine and she had ten minutes of peace before she had to start checking prices of local plant wholesalers for the scheme she'd spent the last few days creating.

She had known Penny's café was popular from the amount of footfall, but expanding to almost twice the covers and utilising the outside space was quite a challenge. The garden wrapped around the building and was fairly long and thin, boxed in by a tall and rather rickety fence. Daisy tried not to panic, but her heart was racing suddenly. She didn't know if she was coming or going right now. She'd wanted to be left alone to re-centre herself, but after a morning of encouraging texts from Maya and Romy and now the interruption from Arthur, who was eyeing up her coffee, she realised that she might as well just start work.

She plastered on a smile and turned to face Arthur. He was so annoying! He was balancing a pile of boxes by his foot that looked like they might fall over any minute and she tried not to stare through the metal balustrades at his firm leg muscles in pyjama shorts. 'I will be in ten minutes. I'm working on some costings for a garden design.'

'Can I grab a cup of coffee?' he batted his eyelashes at her. 'And a croissant if you have a spare?' He eyed the buttery pile of pastries she'd treated herself to because she was feeling glum without Brontë. She had more than she could ever eat. 'The smell of freshly-baked pastry wafted through the windows and I couldn't concentrate on unpacking after that. I brought the empty boxes out so that you might take pity on me,' he joked with what he probably thought was a winning cheeky smile.

Did that really work? She shook her head at the thought of how many women still probably swooned at this man. She was glad not to be one of them. She'd put a wall around her heart when it came to Arthur, and she was happy about that now. But she'd like them to be friends again, she supposed, grumpily.

'My stomach's been rumbling all morning,' he added hopefully.

She rolled her eyes. So much for her ten minutes of peace before work. 'It's not even nine o'clock yet, and don't you have a fancy coffee machine in your kitchen, or an oven?' she asked in exasperation, turning to switch on her computer to keep her hands busy and wishing she'd taken more time to brush the kinks out of her long blonde hair. She really did need to get more organised, and she would have to remember either not to sit on her deck in her short pyjamas, or to get on with putting up that very thickly ivy-covered trellis between the flats. Arthur seemed to think this was a communal meeting place, or a breakfast stop!

Arthur grinned as if helping him would be the most natural thing in the world, which irritated her further, making her wish she could nudge the stack of boxes that he was currently leaning on and watch him fall flat.

'I do have an espresso machine, but it's still in the box. Setting my work desk up by the window seemed more important.'

Arthur was a tech guy and had made a fortune, if her grandad's gossip was correct, but she hadn't really been listening. Her bones ached with exhaustion from a night of tossing and turning at the sounds of the river outside and the unwelcome images of the hot guy next door, but she quickly got up and made the coffee. She didn't ask him how he liked it and poured it into an, "I love my mummy" mug that Brontë had persuaded her to buy, hoping he'd take the hint and get lost.

'Thanks,' he groaned in pleasure as he took his first sip. She didn't like the way the hairs on the back of her neck stood up as if in recognition of that sound. He looked at the croissants she'd reheated earlier from a pack of frozen pastries. She didn't know why she'd put out so many, but knew for certain that it wasn't in the hope he'd see them and want to join her... She frowned and crossly put one on a plate and handed that to him too. He stepped away from the boxes and took the plate, their hands touching briefly. She gasped as a jolt of sexual electricity zapped her fingers and hastily stepped away.

'Who are the costings for? I didn't know you did garden design,' he enquired with interest.

'We haven't exactly spoken for about four years,

Arthur,' she scoffed, sipping her own coffee and enjoying the strong brew she'd selected, hoping he'd hate it. Annoyingly, he was drinking it with pleasure. 'I needed to find something that I could work around having a baby. Most of the work was remote garden design where I just created the plans as a contractor. It was a hobby that came good,' she shrugged.

'Impressive,' he said, seeming genuine, as he happily wolfed down the croissant and gave her a puppy dog look for more. She sighed and held out her hand for the plate, making sure to hold on to the opposite side of it this time.

'Thanks,' she smiled finally, looking at him from under her fringe and deciding a night without Brontë must have put her on edge. 'How come you stay trim if you eat like that?' she joked feebly, shaking her head. He grinned and looked down at his stomach, lifting his T-shirt and showing her very taut abs. She gulped and wished she'd kept her big mouth shut, pulling a long bobbly jumper she'd left on her chair over her head to cover her own nightwear because her legs suddenly had goosebumps. There was quite a chill in the air, but Arthur always made her feel so hot and bothered. It was really annoying.

'Well, when I'm not carrying boxes into my new flat, I like to run along the river. It's what sold me on this place. I can run all the way up to Noah's place. When I used to travel a lot I had to use hotel gyms, but I prefer the outdoors. You might even catch me talking to the occasional tree,' he grinned, nodding towards her open file of notes. 'Who is the client?'

'Penny from the café,' answered Daisy, trying to remember if he'd always been this nosy. 'She's renovating the back of the building and wants an outdoor space for her customers.'

'Wow! That will be great. I hate having to fight my way in for a table. It's even more popular now your grandad's boat is overflowing with customers.'

Warmth and pride filled Daisy. Joe's boat, *Bertha*, had almost been like a ghost ship, but Maya had helped him out with a boat makeover and now the business was flourishing. Daisy just wished that she'd known about the project to save her grandad's precious steamboat and been able to help too. Everyone had kept it a secret. Her grandparents hadn't wanted to worry her about how dire trade was, but surely families should confide in each other? Then she winced, because she hadn't told them how awful Harrison was, or how hard it had been for her to survive. She hadn't wanted to worry them either. She nibbled on her lip and then noticed Arthur watching her. She swept her fingers through her hair, pulling it into a high ponytail with the hairband that she'd left on the table, swishing her hair away from her face. She sat down at her desk after he handed her the empty plate back.

'I'll drop the cup back in later if that's ok? I'm supposed to be on a conference call in a minute and I need to connect my computer back up.'

Daisy had seen how complicated his work computers were. There were loads of them! He had a whole room just for this, with views of the river. She assumed the fourth window was for the master bedroom. Her own bedroom was pretty big, so his must be huge.

'Don't you need to put on a suit or something?' she asked cheekily, eyeing his casual pyjama shorts and white T-shirt combo.

Arthur laughed and put his coffee on the long wooden outer ledge that had been designed into the balcony scheme. Daisy already found it useful for putting down her own cups of tea. 'I'm the boss. I can wear what I like,' he winked.

Her mind flitted to an image of Arthur in a suit and her mouth went dry. She must be thirsty, she thought, and quickly sipped her coffee. Then she frowned. Should she think about some sort of uniform for her own business? Maybe this job would help her find some friends, get her out of the flat more and away from handsome distractions.

She gave him a sharp look. 'I need to get to work too,' she said annoyance clear in her tone again, the friendly atmosphere of a moment ago forgotten. Arthur nodded and bid her goodbye, then left her on her own.

Gazing out across the river, she was determined to leave all thoughts of fitting in with the community again behind – not to mention bothersome, but devilishly handsome ex-boyfriends who now lived next door, The problem was, she didn't know if either were possible.

Chapter Seven

Arthur perched his empty coffee cup on top of the boxes and strode back indoors. He rubbed his chin, which reminded him he needed to shave. He turned his back on the view of the river, which would soon be surrounded by tall grasses like comfrey and great willowherb. His grandad had instilled the importance of plants in him from a young age, so it was not surprising that he still remembered a lot of their names. His sister Maya was obsessed with them too, and they formed the basis of her beautiful jewellery designs.

Daisy was back to stay! He paced around the room before remembering he had a work call soon, so he needed to shake this funk off. He gazed out towards the river as if that might hold the answers to his swirling stomach and uneasy feeling that his world was about to be turned upside down.

He watched a couple jog along the path that wound next to the cruise ships and Joe's steamer, *Bertha. Bertha* was resplendent with a huge black paddle wheel, newly painted golden rails and a soft green awning that had been brought back to life by his sister the previous year. Arthur had helped by scrubbing a few floorboards and sanding the deck, but Maya had transformed the old girl back to her former glory and had repainted, reupholstered and refitted the interior, including the Art Deco bar that now shone with crystal glasses, banquette seating and mirrored shelving. *Bertha*'s steam cruises had since become so popular that as many queued up for them as they did for the Bowen Brothers' sleek and modern river trips. People seemed to enjoy *Bertha*'s chandeliers, strawberry gins and nods to a bygone era as much as the shiny chrome and white upmarket look of Alex and Luca's streamlined boats.

Arthur rubbed his temples, which were starting to ache. He had taken a chance on moving here. His sisters had urged him to relocate near their grandparents' home, so that they could see more of each other, but the last person he'd expected to come face to face with was Daisy! He sat at his desk and tried to concentrate on his work, but he couldn't focus and ended the meeting after an hour.

He turned when he heard a tap on his front door, then grinned when he opened it to find Romy standing outside. Her long blonde hair was dragged back into a haphazard ponytail as per usual and her fitted woolly jumper and jeans were covered in mud. He pulled her into a welcoming hug and then moved back so she could step inside. He watched her eyes darting around and taking in how much he'd organised the flat... which wasn't much.

'Have you literally just moved boxes around from one place to another since last week?' she asked, chuckling.

Arthur rolled his eyes, but she was right, so he could only shrug. He'd been so busy with work, he had barely had time to unpack anything.

'I've sorted out my home office,' he said, humour lifting

his tone. He always felt either irritated or full of love when he saw his siblings. They interfered in his life, but he knew they meant well. Relying on each other as children had created a tight bond and even though he wasn't the eldest, he'd tried to look out for his sisters, as their parents weren't around. Romy stuck her head into the bedroom he'd set up as an office. The flat was designed with lots of blacks, greys and dark blue tones, so it felt calm and a bit stark if he was honest.

'Living on that ramshackle houseboat you've docked across the river isn't your smartest move, either,' he grumbled. He'd said it to her time and again and Romy wasn't listening to him yet either. It was her turn to roll her eyes, but she had brought take-out coffee, so he forgave her. He picked the cups up from where she'd left them on the counter and handed her one, taking the lid off his to inhale the rich aroma. 'Maya and I have both offered to buy or rent you a home, or get you business premises,' he said.

'I'm fine on my boat,' Romy protested.

'It's not safe, Romy,' he argued. 'Those vandals broke into a boat just up the water from you. Yours could be next,' he warned.

'Look, I came here to check out your place, not get another lecture on the suitability of my new home,' Romy said.

"Home', ha! Maya said you could move into the town-house she rents, as she's rarely there,' said Arthur, but he knew Romy was just as stubborn as the rest of them and always did things her own way. Her boat seemed to be a mecca for swans and ducks from the river who nested on the bow. Romy had created a small tearoom for passing walkers and it was already gaining a few regulars who seemed to enjoy getting close to the birds. She was as eccentric as most of his family, so he shrugged and set his coffee down.

'You're like Luca Bowen. He's always going on at me about moving the boat. I like it there and Clara, who owns the mooring and the bungalow behind me, likes me living at the bottom of her garden.'

'I bet she does! She probably feels safer because you're there after the last break-in at that field. Didn't they smash up one of her old sheds for fun?'

Romy ignored him and went to look out of the windows, so Arthur closed his eyes for a moment to re-centre and calm down. 'How are Gran and Grandad?' he asked. Fashion designer to the stars, his grandmother Ettie had dressed royalty before she'd 'retired' but she'd recently been persuaded to dress her best friend, Dame Rosalie Alton, in her most recent movie. Rosalie and Ettie ware constantly creating mischief together, so Arthur tried to stay out of it. Maya's boyfriend, Noah, had starred in Rosalie's most recent film, which had been critically acclaimed.

'They are both causing as much bedlam as usual,' Romy shrugged, but did smile finally as she ran her hand along Arthur's new granite work desk. He'd moved it out of the home office and left it beside the enormous sliding double windows in the lounge. For some reason he liked hearing Daisy move around next door and having his desk there meant he could wander out quickly and speak to her.

'Grandad's mostly been seen talking to those pretty spiky, fluorescent bromelia plants he just bought for his glasshouse,' Romy smiled and Arthur pictured his grandad, Owen, who was an exotic plant specialist with his own niche television show, pulling up a chair to have a chat with his plants. He was obsessed by them and felt his lilting voice helped them grow.

'If he found out about Daisy's new business, he'd park himself on her balcony, talk her ear off and never leave,' grinned Arthur.

'New business?' asked Romy, with interest, brushing her fair hair out of her eyes with her hand and succeeding in making it even more messy. For such a beautiful woman, Romy couldn't care two figs about her appearance. She enjoyed comfort and being amongst animals because humans had hurt her too much, he guessed. One human anyway.

'She runs a gardening business. Did you hear about Harrison?' He tried to hide the hurt in his voice but he could see the sympathy in Romy's face. He'd been so close with Daisy once.

'Maya just told me. I was so shocked! I had no idea what a nightmare he was, though.'

'Nightmare?'

'Um... Maybe I shouldn't have mentioned that. I think Daisy wanted to settle back in and then tell us what happened. It's sad that we lost touch with her over the years.'

He sipped the coffee thoughtfully and wondered, not for the first time, how Daisy was managing to juggle a small child and a new business. He'd been astounded and appalled to learn that Harrison had died. Arthur had shared terse words with Maya the night before, but she'd helpfully pointed out that it was none of his business. Daisy put on a brave face, it seemed, but she'd arrived, moved in and opened the business without any help from anyone. Maya had intimated that Harrison hadn't been such a great husband and dad, and anger burned in Arthur's stomach at the thought of Daisy being in a different country to her family and friends and having to cope alone. He had a whole team of staff to help him run his business and he was single. He couldn't fathom how the hell Daisy managed to do everything, and bring up a small child as well. Arthur tended to steer clear of children, and he definitely didn't want any of his own.

He worked too much and used to travel most days, although that was changing. He had his home office now and had decided only to go into the city or travel abroad for two days a week. There was no point headhunting the best tech team and business managers to run the place while he was travelling to meet clients, if he couldn't rely on them once he was home. His staff were incredible, and worked efficiently as a team. His lively central London offices and creative team had open plan workstations and recreational spaces. Arthur always felt a swell of pride when he walked into the building and saw his company branding, but he was tired. Years of living in hotels had taken its toll. He craved solitude and he was becoming increasingly grumpy, he'd found – a bit like Daisy had been when she'd discovered he was living next door! She'd been full of mischief and laughter when they'd hung around together as teenagers and young adults, but he knew he'd had a hand in ruining that and the guilt and regret hadn't eased with time.

Moving here had been a drastic measure to shake his life up a bit, plus Maya had been pretty persuasive. Something had to change before he burnt out and it all came crumbling down around him. Plus, the headaches were scaring him a little.

'Did you know that Daisy was moving in next door to me?' he asked Romy, who flushed and then quickly walked over to his grey and white kitchen and started opening cupboards, a well-versed distraction technique his sisters both used. If they didn't want to answer a question they'd start poking into his stuff and he'd forget what he'd asked. 'Well?' he said again.

'I can't remember the exact conversation I had with Maya,' his sister dodged. 'Just something about these incredible new flats and that they were selling fast...' she twirled her hair around her fingers until he gave her a pointed stare and she hid her face behind her coffee cup until he huffed and gave up, plonking himself in his black leather work chair.

Working from home had been revolutionised over the past few years and as a tech company, Arthur's team had helped the transition by designing integrated workstations, faster connectivity and work-based applications that encouraged remote team meetings and assisted workflows. His company had grown at an astonishing rate, but the key was his creative ideas. To stay focused he needed room to breathe. Being by the river had always soothed him. His grandad had taught them about river plants like orange balsam and marsh woundwort, and he enjoyed the sound of their names as much as searching for the plants themselves. The whole family was drawn to live by the water as adults, it seemed. He'd grown up beside it and his new flat felt more like home than the many faceless hotel rooms he'd had to spend his time in, however glamorous the settings might be with twenty-four-hour room service and plush bedrooms and lounges.

All work and no play made Arthur a dull boy, he smiled finally, kicking away such maudlin thoughts. He certainly wasn't complaining about his success. He'd been dating a woman named Lilian for a while before coming home permanently, but it had pretty casual for them both. In the end, they'd decided they were better off as friends. He did miss female companionship, though, and Lilian had been fun to be around. In the end the same issues always arose, where she wanted commitment and hinted about settling down, and that had made him put on his sprinting shoes and book more work abroad. Luckily, they'd managed to remain friends, but she had called him a few choice names when they'd split up and she hadn't been wrong, he decided. He'd never promised her anything, but she'd wanted something he couldn't give. They did occasionally still hook up, but he'd recently decided that wasn't one of his best ideas either. The thought gave him the cold sweats. Lilian had adored travelling, parties and the high life, so he had been as surprised as anyone when she'd changed and become obsessed with finding a husband.

'I haven't seen Lilian around much lately,' said Romy, as she tutted and stacked a few food items she'd brought with her in one of his empty kitchen cupboards. 'Don't you know how to shop, Arthur?'

'I have never needed to, living in hotels,' he answered simply. 'Lilian and I aren't together anymore. We decided to cool things off.' Romy stood up and regarded her brother, her head tilted to one side, dark brown eyes focused on him with laser precision, which made him squirm.

'We, or you?' she asked.

'We,' he insisted, but turned away before she could chide him about his inevitable pattern of quick relationships and keeping his feelings in check. Romy joined him on his balcony and they both stared out at the view and watched a woman jog along with her dog for a few moments, her dark hair flying out behind her in the breeze, the little dog racing ahead and then turning in circles to check where she was, before darting off again.

Seeing Daisy with Brontë didn't help, he guessed, as it brought back a rush of feelings that he'd managed to compartmentalise for years. His own unconventional upbringing had taught him that having kids was complicated and that lifestyle wasn't for him. His own parents were doctors who'd worked for a medical charity abroad, so he and his siblings had gone to live with their grandparents as young teenagers. The same way Daisy was pretty much brought up by hers, he guessed. She had definitely spent more time with Joe and Olive, or with his family, than her own parents and that was probably why Daisy and Arthur had connected so well at first. They were a life raft for each other in turbulent seas.

He was happy casually dating some wonderful women, but as soon as they wanted anything serious, he cooled things down. Maya's idea that this flat was perfect for him had seemed like serendipity at the time, but he hadn't realised that Daisy was coming back, or he might have wavered. He was still fuming about the way she had left, even though he'd tried his best not to show it when he'd seen her.

The speed at which Daisy had met Harrison and had moved away from them all had stunned Arthur. Then Joe had proudly shown them photos of his great-granddaughter and Daisy had seemed even further out of reach. It had made Arthur finally move on, though. Now they were both back and he guessed that Daisy must be grieving for Harrison, despite his sister's hints that things hadn't always been rosy. Arthur hadn't liked to push the subject, plus Daisy would barely look at him for some reason, so he was beginning to feel uncomfortable in his own home in case he bumped into her, he thought crossly. She couldn't leave fast enough the night before and he'd tried to open up a friendly chat today, but she'd just seemed uninterested.

He hadn't expected to see her, but he supposed he'd

dreamt of her running into his arms when they finally met again, whilst apologising for eloping with another man. Then he frowned as an unsettling feeling about his own actions came over him. To be fair, he had cadged her food and coffee, but a man needed to eat and her breakfast had smelt delicious. He'd tried not to, but the sight of her long legs peeking out of her silky pyjama shorts under the table, and her beautiful green eyes, even when they were flashing anger at him, perversely made him step out onto his balcony anyway.

'Have you chatted much to Daisy?' asked Romy with interest, stretching her legs out as she propped her bottom against his breakfast bar, leaving flakes of mud fluttering to the ground, which made him tut. He certainly hadn't had a house to be proud of before, but he didn't have a cleaner yet and Romy left trails of mud wherever she went.

'Not really,' he said, honestly.

'Do you want to?' she asked pertinently. Arthur suddenly found his desk drawer very interesting and began sorting through a set of pens, so Romy shook her head at his stubbornness. 'I love you… but you're an idiot,' she added and he frowned.

He hadn't seen Daisy for so long and now he had, he found himself drawn to her again. They'd been pretty inseparable once. He'd made a stupid mistake and everything had changed. She'd been so angry at him for dating other people after they'd had a brief relationship. Touching her and the rush of feelings that had come with it had scared the life out of him all those years ago, and he'd run away from the thought that she might be the love of his life. Being headstrong young adults hadn't helped matters on either side. He'd lacked communication skills and she'd erupted like a volcano. Hurtful things were said and a huge void had cracked open between them. There had been tears, recriminations and accusations from her which weren't true. He hadn't slept with anyone else, he'd just backed off from major heartbreak, but in the end, he'd suffered it anyway when she'd met Harrison about a year later. Arthur had hated himself when she'd left, but that was ancient history now.

He had thrown himself into his work, but in this case, time hadn't healed. It had eased the bitterness he'd felt about the precious opportunity he'd had and lost, but he knew that the life she wanted still wasn't for him. He couldn't give her what she'd needed then and he certainly couldn't now, but it was a weird feeling to keep bumping into his very sexy ex every day. He was a bit short-tempered and grumpy in his staff meeting that morning, until his business manager pulled him up on it. Luckily that turned the meeting around. He was usually a sunny kind of guy, but a black cloud had descended and he'd snapped a few times in answer to innocent enquiries about work. He shook his head to clear images of Daisy's legs, and he stomped about for a bit until he finally managed to shake his mood off. He was being ridiculous. He eyed his running shoes, but his workload decreed that he stay put and get on with it.

Romy picked up her empty coffee cup and threw it into the metal bin in the kitchen that opened automatically as she drew near. Her eyes sparkled with mirth at his love of gadgets and then she gave him a quick hug before she left. 'The next time I arrive, I expect at least one of those boxes to be emptied properly, and I'm sending you a food shop,' she laughed. 'But you can pay for it.'

Arthur shuddered because Romy's idea of food was lettuce, tofu and seeds. He daren't look at the few food items she'd brought with her earlier. Knowing her, they would be the colour of sludge and be there to help cleanse his colon. He felt his stomach turn over, then chuckled, throwing his arm around his sister. He'd towered over her since she was about eleven and he'd turned into a terrible teen. Romy was always on a mission to make them eat more healthily, but he liked his foot hot and fast, a bit like his relationships. He pulled a face as that was becoming tiresome now. He opened the door for Romy to leave and kissed her goodbye, pulling her in for a hug before she left, which made her link her arms behind his waist and rest her head on his chest for a moment, listening to his heartbeat, like she had as a child when their parents had told them they wouldn't be coming back for a while.

'I promise I'll try to clean up and get organised, although by the state of your berth across the water, you're a fine one to lecture me,' he quipped, brushing her hair out of her eyes.

His gran and grandad would surely descend on his new flat soon, he sighed, and Maya's partner Noah would have to be smuggled in at night because he was so famous. His grandad, Owen, was almost as bad, after his gardening shows began airing on television the previous year. Arthur rubbed his forehead and felt that headache looming. He was having far too many of them. It had been the driving force to him finally making lifestyle changes.

It made his head pound even to think about Maya and Noah's situation. He didn't know how they coped. He'd hate having his every movement splashed across the papers, but his sister's relationship with a movie star seemed to be front page news. Often the articles were also about Maya's jewellery designs now, after she'd been outed as the person behind her world-renowned brand. It was a lot of pressure, but they seemed to manage it. Arthur sipped his coffee, grimacing because it was cold.

He wondered how he could put off a visit from his grandparents. They'd arrive with arms full of weird plants and his grandmother would bring something beautifully sewn and bright. He fleetingly thought how much Daisy would love that. Her balcony was already planted like a lush leafy paradise with potted date palms with their long spiky fronds. She'd also lined up some umbrella bamboos with their delicate canopy of deep green leaves and giant elephant's ears plants with enormous bright green leaves with prominent midribs and ruffled edges.

His grandmother, Ettie, seemed to think that making things for her grandchildren was part of her job since coming out of retirement. Arthur's slightly messy flat, including one corner that was piled with boxes, was all masculine lines and he baulked at the thought of a vibrant patchwork throw for his couch or an intricately textured blanket for the end of his all-white bed. Ettie's creations were works of art and worth their weight in gold, but Arthur would have to find a cupboard for them and install some sort of security camera so that he had time to drag them out and put them on show when his grandparents arrived. Luckily, they were busy with their own lives and didn't meddle as much as they used to, but they still liked to cause as much mischief as was humanly possible when they did arrive, he sighed, rooting around in a drawer that was already full of junk after a visit from his younger sister.

Chapter Eight

Daisy couldn't help but smile, holding Brontë's hand as the little girl skipped home. She'd begun the day feeling grumpy because of Arthur stealing her food, but she'd had a really productive few hours afterwards. She'd finalised her plans for the café garden and spoken to some local suppliers about delivery and costs. She knew that Penny might not choose her design, but Daisy was proud of how quickly she'd turned the work around and come up with a solid scheme. Years of scrapbooking and keeping up to date with current trends had served her well. Excitement fizzed in her veins at the prospect of being busy again. The café could be a great addition to her portfolio and garner more work.

Brontë chattered away about her day and her new friends at school. Daisy was relieved that her daughter was so resilient. They swung their arms back and forth as they went and shared secret smiles about how much fun it was to walk through the pretty village together. They did some window shopping, passing the various shop fronts with displays whose subtle tones reflected the colours of the river and were bursting with tempting gifts and sweets. Having to budget in France had meant being creative with their leisure time, so Daisy had found interesting walks around local towns, and at home they had spent hours pressing flower petals between the pages of the hardback books on their shelves. They'd investigate the plants and where they grew, with Brontë seeming to share her mother's passion for the outdoors.

'Look, Brontë,' said Daisy in excitement, pointing to a tiny flower that, against all odds, had grown through a crack in the pavement in front of one shop. Brontë bent down and ran her fingers over the vibrant purple petals of the little crocus, her eyes sparkling in excitement. Its delicate green leaves were just poking above ground and straining to reach some light.

'Can we get some sweets from the sweet shop?' asked Brontë when she stood up, brushing her hands on her school uniform grey skirt. Her winter coat was hooked over Daisy's arm and her bright blue eyes pleaded with her mum, who ruffled her hair and shook her head. The display of brightly wrapped confectionery and a miniature Ferris wheel with toy animals riding it would tempt most people inside, as it looked like a lot of fun.

'Let's go and see Great-Grandpa Joe before we go home. I bet he's got a store of treats in that big cookie jar he keeps hidden behind the bar.' Brontë's eyes lit up and she grabbed her mum's hand and began dragging her along the street and down towards the promenade. Daisy hoped *Bertha* was there, otherwise her daughter would be mightily disappointed, and they'd have to go and visit Penny at the café instead.

'*Dépêche-toi, Maman!*' Brontë called, asking Daisy to hurry up.

Daisy did worry that Brontë might forget her heritage now they'd moved to Windsor. She had been born in France and spoke the language fluently. Harrison's parents, who had both sadly passed away long before Daisy met their son, were French, but had lived in England for most of their lives. The fact that Brontë didn't ask about her daddy was a statement in itself, but Daisy did wish she'd known more about Brontë's paternal grandparents to share with her when she was older. Daisy was determined to take her back to France as often as she could, to keep the connection for her child.

Five years of marriage had clearly meant nothing to Harrison, thought Daisy through clenched teeth. She remembered the day they'd met. She'd been sunbathing outside the trendy little boutique design agency she'd worked at after studying design at college. She found she had a gift for planning spaces and she'd been offered the job in the swish central London studio. Harrison had lied to her that he was a banker and he'd given the impression that he was worldly and wealthy (which had turned out to be true in the end). Not that money had been an overriding priority, until she'd had to scrimp and save to survive and then travel back home with her tail between her legs with an almost five-year-old in tow. She'd made a fairly decent wage back then and her colleagues and boss had welcomed her knowledge as an asset to their team. She'd forgotten what it felt like to be valued, she thought now as she hung her head for a moment.

At least they had security here, which they'd never had when Harrison was alive. It was ironic. She'd never have wished him dead, even at the height of her humiliation, but now he was gone, she felt as if her old self was gradually unfurling and reasserting itself with force. She'd always been a hard worker, with Saturday jobs from a young age, and she'd helped her grandad Joe run his passenger steamboat along the river for a while, but her passion was designing garden spaces that made you feel inspired. Her old flat in France had been pokey and damp when she'd arrived, but by the time she'd worked her magic on it, it had been a pleasure to live in each day. Plants hadn't been something she'd thought too much about at first, but the ultimate transformation of her home had been the indoor garden and the window boxes and plants. The rooms hadn't felt confining, or lonely, after that.

'There's Gigi Joe!' said Brontë, as Joe jumped off the boat and waved to them both, his bushy white beard visible from metres away. Brontë let go of Daisy's hand and Daisy watched her daughter run to Joe and be swung up into his arms for kisses and a big hug. Warmth filled her heart and it cemented the knowledge that she'd made the right choice in returning home.

Moving to the heart of London from leafy Windsor had been a bit of a shock as a young adult, but she'd welcomed the change then. Her overworked parents still lived in the big detached house she'd been born in, situated further along the river. Brontë loved the garden there and her parents invited them both over most weekends – not that Daisy accepted often. London, which actually wasn't very far away, had seemed so daring and exciting at the time. She could see now that she had been young, naïve – and fleeing heartbreak from a blond Lothario with big brown eyes.

Harrison had actually been a timeshare salesman who sold holidays in villas abroad. He'd seemed to work all hours of the day and night, until she found out where he really was, or rather, whose bed he'd been in. He'd clearly been 'working' on his stamina and hip action. By the time she'd realised the kind of person he was, she was pregnant. He'd then persuaded her to relocate to France, he'd alienated most of her friends and family, and made her feel unattractive and stupid. As her pregnant belly had grown, his cruel comments about her appearance ensured her self-confidence had been at an all-time low. Seeing other women at the French hospital, glowing and rejoicing at the imminent arrival of their children, had made the isolation worse. She hadn't been able to keep up or understand their chatter and in the end it had seemed easier to stay by herself and sit in the corner on her own. Harrison had made her world smaller and smaller, and she'd not had the energy to question it until it was too late. Now, going for a job interview with a new acquaintance like friendly, chatty Penny seemed daunting.

'You can do this,' she chanted to herself as she walked towards Joe. Luckily, in France she'd had her beautiful daughter to keep her company when she only spoke a few words of the language and had needed to adapt to a new way of life, with no support from friends, or family. It had hit her hard, and she'd been too proud to admit that she'd quickly realised her mistake.

Visits from her parents had often ended in tears when she'd refuse to come home. Years of tense communication after this resulted in her parents and grandparents missing a huge chunk of Brontë's early development. Daisy carried that guilt, and she was trying to change and not be so controlling with every aspect of Brontë's life – because she'd had to be in the past. Harrison hadn't helped when their daughter had been admitted to hospital with a fever, or given Daisy any time to herself. As a result, independence seemed ingrained now, but she did want to ease up a little and she knew her family meant well. She hugged Joe tightly as she reached him and he kissed her cheek so that his beard tickled her skin and made her laugh.

'I might have mentioned to Brontë that you have a cookie jar of sweets hidden under the bar...' she pulled a face of apology and Joe laughed, his big white eyebrows bobbing up and down. Joe used to wear fluorescent tops and shorts that could undoubtedly have been seen from space, but Maya had managed to tone his uniform down and designed branded T-shirts with an image of the castle nestling amongst the trees and *Bertha's* name underneath it. Joe's top had the word CAPTAIN written on it too, and this always made Daisy smile. She couldn't imagine her grandad anywhere else but behind the wheel of his magnificent steamboat, with her sparkling gold rails with black and white life buoys tied at intervals along the edges.

'I only put the cookie tin there for Brontë's visits anyway,' grinned Joe and Daisy tried not laugh because her grandad was well known for his sweet tooth, even though he was slim and athletic. 'We're here for about twenty minutes before we head out again, if you want to pop aboard too?' he asked and Daisy nodded, following him onto the main deck and then finding a seat under the green awning while Joe led Brontë away to find the sweets.

Trying to find work in France with a newborn had been excruciating, but she'd been determined to bring in extra money somehow. Online work had seemed the best solution. She'd kept her designs simple, but the changes to the spaces were significant. In the end her main customer had agreed to try her designs for a cut-down price, which had been brutal. She toiled away in her tiny kitchen at a small desk by the window. She kept everything immaculately clean, which was hard with a toddler, but Brontë also loved to pot plants and they spent many hours together in the communal garden behind the flat, from the moment Brontë could walk. Daisy had set Brontë up with her own little workstation and gardening apron, flower pots that they had painted together and a bright orange trowel that she adored. That area did get messy from time to time, but it brought Daisy joy to see how much fun her daughter was having with her splodgy mud pies.

Now Daisy grinned at Brontë's mucky face as they strolled back to their flat together after visiting Joe. It had given Daisy a moment to breathe and enjoy watching the ducks paddling up and down the river while Brontë had wrangled more sweets. She was currently hopping about and twirling as they neared home. 'How many sweets did Gigi Joe give you?' Daisy laughed, using the affectionate term they used for Brontë's great-grandfather.

Brontë seemed to be considering how truthful to be without lumping her Gigi in trouble, but then she grinned. 'Not too many!' she said, with a smile, brushing her hair from her face with the back of her hand, which made Daisy's heart squeeze with love.

Daisy wished Harrison had taken as much interest in Brontë as her own family did now. They could be a bit oppressive at times with her education, when she was growing up. Being an only child had meant being her parents' sole focus. They'd concentrated on her education and not so much on her mental health, as they were always at work. She wished she'd appreciated the fact that they juggled huge work responsibilities with caring for her, but she'd felt second best to their careers. She'd pushed them away instead. Now she was determined that her own child wouldn't feel abandoned because her mother had to work. Having a job was necessary and she would find a balance that suited them both. Being a working mum meant Daisy was happier and more secure and that in turn would reflect on her daughter's happiness, she was sure.

She hated that she'd let her parents down and caused them so much worry and pain though. They were probably around more than she gave them credit for and certainly way more than Harrison ever was. It had given her a deeper bond with her grandparents, Joe and Olive, too. That she was forever grateful for.

Daisy had thought Harrison was handsome and exciting, even though there had always been a slight thrill of danger around him. Hastily marrying at a register office when she was pregnant had been a whirlwind, but her errant husband had soon lost interest in both of them. After the birth, he'd checked that his daughter was still alive from time to time, but could never spare an hour to play with her.

Daisy opened the door to her flat and then the one to the balcony, and organised a healthy snack of chopped carrots and sliced cucumber for Brontë while she took things out of cupboards for dinner.

'Are you hungry?' she asked Brontë then grinned because her daughter never refused a snack.

'Always!' joked Brontë as she threw herself on the couch for a moment to take her shoes off.

Daisy heard Arthur moving around outside and found it weirdly comforting suddenly. Arthur might be a womaniser, but he'd always looked out for his friends and family, especially the girls. The siblings had been picked on at school because their parents had moved abroad without them. Maya, Arthur and Romy had started living with their grandparents when Maya turned thirteen. Arthur had been twelve and Romy, just ten. Kids in their classes were cruel about them being left behind. It had hurt them all, but Arthur hid it well and protected his sisters, often getting into scrapes that he took the blame for. He pretended not to care, but Daisy knew the bravado covered his own pain. He loved his grandparents but missed his mum and dad terribly. Maya and Romy adapted well, but Arthur was close to his dad especially and it broke her heart to hear them on the phone and Arthur asking when they were coming back.

As emergency surgeons who worked for a medical charity abroad, it must have broken his parents' hearts too, but their work was important and they visited when they could. Arthur and Daisy had been so similar as children, but as adults they couldn't be more different. Arthur dated everyone he could, from what the gossip columns said, and that turned Daisy's stomach. Daisy was more discerning. She had a child to think about. And who needed a man anyway? She certainly wasn't about to get mixed up with another one until her daughter was at least fifty, she grumbled to herself and then smiled suddenly.

She wondered if Arthur had any handsome friends who visited, because even though she didn't want to date, it might be interesting to have a few more men dotted around to get her used to male company again. Her life had been pretty solitary in France. She hadn't mixed with men other than Nico, as it had always seemed to put Harrison in a mood for a month if she as much as smiled at someone, even if they were as old as her dad!

'Go and get washed and change out of your school uniform, and I'll start dinner,' she said to Brontë as the little girl rushed around checking her toys hadn't been having too much fun while she'd been at school.

'Okay *Maman*,' Brontë sang as she skipped into her room and Daisy sighed, as she loved the soft lilt of her daughter's voice when she spoke in French. Daisy picked up a bag of pasta and shook some into a pan of boiling water, watching a few drops jump out of the pan and onto the work surface as the pasta fell. She smiled because she'd shed enough tears of her own and was determined to start living again.

It was handy moving into a modern flat that she didn't have to decorate. Having a fledgling business, even though it had been online, had also been a godsend. She was planning to settle into the routine, but although she was more than happy to get her hands mucky and get down in the dirt to rebuild Penny's café garden, she did need at least one contractor to help her with the heavy lifting. For Kris' development project, she just had to oversee things and check her designs were followed. With Penny's build, she'd be elbow-deep in mud from the start.

It would give her room to rebuild her finances and put feelers out to the businesses in town to supply plant displays for their shops and offices. She had put most of the money that Harrison had left into a trust fund for Brontë, after using some of it to buy a few basic items, plants for their new home and Brontë's school uniform and shoes. Their little girl would have a world of options when she was old enough to manage her money on her own.

Daisy rolled her neck and then laughed as a small hand crept onto the worktop and snaffled some of the grated cheese that Daisy had been about to put on the table. 'I saw that!' she chided playfully.

Brontë loved cheese and covered her spaghetti Bolognese in it – so much so that you could barely see the meat. Daisy shook her head and made sure that there wasn't too much cheese in the bowl and then ruffled Brontë's already messy blonde hair. It usually hung in a straight curtain to her shoulders, but Daisy had started braiding it into French plaits when she was four to keep it out of her eyes when they were digging in the mud, and she seemed to like that style for school. By the time she got home the neat braids were more than a little bit frazzled at the edges, but to Daisy that meant that she'd had a good day and hopefully done lots of exploring and playing with her friends in the playground. Daisy's own almost straight hair – apart from an annoying kink at the end – was often tied up in a high ponytail that swung over her shoulder, but now she was home she might start adding some tonged curls. She'd not thought much about her appearance for years, but suddenly she had the urge to primp a little and she definitely wasn't doing it because of the very annoying and sexy blond Adonis next door.

Chapter Nine

The sun was barely up, but Maya enjoyed a rare moment of solitude while she waited for Daisy to order a coffee and join her. It was becoming harder and harder to wander around freely now that people knew that she was the mystery designer behind the previous year's smash hit jewellery brand, No. 1 Ethereal Lane. Not only that, but she'd begun dating movie star Noah Benedict. She smiled secretly to herself when she pictured waking up beside him in tangled sheets, his body glistening from a night of passion. She really couldn't believe how much her life had changed in twelve months, but she was growing into the role that had been thrust upon her – local celebrity!

She'd often wondered how Noah felt, with paparazzi jumping out of bushes and watching his every move. Now she knew, although locals pretty much left them both alone. She recalled the first time they'd locked eyes, after he'd spilled her coffee over her while he was running from a group of fans seeking selfies with their idol. She chuckled and held her empty cup up to Daisy and her friend called over, 'Do you want a refill?'

'Yes please! I'm still not awake yet, even though it's after 8am. Where's Brontë?'

'She begged me to let her go to breakfast club,' said Daisy, but she bit her lip and didn't look as if she liked that idea.

'I'm sure she's having a great time!' Maya reassured her. So many things had changed for Daisy in a very short space of time that Maya worried about her. She never asked for help and was a pretty closed book. Maya was determined to change that.

Dating Noah meant that all of Maya's secrets had been spilled in the national press and she weirdly felt unburdened by it. She didn't have to hide her true self anymore, but she did have to hide from the endless stories speculating about the relationship. Was it serious, was he going to dump her for the stunning co-star in his latest film? She sighed and rubbed her temples. Dating someone famous wasn't easy.

She thought about her brother. His face had been splashed across glossy gossip magazines, too. Arthur brushed it off because it wasn't headline news, but he was a handsome and wealthy bachelor and people liked to speculate about the person who would finally tame him. Maya laughed at that. Arthur was a free spirit and was more driven by his business than by any woman he had met so far. Being his sister, though, she knew his deepest secrets, even if he'd forgotten them himself. A certain curvaceous blonde bombshell returning from France might snap him out of his recent self-imposed isolation, she hoped, which was why she'd set them up living in flats next door to each other. She just hoped that her meddling didn't backfire.

Daisy pulled a seat out next to Maya and kissed her cheek in greeting but Maya pulled her in for a proper hug.

'We missed you while you were in France,' she said carefully.

Daisy hung her head, her long blonde ponytail swinging over her face. Maya brushed it gently away and smoothed her fringe from her striking green eyes. 'I'm sorry,' mumbled Daisy.

'That wasn't a criticism. I'm ecstatic that you're back and that we get to see more of each other!' She read the room and changed the subject. 'How funny that you and Arthur both decided to move home at the same time.'

'I wondered about that too...' said Daisy, raising an eyebrow in her friend's direction.

Maya suddenly decided they needed sugar in their coffee and got up to grab some sachets from the counter, before returning and changing the subject, wishing she'd kept her mouth shut!

Maya smiled her thanks as one of Penny's staff placed tall glasses of frothy coffee in front of them and took away Maya's previous cup. 'Penny makes the best cappuccinos! Just don't tell Romy as her coffee boat is just across the water and she'd kill me,' Maya joked.

'Romy loves the coffee here, too,' grinned Daisy, finally looking up.

'She comes here for a rest,' smiled Maya. 'Her boat is a lot of work.'

'Penny says that this place practically runs itself, but she's a whirlwind. Her new pastry chef is drawing in even bigger crowds too.'

'She's definitely upgraded,' Maya nodded towards the incredibly intricate cakes displayed in huge domes and the glass cool counter by the till. 'And not just the cakes either,' she joked. 'She said her new baker is jaw-droppingly hand-some and he's clearly good with his hands,' she joked and

Daisy almost spat out her drink. 'Penny used to buy in all her stock. Not any more. This place will be packed to the rafters if he keeps making such divine cakes. Plus, it smells heavenly in here... all that butter, cocoa and caramel.' Maya closed her eyes and inhaled the sugary scent for a moment.

Daisy laughed and gazed around the pretty coffee shop. There were pristine square wooden tables and high-backed chairs that had flower patterns on the seat pads. An abundance of leafy plants was dotted around in deep blue ceramic pots. Maya wondered if she was hoping to catch sight of such a talented hunk. She hoped not because Maya had dastardly plans for her friend and any distractions would make them crash and burn. Maya smiled and took Daisy's hand for a quick squeeze before letting her go.

'Thanks for introducing me to Penny, Maya,' said Daisy. 'You're one of the few people I stayed in contact with while I was abroad. Mum and Dad hated Harrison, and although I knew they were right,' she paused, 'I had to come back when I was ready, and not before.' Daisy's hands wrung in her lap, so she picked up her canvas tote bag for something to do, then put it down again after retrieving a lipstick. She bit her lip and quickly shoved the lipstick into her jeans pocket.

'Sorry. I've decided I need to take a bit more time and effort with my appearance, so I packed a new lipstick in my bag. It's a deep red and far too bold for me, so I keep picking it up and putting it down for some reason! It feels like war paint,' she sighed. 'No one even knows about Harrison, but I keep thinking everyone is staring at me.'

Maya's skin prickled with anger. 'Daisy. You're perfect as you are. If you want to wear a vibrant red lipstick, then wear it. If you want to put it on now, go for it! If it makes you feel empowered, then slap it on, but changing the way you look isn't going to make you feel more settled about coming home. It's been a huge upheaval for you and you're just finding your feet.'

Daisy's lip wobbled and Maya took her hand again. 'Give yourself time to feel at home here. It's only been a short while.'

Daisy drew in a huge breath and closed her eyes for a moment before speaking. 'I know Harrison left me a while ago, but I needed time to find enough courage to come home, even though I've wanted to for ages. Being on your own is tough.'

'You more than survived!' said Maya. 'You thrived – despite Harrison.'

'I wanted to prove I was worthy of my family before I felt I could come back. I know I let you all down.'

'You didn't!'

It was Daisy's turn to take Maya's hand now. 'I know I did. I pretended everything was fine when it was far from it. I should have asked for help... I'm sorry,' she said, putting her hands back in her lap and fiddling with the edge of her denim shirt.

'Well, you managed to get a job that included a beautiful flat, so now you have your own home and a great base to build from,' Maya assured her.

'You got me that job!' said Daisy in exasperation.

'I just told you about it,' reasoned Maya. 'I couldn't have asked just anyone. It had to be someone with the skills to *do* the job,' she added and Daisy's forehead creased in thought.

'It's scary, though,' sighed Daisy. 'Harrison was never there, but at least in France I could pretend to everyone here that everything was rosy. I've put most of the money he left us in trust for Brontë, but had to use some for our new home,' Daisy said in a hushed voice, her eyes darting around them, as if she were a criminal. No one was paying them the slightest bit of attention. 'He was a complete miser in real life. I couldn't believe it when I found out how much money he'd stashed away, or what he was spending on other women.'

Maya gave her a sympathetic glance. Any mention of Daisy's ex made her want to kick something, or him. 'I'm sorry you had to go through that,' she said, tears now filling her eyes. 'Romy and I both had disastrous relationships around the same time, so you weren't alone in feeling like you'd made a mess of your life, or not asking for help.' Maya leaned in conspiratorially. 'Romy still needs our help, but won't take it,' she shrugged.

'You're happy now, though?' asked Daisy. Maya's face lit up at the thought of Noah, which said it all. Daisy laughed as her friend blushed. 'I need to meet him!' Daisy grinned.

'Come to dinner!' said Maya excitement bubbling in her veins. This would be a great excuse to get Daisy out and about. 'It's just along the river. I'll come and collect you in my boat.'

'Oh! Um... Brontë. I couldn't leave her.' Maya brushed that off.

'Bring her! Or if you'd like an evening off, Joe and Olive have been champing at the bit to look after her again. So have your parents! They haven't stopped gushing about how proud of you they are.' Daisy frowned and Maya nudged her shoulder. 'Daisy. You pretty much single-handedly brought up your child in a foreign country, with no resources.'

'But...' Maya waved Daisy's protestations away.

'You refused to ask for help. You are so like your grandad,' she joked and Daisy spluttered her drink. 'You know I had to trick him to take your gran on holiday after her hip operation so that I could revamp *Bertha*. He'd never have gone otherwise.'

Daisy's eyes glittered with unshed tears. 'I can't explain how much that means to us all, Maya. You saved his business, now you're doing the same for mine.'

Maya sat back in shock. 'You did this all by yourself,' she argued. 'I can't design a garden.' She finished her coffee and put the glass down. 'You aren't alone anymore, though,' she said fiercely.

Daisy flushed and signalled to a passing waitress to bring them cake. Two plates arrived with squares of delicate filo pastry, sandwiched between smooth vanilla-scented *crème anglaise*, drizzled with icing and chocolate. Maya's mouth watered and she used a fork to take a bite. She sighed in bliss, before shoving two more heaped mouthfuls in, while Daisy savoured each buttery morsel.

'It's our pastry of the week,' said Penny, appearing out of nowhere, dressed in her usual jeans and smart branded top. 'It's something new I'm trying and I got Fred to bake loads of them,' she grinned. 'He keeps saying that he's only got one pair of hands.' She waggled her eyebrows and grinned childishly, making Daisy laugh. 'He's so gorgeous,' Penny whispered under her breath as she hunched down beside them, then decided to pull out a chair and sit down. 'Half my staff are acting like they've never seen a good-looking man before, and even I have to keep fanning my face because I go bright red every time I see him. And I'm his boss!'

'I can see why he's so in demand,' said Maya, through mouthfuls of the light and delicious confection. 'I need to take some of these home for Noah.'

'Home?' asked Daisy with a twinkle in her eye. 'I

thought you still rented the town house just across the river?'

'I do,' said Maya as her skin warmed up, going a bit pink. 'But I tend to spend most of my time at Noah's now. He asked me to move in with him last year, but it isn't official yet because I've been holding on to my place. Our schedules are crazy, so it works for us.' She covered her face with her hands for a moment to hide her blushes. 'I was kind of hoping that Romy might take up my offer and live at my old rental, but she won't leave that boat. Arthur hates it because he worries about her safety. We both do.'

'Why?' asked Daisy, alarm in her tone.

'There's been a few break-ins on that side of the water. Boats, mostly – and an old shed. We think it's kids, but we wish Romy wasn't so stubborn.'

'I think we all have that problem,' laughed Daisy. 'I'm sure she'll do what is right for her. She can look after herself,' she added reassuringly. Maya knew she was right. Woe betide anyone who got on the wrong side of her sparky sister.

'Noah has set a design studio up for me in his guesthouse,' said Maya, thinking back to their original conversation. 'I look out over the river all day and watch the world go by, a bit like I used to when I helped your grandad out on *Bertha*.'

'That sounds divine!' said Daisy.

Maya grinned. 'The first time I stepped into Noah's guesthouse, I wished I had a studio with that view.'

'Even though your own house is just down the river?' teased Penny.

'The guesthouse wall nearest the river is glass, so it's like being outside, but indoors. It's heavenly,' sighed Maya dreamily and Daisy nudged her shoulder playfully.

'So is Noah, I hear,' laughed Penny as she got up to assist a customer. Daisy smothered a giggle with her hand.

'*Bertha* looks beautiful now,' Daisy chipped in. 'Grandpa Joe sent me photos, but she's even more stunning in real life. She's like a floating masterpiece. You've brought her back to life.'

Maya had heard this many times now, but it still thrilled her to know people appreciated the effort it had taken to bring the huge steamboat into the modern age without destroying her history.

Bertha had been given a complete makeover with new lighting, seating, awnings and the beautiful wooden and granite bar. Even Arthur had turned up to scrub the inside clean when she'd asked him. Maya was kind of hoping that having Daisy and Brontë living next door might stop him working so hard, if they became friends again. She knew he'd been having headaches and refused to slow down.

He had been dating Lilian fairly recently, but she was a huge party animal and Maya got the feeling that Arthur was tired of that now. She hadn't heard him mention Lilian's name for a while. Arthur wasn't one to brag or moan about his relationships, so his sisters literally had to drag information out of him by pinning him to the ground as they had as children, until he slapped the floor to signal he gave up. Arthur was very protective over her and Romy – and Daisy too – and he usually ended up letting them run rings around him until he'd had enough. She and Romy tried not to tease him too much, but the way women had always fallen over themselves to get his attention or date him was perfect fodder for pranks. Half their friends had been in love with him, including Daisy, Maya knew. But Arthur had been too restless then to stick around for long and had broken her heart.

Their upbringing, away from their parents, had been unusual, and that was something they'd all had to deal with in their own way. Their grandparents certainly made up for it with their bonkers behaviour. She rolled her eyes heavenward at the thought of the endless parties in their huge garden by the river, and the guests coming and going. It had been an adventure for the three young siblings, but a complete change of pace from city living and their old routine in the compact terraced house they had grown up in.

Daisy had lived abroad away from her own parents too, and she had managed. Maya could see the toll that it had taken on the once carefree girl, but she was back with her family now and they would all rally round for her.

'Was Arthur in when you left? I thought I might as well stick my head in at his place if he is.'

Daisy frowned, as if she didn't want to think about Arthur, and Maya hoped he hadn't annoyed her already. If he had, she'd give him a sisterly piece of advice about upsetting his neighbours. Arthur didn't often remember to think of how his actions affected others. He just made big brown eyes at them and they gave him what he wanted. Plus he was so messy! It drove Maya crazy. She was very organised, and a bit anally retentive. Romy didn't care a jot either way and seemed to be at home in most places. Arthur pretended to be a lone wolf, but inside he was a loveable puppy who put up with his unorthodox family with good grace. Maya turned her attention back to Daisy, who grumbled, 'He comes and goes, mostly stealing cups of coffee or my breakfast.'

'Hmm,' said Maya. It didn't surprise her. Arthur was often too busy to cook for himself and could go for days without surfacing if he had a big technical job for a client.

He had an office in the city with lots of staff, but he liked to hide away and work from home when he could. Maya was worried he was becoming a bit of a recluse, but he had always previously managed to get dates easily enough, so she shrugged that thought off. He could probably do with a reprieve from the demands of his old lifestyle. 'Do you remember when Romy and I used to dress you and Arthur up as a bride and groom?'

Daisy smiled at the memory. 'Yes. The veil was huge and I kept tripping up on it. Plus, you made Arthur wear one of your grandad's bow ties and he kept trying to take it off. He was so embarrassed!' Both women sniggered and then looked up. Arthur himself was striding through the door of the café, clearly looking for coffee before he went back to his flat. His eyes narrowed when he saw them sitting so close together and giggling. To Maya's surprise, as he was so often in a hurry, he strode over and pulled out Penny's vacant chair to join them. Daisy seemed equally bewildered and slightly uncomfortable. Something had definitely gone on there, mused Maya with gut-wrenching certainty. Bloody Arthur.

People were beginning to come in now, but it was still early for the river cruises, so there were just a few school mums and some workmen sitting at tables and chatting, or reading that day's newspaper. Arthur looked handsome in dark jeans and a soft blue shirt that was folded up at the elbows. Daisy's face was flushed, but Maya didn't know if that was because she was flustered at what they'd been discussing, or if Arthur had managed to upset her in some way. A few people were glancing at them and Maya tried not to notice. It had been hard getting used to being recognised everywhere, but she was adapting, and most people left her alone.

Before she had been outed as the designer of No 1. Ethereal Lane, she'd led a quiet and unassuming life, with days sitting on *Bertha* and drawing the plants by the river, which she transformed into delicate pieces of jewellery. Her latest piece was a royal fern with clusters of arching green fronds and circular spores at the tips, crafted from white gold and diamonds. Once the story of her true identity had broken, she had needed to make adjustments to her routine, but not as many as she had feared. The news had also brought her Noah, which she'd be eternally grateful for, so it wasn't all bad. She was used to her little brother being stared at, though. The gossip columns called him a local heartthrob, which made her smirk because she knew what an absolute pain he could be when he wanted to.

'Hey, ladies,' said Arthur. He offered them both a smile, but Maya could see that it didn't quite reach his eyes, which made her frown in concern. 'Can I get you both anything?' he asked, taking note of Daisy's half-finished drink. 'I also need to settle up my tab with you, Daisy. I know I've been drinking gallons of your coffee and eating your food, but my latest project has meant a lot of late nights and early mornings.'

'I'm okay, thanks,' said Daisy, her skin still flushed.

'Moving home in the middle of a huge project has been a pain in my backside. Sorry,' he said to Daisy, before smiling at Maya.

Maya had spoken to Romy about some sort of intervention to get Arthur to rest more. Maya had baulked at interfering at first, but once Arthur had checked his expensive watch and then jumped up to order himself a coffee, her eyes met Daisy's over the rim of her own cup.

'He looks tired,' noted Daisy. 'I've been burning the candle at both ends to get Penny's design and costings finished, so I can relate to his exhaustion. Having a beautiful coffee shop a few doors down helps. Sandwiches on tap,' she joked. 'Plus, like he said, he steals breakfast from me most days. I don't think that man knows how to shop or put bread in a toaster!'

'You're both working too hard,' commented Maya, draining the dregs of her coffee. 'How's Brontë fitting in at her new school?'

Daisy's eyes slid to the other school mums who were dotted about, sitting at tables chatting happily, and she lowered her voice. 'She's loving it, it's just me who is not fitting in.' She tilted her head towards a table at the back of the café, 'They have tried to invite me out, but mostly I'm worrying about Brontë and not concentrating on important gossip.'

'That's not good,' said Maya sympathetically.

'I feel like they're staring at me and wondering why the hell they invited me. The fact that I won't gossip about you or Arthur seems to be another issue,' she added sheepishly. 'They've seen you and me out together before.' Maya sighed and brushed her dark hair back behind her shoulders with her hands. 'I mean,' giggled Daisy suddenly, with a wink, 'Am I not impressive enough on my own? Do they need to find out about my famous friends first?'

'Sorry about that, but thank you just the same,' smiled Maya, whilst cringing inside. Friends locally were often approached for stories about Maya and her family. Luckily none of them had the slightest interest in betraying their friendship. Maya had been hurt the previous year, by an ex of Noah's who'd enjoyed making up and selling stories about Maya's relationship.

Arthur wove his way through the tables and sat back down again, his shoulders drooping. He smiled at them both, but his usual easy charm was lacking. Daisy and Maya exchanged glances. 'Um... look,' Daisy apologised. 'I need to get back to work. I'll see you both later.' She got up and started shrugging her coat on over her shirt. Arthur gave her a tired smile and she offered him one back.

'I'll come back with you and help organise your flat,' Maya said to her brother. 'You look exhausted.'

'Thanks, sis. You'll make it too clinically clean though,' he joked lamely. 'Maya is such a neat freak,' he added, winking at Daisy.

'I have to be, for my work,' scolded Maya primly. 'I like things to be in order. How the hell you can ever find anything is beyond me,' she threw up her hands in exasperation.

'Me too,' said Daisy. 'Organisation helps me keep my mind focused and clear. Otherwise, all I can think about is clutter,' she pointedly looked at the scrunched napkins surrounding Arthur on the table and Maya sniggered.

Arthur shrugged good-naturedly and clearly knew he was beaten. 'Okay. Let me grab some sandwiches and we can go back to the flats. Maya can organise my life while Daisy and I work and eat lunch. Do you want to bring your computer round and work on the breakfast bar in the kitchen?' he asked Daisy, who looked confused at the offer.

'It means Maya might stop and chat and not spring-clean every single surface and drawer, and I can finally try and work out the last piece of coding I need for a customer's application,' Arthur continued. 'It's eluding me and I think I need company. It's why I came here, but I think this many people might be a step too far.'

He glanced around at the café, which was now bursting at the seams with customers. A few were already eyeing up their table now that Daisy and Maya were getting to their feet. One lady looked like she might throw herself across the surface of it, as a man sidled up and put a hand on the back of Daisy's chair. Both Maya and Daisy exchanged glances and then packed up to leave. This was as close as either of them had ever got to hearing Arthur express a need for help. Before he had a chance to change his mind, they were both ushering him to the counter to get them all some lunch, and away from the fight that might at any moment break out over their vacant café table.

Chapter Ten

Daisy wriggled her toes as she sat on the bench seating that ran up and down *Bertha*'s bow. She'd quite enjoyed co-working with Arthur and Maya. Maya had ended up forgetting about the cleaning after twenty minutes and sat with a sketchpad, drawing the view of the river from the balcony. It seemed she carried a pad everywhere with her. Daisy had retrieved her computer and the three of them had enjoyed a companionable lunch and actually had a productive afternoon. Arthur had cracked his coding issue and was full of smiles by the time they'd left, while Daisy had worked out a plan for approaching new customers in the high street. She tried not to think of how much her cheek had tingled after Arthur had kissed them both goodbye.

Today, Joe was entertaining Brontë while his team of staff ran the cruise. It was a revelation to sit on board and to see Maya's genius close up. Daisy had seen the boat steam up and down the river numerous times since she'd moved back, but standing on board was like an out of body experience. The ceiling above the bar was now crammed with the golden signatures of famous visitors and the cruises were sold out most days. Daisy was proud of her grandad for being forward-thinking, and not baulking at the updated design of this floating piece of history.

She loved the way Maya had hung chandeliers in the bar. The panelling shone and the sage green velvet seating that ran along each wall was sumptuous to touch and soft to sit on. The back of the bar had smoky backlit glass shelving, housing rows of bottles of alcohol and fancy cocktail glasses that looked vintage. There were lots of leafy ferns creeping down from the top shelf with their wiggly fronds.

People were milling around and enjoying the canvases that Maya and her friends, like those from Mason's art group, a local organisation for the homeless, had carefully created for the walls. They were so popular, they were regularly sold and replaced. Daisy walked closer to one piece and pictured the deep green and blue hues of the watery scene in her own kitchen. She noted the price and went to talk to Roman the barman, who was serving drinks, his dreadlocks tied back with a thick red hairband. He smiled when he saw her and she grinned back. Roman had worked for her grandad for years and you couldn't help but love his easy manner and cheeky grin. Also, he was gorgeous! He towered over Daisy at six feet tall and was an outrageous flirt. The Bowen brothers, Alex and Luca, were just as bad, with their twinkling eyes and cheeky smiles and she was quite enjoying being surrounded by such beautiful men for a change. She'd never had siblings of her own, but Maya, Romy and Arthur had filled that void. Since she'd arrived back from France, Roman had become family too. 'Can you save the middle artwork over there for me?' she pointed to the one she coveted.

'I think that one is sold...' he teased, his eyes creasing up with humour. She tutted and pouted, so he gave in. 'I'll put a sticker on it for you.' He blew her a kiss and she pretended to catch it in her hand and hold it to her heart, which made him laugh. 'You probably get a family discount,' he added.

'I don't need a reduction,' said Daisy, looking at the brushwork again and feeling the fizz of buying something new for her home. 'I know the artists from Mason's art group are mainly homeless. Maya said the sales of their art are really helping?'

'They are,' Roman agreed as he expertly made three *Bertha* specials of gin and strawberry lemonade and handed them to a customer, who thanked him with a smile and a nice tip.

Daisy noticed that people were looking at the art as much as the view. Now that Maya had been exposed as a famous jewellery designer, Daisy supposed that *Bertha* herself must be worth a fortune, as Maya had painted a small mural above the bench seating when she remodelled the boat. Daisy knew the Bowen brothers and her grandad had upped security all around the boats, though to be honest, it wasn't as if *Bertha* wouldn't be noticed if she sailed away when she wasn't supposed to. She was a spectacle!

Daisy popped behind the bar to give Roman a swift kiss on the cheek and then wandered back outside as the boat got ready to leave the dock. Her mind was working at full pelt because as customers queued up to board the boat, the long patch of concrete that children ran along while their parents waited in line had captured her imagination. She wondered who owned it. She immediately had loads of ideas about redesigning the space to benefit the boats berthed along this stretch of the river. It could look amazing when people strolled by on the other side of the water, and would entice people over.

She enjoyed the view out across the water as Joe sat Brontë next to him and moved *Bertha* into the centre of the river, and was interested to see the house now drawing a lot of attention on the cruise. It was Noah Benedict's home, situated beside the water. Maya lived there most of the time now. Although she had an open invite to visit, Daisy hadn't been yet and was as curious as anyone to see how a film star lived. She was still too bashful to accept Maya's invitation. Now she felt a thrill of excitement as the steel and natural wood building came into view.

She knew from talking to her friend that the wooden outhouse housed a full-size swimming pool, a fancy bedroom and now a studio for Maya. The gardens that ran up to the house were full of mature trees and beds of rose bushes and hebe shrubs that Daisy bet would look amazing in the summer, with their evergreen leaves and purple and pink fluffy flowers attracting bees and butterflies. The mowed lawns were immaculate. Maya had promised Brontë a swim in the pool, so Daisy would have to take her there soon. Strategic planting gave Noah some privacy from prying eyes, and the sight of the multitude of plants made Daisy itch to get back to her beautiful new flat and the big bright desk she'd set up. She adored watching the water and she could imagine sitting there and designing a multi-functional outside space to service the boats and their customers.

She sighed and remembered that she didn't need to work every spare hour now. She could listen to the sound of the birds singing in the trees, just enjoy the scent of the early spring flowers along the riverbanks and the feel of the sun on her skin. She grinned to herself and then noticed a man with dark hair and black modern glasses that framed his deep blue eyes watching her with interest. She flushed and peeked at him from under her lashes. He caught her eye and grinned and she tentatively smiled back. Was he flirting with her or just being friendly? She bit her lip and then turned back to the view, deciding to go and buy another of Joe's famous strawberry lemonades from the bar and to check in with her daughter. It was taking some time, getting used to trusting anyone else with Brontë, but her daughter didn't seem to have any problem spending time away from her mum.

Daisy glanced back at the good-looking man, but he was chatting to a gentleman next to him and she quickly slipped away before she scared him. Her grandad might ban her from his boat if she kept staring at every handsome customer. Her hormones seemed to be having a party lately. After years of staying in alone, she was suddenly hyper-aware of any attractive man who walked past her in the street. It was getting ridiculous. Maybe she needed a few dates to remind herself she was still human, she pondered.

After thanking Roman for her drink and heading back out to the deck to enjoy the last few minutes of the outward-bound cruise, she brushed past the same man she'd just seen outside. 'Sorry!' she said as she almost spilt her drink on him.

He laughed and smiled, his eyes dancing. 'I think that might have been my fault,' he said graciously. 'I was just looking for the pretty woman who I'd seen on deck.'

Daisy's face flamed and she gulped. 'Oh!' She was at a loss for words for a moment – definitely flirting earlier, then. 'Where is she?' she joked lamely, looking over her shoulder. He grinned and held out his hand to introduce himself.

'I'm Fred,' he offered with a smile. He was wearing jeans and a dark grey long-sleeved T-shirt, and gave off an arty, trendy kind of vibe. Daisy's eyes would have followed him across a bar and she enjoyed the feeling of her palm in his as he shook her hand. 'I'd love to take you out for a drink, if you ever have time?' he asked cheekily, just as Brontë bounded into her legs and wrapped her arms around her backside, almost knocking her over.

'*Maman!*' she squealed in delight. 'Gigi Joe has been showing me how to steer the boat and he let me have a glass of strawberry lemonade!'

Daisy felt her heart melt. 'I can see that from the berries all over your nose,' she laughed and rubbed them off with her thumb, turning and giving an apologetic smile to Fred, expecting him to have already moved away. Instead, he introduced himself to Brontë too and shook her hand formally, which made Daisy smile.

'I work at Penny's café,' said Fred. 'I think I've seen you in there enjoying a coffee?'

'The pastry chef! I seem to spend most of my time eating your delicious cakes,' she grinned.

Brontë looked up at Fred, her big blue eyes slightly wary at first, then going wide at the mention of cakes – her favourite thing to eat. She held on tight to her mother's hand, but he had clearly piqued her interest. She was now giving Daisy a pleading stare to suggest they went immediately to the café and sampled some.

Fred seemed to recognise the look as well and laughed. 'I've got a day off today, but the next time you both come by, I will personally deliver you a slice of my very sticky chocolate cake,' he promised Brontë and she licked her lips in anticipation, making them all chuckle.

Daisy ruffled her daughter's hair. 'I'll be working there as well soon.' When she saw she'd surprised him, she laughed. 'I've just won the contract to redesign the outside space and the interior planting. It's a fairly unusual space, as it runs around the back of the café, and that's my speciality,' she added with pride, realising this was true. Most of her online design jobs had been for spaces she knew other people didn't want to get involved with because the angles, or buildings beside them, were tricky. Fred's eyes lit up at the mention of them working alongside each other at the café.

Daisy noticed that *Bertha* had slid into her space along the promenade. Fred noted the movement too and turned back to face her. 'I look forward to seeing you at work, then!' he said with a smile that made Daisy's stomach turn over. He was handsome, in a sexy geek kind of way.

Funnily enough, Arthur really was a tech geek but he looked more polished, like a model. She thought of geeks as people like herself, creative dreamers but with an edge to succeed. She knew the word could be used as an attack. Harrison had called her geeky, for continually having her nose stuck in garden design books, but despite that she had always thought of it as a compliment. It had given her a twisted sense of victory over him in the tiniest of ways. It made her quite sad now to think back to it, as she must have been desperate to gain some semblance of control. But that obsession with plants and design meant she would have a healthier bank balance soon, and she'd also be spending a few weeks working alongside a hot pastry chef while he baked her tempting morsels.

She felt her skin flush as Fred kissed her cheek and bid them both farewell. Then Brontë spotted Joe and ran to take his hand again. Daisy grinned and decided that things were certainly looking up.

Chapter Eleven

Arthur could hear Brontë playing in the little garden on her balcony. She was a cute kid and he found he quite liked listening to her enjoying herself, or talking to her toys. She had a particular favourite, Mr Bear, who was worn out from cuddles and only had one ear. Brontë often told the toy about her day and her friends, or pretended to share her dinner with him if she ate outside. Arthur had seen Mr Bear with ice cream all over his whiskers, so he'd clearly actually shared the puddings.

He grinned, recalling his sisters feeding their toys biscuits and cake at various tea parties in his parents' tiny garden in London. His dad had despaired and was forever washing both children and toys in the bath, but his grandmother loved tea and cake and often joined in with the party when she visited. Arthur was sure he got his aversion to straight lines and clear surfaces from his grandmother, who adored clutter. Luckily his grandad was a perfectionist with his plants, and he craved space and order, so most of their house was pretty organised, although he would happily fill the whole place with exotic blooms. A few rooms were chaos, but it had been a wonderful mix of them both.

When Arthur had found out that Daisy had moved back, he'd been pleased for her because she had been so close to her grandparents especially, before she'd left. His anger at her decisions had been hard to shake. They'd been good friends as kids, but had drifted apart when they'd both started dating other people. For some reason neither of them talked about the time they had spent together and it certainly made Arthur feel uncomfortable because he could remember how it felt to hold her in his arms. It had scared the hell out of him. He'd messed it all up by taking one of her friends out on a date to put space between them, while he tried to think about how he felt. Unfortunately, that had been his biggest mistake.

He guessed he'd always assumed they'd end up with each other because they did everything together, but Daisy had then dated a guy from her design course at college and Arthur had ended up going out with someone he met online on a dating app that he'd joined for fun. It hadn't lasted, but the chasm between him and Daisy had never quite reset. When he'd heard about Harrison, he hadn't been happy, but his sisters had told him to keep out of it. Unfortunately, by the time Arthur had decided he'd waited long enough for this nonsense to end, she'd announced her pregnancy.

Harrison was six years older than them. Arthur had already heard of him by reputation, and nothing that had been said about him was good. Arthur had been protective of Daisy – fiercely so at the time, he remembered. She'd cut off contact when she went abroad, but even before that, things had been distant, as if his friendship meant nothing to her. Her news had blown his world apart and he'd retreated in defeat and licked his wounds by staying away from home, partying, building his own reputation as a bit of a ladies' man and becoming so successful that he didn't have time to remember the pain. It had hurt, but he'd moved on. He'd put all his energy into his work and now he had little time for much else, which suited him. He enjoyed dating when he had the energy, but it usually got complicated when they caught feelings, whereas he was always clear from the start that a relationship wasn't for him. He'd never met anyone who'd made him want to change and he was happy with that.

He heard Daisy go outside and help Brontë make a sandcastle with the new sandbox that Daisy's parents had brought the day before. Arthur wanted to pop his head out and say hello – but then Daisy might think he was being a creep and listening out for her. It was pretty hard not to hear, mind you, as the building was modern and they'd used every bit of space, even extending the balconies to make them brush up against each other. Other flats did have frosted glass partitions between the balconies, though, he'd noticed the day before. He'd meant to ask about that, but had been inundated with work. There was one between his flat and the next one along, just not between his and Daisy's. He was sure it was just an oversight in the new build, but in a way he'd got used to seeing Daisy over the barrier. He guessed that Daisy might make a complaint, as the last thing she needed to see every day was his ugly mug, but maybe she hadn't noticed yet either, as her flat was the first one on this floor.

The shiny, cool and muted new interior of his flat suited him well, as he hated fuss or frills, even though he was messy. He was used to his bed being made every day at the hotels he'd stayed in, but vowed to become tidier for his own sake... looking at piles of junk wasn't conducive to inspiring creative work.

'I think Mr Bear might need a wash after he's been to the beach,' he heard Daisy say to Brontë and he could imagine Brontë's pout of resistance, which made him chuckle.

'He likes the sand in his hair,' retorted Brontë and Daisy's laugh made Arthur's breath catch. He walked up to his lounge windows, but didn't go outside.

The exterior of the building was clad in natural wood. It fitted in perfectly beside the river and would weather beautifully into a silvery tone with age. The views across the water had sold the place to him, though. He could see Joe's steamboat come and go, and he could people-watch, without having to be amongst them. The other two cruise boats, owned by Alex and Luca Bowen, were berthed by the riverside. People booked river cruises from the little ticket office on the dock and often wandered into the café for refreshments, or to wait for their ride.

It soothed his soul to watch the ducks and swans meander up and down in the rippling water, while the comings and goings of people and boats fuelled his creative ideas. He wondered if he should introduce water to his offices on virtual screens to relax and inspire his workforce, and stored that idea away for later. He might even ask Daisy if she could create a few little oasis spaces, like the one she'd made on her balcony. It didn't take up that much room and the difference it made to how he felt walking outdoors every day, even though he had a magnificent view of the river, was testament to her design. The plants weren't even on his balcony, but the sight of the lemon tree she'd potted and the huge date palms and strategically placed tree ferns soothed his soul. He guessed growing up with his grandparents' wild garden further down the river had made him crave open space, even though he was often in the city, or holed up in a hotel room in a different country.

He could see how this place worked so well for his sister Maya and why she'd sat on the bow of *Bertha* for years and sketched her jewellery designs. She was too well-known to do that now, but he could understand the appeal. His central London office was surrounded by endless skyscrapers, which didn't inspire his imagination, and now he wondered about his staff. He found himself working from home more and more lately for his biggest client. Suddenly the water and its surroundings were re-energising his tired brain and he was able to get his workflow back again.

He hated to admit it, but Maya had been right. Being home and near his family and old friends did hold a certain appeal – and so did his new next-door neighbour...

Chapter Twelve

Daisy blinked and tried not to panic. Planning meetings with Penny were like a bucket of cold water to the face, it seemed! She spoke quickly and waved her hands around a lot to express herself, but luckily it was all due to her excitement about Daisy's beautiful garden design ideas. She didn't sit still, and threw even more ideas into the mix, almost giving Daisy a heart attack. Then she calmed down and brought frothy coffees to the table. She adored all Daisy's suggestions for the narrow space behind the café, and Daisy was buzzing and now a tiny bit terrified.

It was still too early for the school run, so she decided to stay at the table after Penny had left and treat herself to a slice of Fred's cake of the day, which seemed to be lemon drizzle with delicious-looking white icing. The zingy, fresh scent made her mouth water as she approached the front of the queue and the hum of conversation soothed her frazzled nerves. It was a good job she'd be doing so much exercise soon with the garden build, as she was using cake to overcome her anxiety about how much her new client believed in her.

Arthur paused as he reached the café door and frowned as he overheard some of the local school mums gossiping behind him. 'Did you invite Daisy to join us?' one asked with a titter.

Another laughed and then leaned in conspiratorially, but still spoke loudly enough for him to hear. He listened before he had to move inside. 'No,' said the one with long, poker straight dark hair. 'She doesn't really fit in with our vibe and apparently she's just a gardener. She told me she was a designer, so she's already telling fibs,' she tutted, as she straightened up and caught sight of Arthur. Her face suddenly lit up and she smiled at him and ran her fingers through her hair.

As he walked in, the group of mums followed behind and rushed to grab a table that they all crowded round. Daisy looked up from where she was sitting and gave them a weak smile before turning back to her tall glass of coffee and plate of lemon cake. She felt a bit stunned that they hadn't come to sit with her as she clearly already had a table, but if she was completely honest, she wasn't sure they were her kind of people anyway. She quickly retrieved her bag and placed her brand-new notebook, which had a leafy green image on the cover, on the table and her new recycled wooden pen on top, so she would look like she was working and didn't feel embarrassed to be sitting on her own. She'd occasionally popped into cafés with Brontë when she'd been smaller and had been fine with no other adult to converse with, but that seemed a bit of an anomaly here. People grouped together most of the time. She was sure she'd find new friends eventually and had spoken to one or two old ones, but most had moved away or were busy with their own families or jobs now.

Daisy had already realised that Imogen, the woman who seemed to be the spokesperson for that particular huddle and was one of the most dominant mums in the playground, wasn't interested in her inventive garden design business. The fact that Daisy wasn't a yummy mummy in swish designer clothes didn't help. She mostly wore old jeans and a white fitted T-shirt. She usually swung her hair up into a tight high ponytail, because she knew it made her cheeks pop, but it could also make her look much younger than her twenty-nine years of age. It seemed school mums could be competitive over all kinds of areas, including who looked the oldest. Poor Henrietta, who had a child in the school year above, had clearly tried some kind of facial fillers to keep up with the younger school mums and now looked permanently startled. The school grapevine said that she'd tried to keep it a secret and had visited some dodgy practitioner down a back street abroad, instead of a professional one locally, and now she'd given the gossips even more fodder.

Daisy hadn't noticed Arthur had come into the café until he was standing right in front of her. She darted a glance around at the rest of the clientele when he asked if he could join her, and then he sat down before she had a moment to stutter an answer. He was looking good in dark suit trousers and a white collared shirt, and he placed his own cup of coffee next to hers and eyed up her cake. She pushed it in front of him and he took her fork and gratefully ate some of it, moaning happily. Her stomach contracted at the sound, but she refused to flush in front of the other school mums.

'Did you forget breakfast again?' she asked. 'I can't

believe I'm giving you some of my cake. I haven't even touched it yet,' she smiled and he grinned, making her heart beat faster and her insides go all mushy.

Arthur stole one more bite. 'I had an early meeting in town and then got the first train back. My initial thought was to grab a bacon sandwich, but my urge for coffee was stronger.'

Daisy frowned. 'Where's the sandwich, then? Did you eat it on the walk to the table?' she asked incredulously. Arthur darted a glance towards the swarm of mums at the other two tables and then looked back at her. 'You didn't need to rush to sit with me because they wouldn't,' she added indignantly, about to get up, but he gently caught her arm and placated her. She sighed and gave in, filching the cake back before he ate it all and using the same fork, which seemed oddly intimate. His eyes grew dark as she placed the fork in her mouth and almost groaned at the sharp but delicious hit of lemon. 'Oh my God. This cake should be illegal, it's so good,' she joked, trying not to look at the dark pools of his eyes and remember what it felt like to have them solely focused on her.

'I decided I just needed cake when I got up there,' Arthur explained. 'But when I saw the slice in front of you, it looked big enough for both of us!' he teased, snaffling the last bite when she'd literally barely tasted the cake herself. Wow, he was annoying, but she had to admit it was nice to have an almost-friendly face to sit with when faced with a roomful of school mums. There had only been one table of them at the start but now there were three, all getting up to go and chat to each other.

'Well, it seems like you're a big hit,' said Daisy sarcastically, tilting her head to make him look to his left. He was clearly a subject of curiosity, because although no one had invited Daisy to sit with them, they were all looking her way now that Arthur had joined her. They were giggling like schoolgirls and Daisy's sense of humour began to return. Poor Arthur, she smirked, not feeling that sorry for him because he'd stolen most of her treat.

Arthur ignored her comment and didn't bother to look round. His sole focus seemed to be Daisy, for some unnerving reason. She supposed they had become kind of friends again, which was weird because they'd been inseparable once, then he'd broken her heart, and she'd vowed never to get close to him after that. He was familiar, though. She guessed that she thought of him as a surrogate brother or something, now?

'I have been meaning to speak to you anyway,' said Arthur, putting her napkin down after he'd brushed the crumbs off his face with it. She frowned and put it on her plate. 'Your balcony looks amazing and I'd love you to do something similar with mine...' when she was about to speak, he stopped her, by putting his hand on hers on the table but she quickly slid hers away before anyone saw.

Her outside space was a little haven, but she'd assumed he'd get an interior designer in, and then an exterior one if he needed it. His place was messy but sparse when it came to furniture. Excitement began to fizz in her veins as she pictured how lush his balcony could look and how much fun it would be to design, as it was twice the size of her own space.

'I'd adore that! I'm starting working on the garden here tomorrow, but I can begin your design straight after. What's your budget?' When he named a figure that almost sent her cross-eyed, she sat back and then took a huge sip of fortifying coffee, wishing it was wine. 'Look, as much as I'd love to take your money, you won't need to spend that,' she grinned and he seemed surprised.

Did this guy overpay everyone? She'd have to get him in shape and make sure he wasn't being ripped off. Then she remembered that he employed thousands of people and ran a successful business, and her eyes narrowed. 'Is this charity?'

Arthur sat back, his eyes wide and innocent as he protested how wrong she was. 'I just have no idea about garden design. It was a guestimate,' he said, holding his hands up to defend himself from her fiery gaze. They grinned at each other suddenly and the tension eased. They had enjoyed a few feisty arguments when they were together, but the making up afterwards had always been worth it, she remembered, her skin warming up.

'Okay. I believe you,' she grudgingly admitted, looking at the crumbs on the plate and wishing she had some cake left.

'I've also been thinking of creating mini oasis areas at my headquarters... kind of like little green creative spaces to inspire my teams to think outside the box. What do you think?' he asked.

'That's a great idea! I wish all businesses were as forward thinking.' She could have hugged him, but the school mums were pretty much all staring at her now. She stared back, which made them turn away and start speaking again, but in hushed voices. 'I'm not sure how I can juggle that with Brontë, but I can certainly visit your office and make the designs. If you like them, someone else can fit them if I can't.'

'We'll work it out,' he grinned, his smile infectious. 'I'm sure Brontë might enjoy a visit to a big city and if not, your family or my sisters are always talking about wanting to see you both more. They'll help, I'm sure.' A shadow fell over Arthur and they both turned their faces to look behind him. Fred had appeared from the kitchen, looking dapper in black jeans and a black branded café T-shirt that suited his slim frame. His smile widened when he saw Daisy.

'How's Brontë?' he asked and she flushed and noted Arthur's raised eyebrows and the craning necks of some of the school mums.

'She's great, thanks!' said Daisy, deciding she might as well enjoy being the centre of attention because they'd all been ignoring her at the start. 'She's still at school, but I'll tell her I've seen you and she'll probably want to pop by for some cake,' she tried to joke, whilst feeling Arthur's eyes fixed on her every movement. He was overplaying the protective big brother thing now.

Daisy could feel her skin flaming when Fred produced a huge slice of Victoria sponge cake from behind his back with a flourish, just for her. 'I kind of noticed that you didn't get to eat much of the last cake,' he said cheekily.

Arthur's eyebrows shot up into his hairline at the fact that Fred had clearly been keeping an eye on Daisy as well, but maybe for different reasons. She smothered a laugh at the look on Arthur's face. 'I've saved another slice for Brontë, so feel free to pick it up on your way home from the school run.'

'Wow! Thanks, Fred,' she smiled up at him, taking the cake and placing it in front of her reverently, nudging the empty plate nearer to Arthur, who wasn't looking so happy suddenly.

'Where's my free cake?' asked Arthur with a growl, as he watched Fred walk back into the kitchen. Lots of the women in the café also turned their heads to follow the confident chef's saunter. Arthur glanced at his watch. 'Can

I come and get Brontë from school with you? I need to stretch my legs.'

Daisy baulked as she was about to swallow a bite of the Victoria sponge cake. Her mouth was already watering to taste it and she frowned, as if she'd misheard. She looked at the clock on the wall behind the serving counter. She still had fifteen minutes before she needed to head off on the school run, but Arthur wouldn't know that. She put down her fork with genuine regret and then slapped Arthur's hand as he tried to pick it up and steal some. 'It will create loads of school gossip if I arrive with you.'

'Ouch!' he protested. 'Do you care?' he challenged.

'...Not really,' she admitted with a small smile, giving in and handing him her fork so he could sample the cake first, but he broke off a piece with the fork and held it up for her to taste. She blinked a few times in shock, but felt she had no choice but to take a bite. The cake was heavenly. She closed her eyes for a few seconds and savoured it. When she opened them, Arthur was watching her. He tasted the cake himself with the same fork again, which made her wriggle a bit in her chair. She couldn't take her eyes off him. Then she blinked again and the spell was broken.

She licked her lips and dabbed her finger into a few crumbs on the plate, eating them for something to do. 'Um... okay. Maybe we should take the rest of the cake for later. Brontë would never forgive me if she finds out I've been here without her and I won't have time to do more than pop in and grab her cake from Fred, which might seem rude,' she winced, but Arthur shrugged and grinned. 'But I start work here tomorrow, so she'll have plenty of time to come here then,' she added – and just like that his scowl was back.

Chapter Thirteen

I t had almost felt like an out of body experience to walk through the main road of the town and up to the primary school with Arthur, the previous day. The gaggle of other mums weren't far behind and she'd been able to feel their eyes on her back as she progressed up the hill. They strolled past the little shops on the main street. There were hanging baskets overflowing with plants outside some stores, Daisy had noted. She'd already pencilled in dates to speak to a few owners about maintaining them, and adding indoor plant installations to bring the outside in and match the historic shop fronts. She'd been happy to learn that many of the people she'd spoken to didn't have time to maintain their own shop exteriors or interior plants, so they'd been really receptive to her ideas from initial telephone enquiries.

'Arthuuuur!' Brontë had squealed in delight when she'd seen him, and she'd run towards him with open arms. Daisy had not known where to look, but he'd swung her up into his arms as if it was the most natural thing in the world. Arthur hated children, or the thought of them anyway!

Daisy knew that from the way he always shied away from topics that involved them, unless it was about Brontë, whom he seemed to tolerate quite well. Daisy had turned to see the surprised faces of the mums and dads behind her and that had made her cringe inside. Now she'd be an even bigger focus of gossip, over why Brontë was so happy to see the town's most eligible bachelor, and why he was hugging her as if he was family. He'd even taken the little girl's hand and her school bag, and listened to her chatter as they strolled home. After a quick detour to grab her cake and say thanks to Fred, Brontë had rushed indoors to devour her treasure.

'Bye, Arthur,' Daisy had said in a quick and rather uncomfortable farewell. Then, once she was inside, she'd leant her body against the closed door, letting out a woosh of breath to try and find some relief from the tension she'd carried for the previous hour or so.

Were they now friends again, or just ex-door neighbours? She still wasn't sure. Then she remembered the big fat contract he'd offered her and her heart skipped a beat. They were colleagues now, or they would be if she could get her pricing right, so she would have to make sure that she was polite to him and try not to think of kicking boxes out from under his feet whenever he stole her food.

Designing green spaces for a huge office block might have felt terrifying a couple of months ago, but Penny's response to Daisy's designs and the overwhelming demand for her interior and exterior plant services could literally fill her books for months. She also really wanted to find out more about the green space by the boats. She wandered over to the lounge windows to look out across the river. It was weird how much her life was changing, but she was determined to feel more empowered than scared, however

114

much her hands shook when she'd made the cold calls. The gardens surrounding the flats she lived in were shaping up nicely too. The pathways had been installed and the informal wooden seating she'd dotted around to inspire relaxation and conversation between tenants was already in place on the newly-laid grass. She was starting to enjoy the thrill of running her own business.

The doorbell pealed and she wondered who on earth it could be. Not many people visited her without calling first, other than Arthur, who usually stuck his head across the balcony as they were both in the habit of leaving their double doors open. She often took two coffees outside if she was working there as the smell would always bring him outside for a quick chat and then he'd take his drink and immerse himself in his work again. He'd had to travel abroad the week before, but he seemed to be at home a lot otherwise.

A huge smile lifted her face as she opened the door to Romy – Maya and Arthur's little sister. She wasn't that little now, at the age of twenty-seven. She was a striking blonde with deep brown eyes and a lithe frame. She always seemed to wear jeans with mud stains or paw prints on them and she invariably had straw sticking out of her hair from one of the animals she cared for across the water.

'Romy! Come on in!' Daisy leaned forward and put her arms around her friend in greeting. Romy hugged her back just as hard and then followed her inside.

'Coffee?' asked Daisy, already putting the milk in the frother, as Romy drank gallons of the stuff. Maya sometimes joked that Romy wouldn't be half as feisty without the amount of caffeine she consumed, but Daisy remembered how outspoken she'd been when they were little. She always won an argument, especially if it was about an injured animal or one of their household 'pets' – if you could call the snail and tailless newt that Romy had rescued pets.

'Yes please,' sighed Romy, inhaling the heady scent of the coffee as Daisy handed her a cup. 'I need at least four cups a day to wake myself up,' she winked at Daisy as if she'd been reading her mind. 'I wanted to apologise for not coming round sooner. I picked you some wildflowers from the meadow behind my boat, but the goat I'm keeping in my landlady's garden for a few days ate them! Sorry,' she said again, as Daisy laughed.

'Understanding landlady! Only you would tell me my flowers had been scoffed by a goat,' giggled Daisy.

'She rents me the berth at the end of her garden for the tearoom.' Romy looked at Daisy's desk, set out with her computer, and pulled an apologetic face. 'Am I disturbing your work? Maya told me about the garden design job for the café.'

'I needed a break,' Daisy said with an easy smile. 'Plus I've been meaning to pop over and see you too. Sorry.' Romy took her hand and gave it a squeeze and Daisy led her to the table outside. It was a mild day, the sun was showing its face and warming the air.

Brontë rushed in with a squeal of delight, hugged Romy around the legs and then explained about the special cake Fred had made her and how she needed to get back to it, with a very intent expression on her little face. Romy laughed and nodded. 'I understand the seriousness of time alone with cake,' she said as Brontë happily returned to her room after another quick leg hug.

'She's as adorable as ever!' Romy looked around the balcony garden in awe and then she put her cup down and hugged Daisy again, so that all the air was knocked out of her lungs. 'Daisy, this is incredible! I'd spend all day out here if this were mine.' She walked around touching the plant leaves and crouching down to examine the red and yellow tulips that were poking their heads above ground in two tall earthenware pots.

Daisy knew the whole family loved plants as much as she did. Romy's grandad, Owen, had made the eclectic collection of exotic plants in his garden magical and mysterious to them all as they grew up, which made them want to explore and discover. To Daisy, plants and nature brought so much joy to her life. It was surely magic.

Daisy twirled around and then laughed. 'It was the first thing I did with the flat, because we didn't have outside space in France. Arthur wants me to design a scheme for his place next door.'

Romy raised her eyebrows at this. 'Is he in? I really should pop and see him as well, I guess. My first thought was that I hadn't seen you in ages,' she grinned, her eyes sparkling with mischief. 'Is he annoying to have as a neighbour? He would drive me nuts!'

Daisy looked at Arthur's balcony and realised that he must be busy, or on a work call, because his door was shut and he hadn't already joined them for coffee. She wondered what he'd do if he ever saw she had company – but knowing Arthur, he'd join in anyway!

When they were settled opposite each other on the couch in her lounge, Daisy broached the subject of where Romy lived, in the big ropey-looking boat that she'd docked at a little jetty across the water. 'Is it comfortable?' she asked. 'How do you manage the tearoom, and what about the flocks of the birds that seem to have made a home on the outside? Sorry about all the questions, but I can see you across the water from here. I've kept meaning to walk round,' she said. 'It's just been hectic with settling Brontë into her first school and building my business. I can't wait to visit.'

'I only serve drinks, teacakes and hot buttery toast, but people seem to love it,' Romy said. 'The local kids want to see the birds close up and they find it hilarious when the temporary goat, Jeremy, eats their clothes. Even the mums don't seem to mind! The place is mobbed most days with dog walkers who amble along the riverside. I made the mistake of setting up a dog station and now I have hordes of them every day.' Romy rubbed her eyes and blinked a few times as if she was still stunned by the popularity of her business.

'Isn't that a good thing? And don't the dogs scare the birds away?'

'They don't seem to. I certainly wouldn't pick an argument with a swan, however big I was. Their beaks are ferocious!' Romy laughed.

'I'm adding a dog area to Penny's café. Does she mind about the tea boat, as its not far from her café?' Daisy had wondered about this when she had been looking into local competition for Penny's place.

Romy stared out to where her boat was sitting in the water and sighed. 'Penny doesn't mind at all. My place isn't in competition with hers. It's a bit of a mess to be honest,' she admitted. 'I'm dying to spend more time with Brontë, but I will have to do something about the state of the boat first. I've leased the berth for five years and need ideas to stop everyone moaning about the eyesore, but it's getting me down. Looking after the birds takes up as much of my day as the tearoom. I thought I'd have more time to walk along the river myself, after years of working all hours and being on call at the vets where I used to be a partner.

Now people keep bringing me injured animals and asking me to check their dogs' ingrown toenails while they wait for their coffee! How can a beaten-up old boat be so popular!' she scrunched up her nose in disgust. 'I came here for a rest!'

'Oh Romy. I'm sorry. I didn't realise. I've been so wrapped up in my own troubles,' Daisy said sympathetically.

'It's not your fault. Your husband died! You have every right to need time to heal. My relationship broke up was because he was still married to his work – and his supposed-to-be-ex-wife!' Romy seemed suitably satisfied by Daisy's gasp of horror. 'He was my partner at the vets I worked at, and he was full of big declarations of love. He forgot to mention he was still servicing the wife he'd told me he had separated from ages ago – and not just with advice about their pets,' Romy spat out.

'Oh Romy,' fumed Daisy and Romy smiled. Daisy did wonder if Romy left any room in her life for finding new love, now that it was rammed full of wildlife and rescue animals, but perhaps it wasn't the moment to dwell on that now.

'I wonder if it was more lust than love, but it hurt like hell at the time. I just don't fit in anywhere, except with my own very madcap family, of course!' Romy joked.

'Me neither,' said Daisy, morosely. 'The other school mums don't seem to think I'm cool enough to hang around with. Arthur decided to be my knight in shining armour earlier and walk Brontë and me home from school, after they didn't sit with me at Penny's café. The problem is that now I'm the hot topic of playground gossip!'

Romy's mouth hung open. 'How rude!' she said with fire in her tone, and then snapped her jaw shut and frowned. 'Did you say Arthur did the school run with you?' she questioned in disbelief.

'Um...' Drat. Maybe Daisy shouldn't have mentioned that. 'He said he needed to stretch his legs, but I think he was just keeping me company.'

'The problem is that where Arthur goes, gossip follows,' said Romy. 'It's not his fault, but women throw themselves at him! I just don't get it.'

'Nor me...' added Daisy quickly, not quite meeting Romy's knowing stare. 'Tell me more about what's happening with the tea boat. Maybe I can help?'

'That would be amazing,' said Romy, 'but I need to leave any renovations for a while so as not to upset the birds. They were there first. Changes in their environment might cause stress. I'm definitely going to do something to it next year, but for now I'm concentrating on making enough from the tearoom to support them as well. They need feeding up. There aren't that many of them, but as soon as I send one back into the wild, another one turns up.'

'So, who is bothering you about the mess?' Daisy asked.

Romy paused and contemplated before answering, putting her empty cup back down and eyeing a plate of biscuits that Daisy had just put on the table.

'Help yourself,' said Daisy, pushing them towards Romy in the hope that she'd decided she could confide in her. Her friend hadn't changed. She was still the same wild and self-sufficient individual she'd always been. Daisy wished she could be more like that. Harrison put an ocean between her and her friends, but even though she was now back she still felt like there were mountains to climb. Some of her old crowd had moved away and most had made new friends of their own. She didn't like to just throw herself on their mercy and apologise for dropping them, because she could never admit why she had done it.

Outwardly Harrison had been charm personified, which was the reason she'd fallen for him in the first place. She thought back to the tight-knit friendship she'd had with Maya, Romy, and Arthur too back then, and her heart broke a little at how much she'd let them down. Maybe she could do something nice for each of them and it might go some way to repairing the damage she'd done by cutting communication? She could start with tidying up the outside space along the jetty beside Romy's tea boat in her spare time.

'Do you know the Bowen brothers?' asked Romy with a snarl, which made Daisy turn and pause.

'Alex and Luca?'

Handsome Alex and Luca Bowen owned the other boats that ran along this stretch of the river. Maya had mentioned casually that they liked to flirt with anything that moved, and she wasn't wrong. It felt weird when Daisy's grandad had introduced them and they'd looked her over appreciatively. She'd almost forgotten that she was a woman as well as a mum. Her child had been her sole focus for so long that she didn't know how to behave and had blushed and stumbled over her words. Alex had winked at her and Luca had grinned and offered her a cruise on a proper boat, with a chuckle. She'd known they were joking and that there had always been friendly rivalry between the local boat companies, but she hadn't realised how heart-stoppingly gorgeous both men were, with dark good looks and lithe toned bodies. Not that she'd noticed... No wonder their cruises were always fully booked.

'That's them,' said Romy, breaking into Daisy's thoughts. 'Luca has a real problem with me for some reason. He can't seem to leave it alone. He thinks the boat is a blot on the landscape of his tours and he's forever stalking round and sticking his nose in my business.'

'That's awful!' gasped Daisy, scandalised. 'How dare he do that?' Romy's eyes sparkled at the fire in Daisy's. 'The land is legally leased and he's trespassing if you don't invite him in.'

'It's a tearoom, so I can hardly ban him, but he's just another thing I could really do without when I have birds to care for and copious amounts of teacakes to bake. Clara, the lady I rent the land from, loves having me there. She's quite a character.' Romy said.

'So, what's Luca's problem? I don't understand.'

'She likes having me there for the company, but Luca hates the messy boat being seen from his river tours. And I think he kind of enjoys the verbal sparring,' Romy shrugged. 'Clara just says it's her land and she can rent it out to whoever she likes,' she rubbed her temples and Daisy got up to make them fresh coffee. 'She owns the bungalow next to my dock. She comes to the boat for a teacake most mornings. She adores the place! We spend ages putting the world to rights and she's a bit like a surrogate grandmother. Not that I need another one with my very own Ettie,' she grinned. 'She's such a handful!' Romy followed Daisy as she bent to stack the dishwasher and propped her backside on the small island unit in the open plan all-white kitchen.

'Joe told me that Ettie held a dance class for her friends by the side of the river, but it was more like a festival with loud pop music. Apparently, they all wore luminous leggings and hairbands and everyone ran to the starboard side of the boat to see the spectacle. Joe wondered what on earth was happening. He said he should have known it was Ettie and her shenanigans,' Daisy snickered.

'That sounds like Gran.' Romy shook her head in exasperation, wandering around running her hand along the kitchen counter and admiring the plants. Daisy had softened the room with trailing plants and had stuck lots of Brontë's artworks around because they always made her smile. The picture of the river that Daisy had bought from *Bertha's* bar hung by the dining room table, making her think of her grandad every time she saw it.

'What's Clara like?' asked Daisy.

'She's amazing,' answered Romy. 'She adores the birds, even if they wander onto her land. I've got a duck with an injured wing who came from an old people's home. A resident had smuggled him into his bathroom after finding him loping around the communal gardens. The duck was swimming happily in the tub for a few days before staff discovered him,' she grinned and Daisy burst out laughing.

'I'd love to meet them all, including Clara. I can advise you about hedging and things you can do to give yourself more privacy, if you'd like?'

'The problem is that I know the boat looks like a dilapidated heap, a bit like me,' said Romy self-depreciatingly, glancing down at her dirty jeans and oversized sage green hoodie. Her long blonde hair was tied into two bunches and she looked much younger than her twenty-seven years. She was lithe where Daisy had soft curves, but both were fit and toned from hours of working outside.

Daisy would never think of herself as a knockout, but she knew that she brushed up well. Romy, on the other hand, was stunningly beautiful, even though her hair was always a mess. She had her father's dark brown eyes and dark lashes, and her mother's high cheekbones and elegant movements, even though Romy tended to stomp everywhere these days. Daisy would never squeeze herself into a tightly fitted dress for a night out, but she did like off-the-shoulder tops that swept across her chest and she was a magpie for jewellery in the shape of leaves, or petals. She'd love to own one of Maya's No. 1 Ethereal Lane pieces, but the thought of the cost of even a small item made her eyes water.

Daisy tutted at Romy and handed her a fresh coffee which she took as if she'd never seen one before. 'You always look beautiful.' She did, even when she was in a huff, and her inquisitive eyes and long sooty lashes meant she didn't really need make-up, not that Daisy had ever really seen her friend all dressed up.

'Food?' Daisy asked, glancing at the clock on the built-in oven and deciding she might as well have an early dinner with Romy. 'I can make us all some roasted vegetables and pasta with a spicy tomato sauce? I've got some left over from yesterday.'

Romy licked her lips and Daisy laughed and called Brontë to the table. A little blonde head poked itself around her bedroom door and then her eyes sparkled when she saw the plates of food Daisy was taking out of the fridge to reheat and she ran to join them.

'Do you forget to feed yourself when you're looking after all those animals?' Daisy asked Romy. When her friend flushed, Daisy turned on the oven to warm the pasta bake. 'Honestly! You're so much like Arthur. He always forgets to eat when he's working.'

'How do you know that?' asked Romy, waggling her eyebrows suggestively at Daisy, who rolled her eyes heavenward.

'It seems to me that he doesn't have time to open his oven, switch on a kettle or make his own lunch, so whenever I have food out on the balcony, he is like a sniffer dog!' said Daisy in annoyance. 'It's why we bumped into each other at

Penny's café. He has to grab sustenance from other places, or I'll hit him over the head with my breadsticks for all the food he steals from me.'

Romy grinned and didn't seem that surprised. She reached out for the steaming bowl of pasta Daisy had just heated up and bit into the crusty French bread she'd put on a plate next to it, crunching happily on the buttery deliciousness.

Daisy recalled her meeting with the Bowen brothers, but then her thoughts jumped to another man who was too handsome for his own good. There might have been more than a flicker of a spark between herself and Arthur when they were younger, but then Arthur had gone on to date so many of their mutual friends afterwards that she'd got fed up with waiting for him to realise what they had was special – a love connection. Clearly it wasn't, as far as he was concerned.

The last thing she wanted was to get into another relationship, anyway. She had to put Brontë first. Neither she nor her daughter were used to men hanging around, so it took some getting used to, having a neighbour who treated her home like his own, even if they were becoming friends again. He was annoying, but she also hated to admit that having an old friend so nearby was making her feel more at home.

Her parents had visited her in France from time to time, but Joe and Olive could never leave the boat. It didn't matter now she was home, but it crushed her a little to realise what Brontë had missed out on. Harrison might have been an absent father, but Gigi Joe was wonderful and her own dad tried his best, even if it had taken a while to understand how hard her parents worked to provide for her. She should have held onto that and come home sooner, but she'd felt that she'd caused too much of a rift by backing away from them and it mortified her to return home under such a cloud.

All she wanted to do was to work hard and build some security for herself and her daughter. She didn't need anyone else for that. She'd been on her own for so long at that point that she'd almost forgotten that she was ever married. Harrison clearly had. The problem was that she suspected he'd checked out of the relationship the minute she'd told him she was pregnant, and only dragged her to France with him so that she couldn't connect with anyone else. He hadn't wanted her, but he hadn't wanted anyone else to have her either, especially Arthur whom he'd disliked with a passion.

Chapter Fourteen

Daisy tapped on the balcony, their new calling signal, and waited for Arthur to appear. When he stuck his head out of the door she grinned. He looked like he'd been dragged through a hedge backwards. 'Are you okay?' she asked, trying not to laugh. He frowned and then quickly ran his fingers through his hair and pulled his rumpled grey T-shirt down, which made it caress his firm chest. Daisy tried not to stare, but she was only human.

'Were you serious about me redesigning your balcony and green office spaces?' She held her breath while she waited for a reply, but then had to let it out because he was clearly distracted. 'Don't worry. I can talk to you about it later.' She offered him the coffee she'd been just about to drink. He padded over in bare feet and gratefully accepted it, sipping it with a sigh. 'Have you actually turned your kettle on yet?' she asked.

'Too busy,' he responded, rubbing his eyes with his spare hand and leaning his backside against the outer balcony edge while he looked at her, which made a shiver run down her spine.

'What about putting in a divider between our properties?' she asked, as she tilted her head towards the other side of his balcony and the glass that separated it from the flat next door. 'I don't know why they missed the one between our flats. Shall we do something about it? We can ask the developer, or I can make you a wooden one?'

'I quite like the open space,' he said distractedly while he searched his jeans pocket for something and then brought out a pen that had a well-chewed lid stuck on the end. Daisy shook her head in disgust, but couldn't help but smile. Arthur was such a contradiction of productivity and chaos. They had spent quite a few evenings out here chatting over a fancy glass of wine – supplied by Arthur. They'd enjoyed some good debates and, although Arthur was still a flirty playboy and she was a bit serious and grumpy around him, they were both gradually lightening up. He pinched the bridge of his nose and looked out over the river. 'I'm a bit stressed and under pressure to deliver some tech for a new client. They want shortcuts, but mistakes can be made by cutting corners, so I'm standing my ground,' he said, pushing off against the barrier and handing her the empty coffee cup back with a nod of thanks.

'That's admirable,' said Daisy. 'Lots of people would do whatever they could to appease a pushy client.' Arthur watched her and his face suddenly lit up.

'Would you?' he asked cheekily. 'Will I be your boss if you redesign my balcony and office spaces?' He grinned mischievously.

'Certainly not!' she said pertly and he laughed, finally straightening up and seeming half-human. They both heard a sound and turned to see Brontë come outside and join her mum, slipping her hand into Daisy's while she hopped from foot to foot.

'Hi Arthur!' said Brontë, letting go of her mum and pressing her little face into the balcony, so that he had to crouch down to talk to her. Daisy tried to draw her away, but he waved his hand for her to leave it.

'Hi Brontë,' he responded with a smile. 'No school today?' Brontë giggled into her hand and then looked up at her mum, her blonde hair falling over her eyes, so Daisy brushed it out again with her fingers and clipped it back into place with the hair slide that was almost falling out.

'It's Friday, silly!' said Brontë and Arthur stood back up and winked at Daisy. 'I've already been at school all day. Now it's almost the weekend.'

'Goodness!' said Arthur, pretending to be shocked. 'Is it really? Where has today gone?'

Brontë looked under the outdoor table and then under a small golden plant pot, before responding. 'Well, it isn't under here,' she shrugged theatrically, and they all laughed. 'Can I come round and see your flat?' she asked candidly.

'Brontë!' gasped Daisy. 'Arthur is still at work.'

'It's okay,' said Arthur quickly. 'I really could do with a break – and you can show me how to turn on my coffee machine.' Daisy rolled her eyes in exasperation. 'How can a tech guy have no clue about household appliances?'

'Come round!' said Arthur, suddenly animated, which made Daisy pause for a moment. Brontë was a regular five-year-old who made mess and found most things interesting. She'd have his flat turned inside out in seconds. She went to get Brontë, but she'd already raced to their front door and was trying to pull it open. Luckily it was a fire door and quite heavy. She took hold of her daughter's hand, giving her a stern stare to ask her to slow down, which didn't work, so she gave in and let Brontë run towards Arthur's door and knock on it. He opened the door with a flourish and beckoned them both inside.

'I don't know why I was worried about my five-year old making a mess!' said Daisy as she looked around. There were piles of papers everywhere. Half the boxes from the move were still dotted around, some with the contents spewing out as if he'd rummaged inside to find something and given up.

Arthur took her comment in good humour and shrugged boyishly, which did something to her insides. 'I need to hire a cleaner,' he said honestly.

'Or pick things up yourself,' said Brontë candidly and Daisy couldn't help but feel proud of her child.

'Sorry, Brontë,' said Arthur solemnly, hanging his head for a moment. 'I promise I will try harder. I've been very busy with a new project at work and it hasn't left much time for unpacking, or cleaning either.'

Brontë stared at him with her innocent, big blue eyes. 'Mummy's busy too *and* she has a new customer,' she said proudly, looking at her mum with a big grin. 'But our flat is tidy. She works while I'm at school and tidies the rooms at night, and we don't have a cleaner.' She arched an eyebrow at Arthur and Daisy could see he was trying not to laugh.

'Good point, Brontë. I'll try to keep up with your mum. She is a bit of superwoman, but I could do better.'

'Sorry!' mouthed Daisy over the top of her daughter's head. Arthur sat on one the dark blue suede oversized sofas placed in the middle of the open plan room to designate the lounge area. It was the most relaxed he'd seemed in ages, even with a five-year-old in his flat and a deskful of work. Brontë chewed her lip while staring pointedly at a fresh box of printer paper and a stack of coloured pens that were in a silver pot on Arthur's beautiful desk.

'Brontë,' warned Daisy, knowing how much her daughter loved to draw. 'Wait until we get home and you can get your paintbox out on the balcony desk.'

'It's okay,' said Arthur, pulling out his desk chair and putting some sheets of paper and a handful of pens out on it for Brontë, who squealed in delight as it was a swivel chair and he spun her round twice first. Then she frowned in concentration with her tongue between her teeth and began to draw. Daisy winced as the desk was made of a single slab of granite and looked like a work of art. She rushed forward and grabbed a few sheets of the newspaper that had been sitting in the metal bin by the side of the desk and slipped them under the drawing, while looking at him as if he was mad, but he shrugged and moved towards the lounge windows.

'I saw out of the window that you were building sand-castles. I haven't been to the beach in a while,' he commented wistfully.

'I made a castle and *Maman* helped me make a draw-bridge out of sticks,' said Brontë proudly, puffing out her chest. 'She let me add a moat and we put a little boat that great-grandpa Joe gave me on it. It sank...' she said with disappointment. Both Daisy and Arthur shared a smile.

'I think the sand needed a drink, but perhaps we should add a plastic tub underneath next time?' suggested Daisy. Brontë tilted her head to one side while considering this and then nodded her consent to a good idea.

Daisy looked out of the window and across the water. She could see Romy's tea boat to the far left and Maya's house to the right. The main selling point of the flats were the views up to the town and across the water. The other cruise boats and *Bertha* were docked in front of the next few flats, which were great for anyone who loved a bustling river scene.

'Sorry. I couldn't help but notice the new sand pit, but I can put up that screen you mentioned if that would make you feel more comfortable? Or put film across the bottom of the windows,' Arthur offered chivalrously.

'And ruin your view of the river from your desk? It's ok,' said Daisy, and she meant it. It had been hard adapting to such openness here but she'd discovered that she quite liked knowing that she could pretty much call Arthur at any time of day or night and he'd come running. 'It's not as if I'll be laying out there in a bikini, and Brontë is just getting used to enjoying our own outside space.'

'Shame about the bikini,' he winked as Brontë wandered over to stand on her tiptoes and look out at the view with interest and Daisy flushed.

'Thanks for coffee earlier. I probably would have forgotten to surface,' he said, and she walked purposefully into the kitchen area, which was sleek and slate grey with fancy marbled surfaces. She ran her hand along the countertop and enjoyed the cool feel of the stone. She picked up boxes containing a toaster, kettle, and coffee machine and got them all out of their packaging, neatly packing the remnants back inside and stacking the boxes by the recycling bin. After about twenty minutes, she had everything in perfect working order and had even stuck some bread in the toaster for him. She paused when she turned because he had pulled up a chair next to Brontë and was writing some notes while she chatted away about her school friends and carried on drawing. Daisy felt the breath whoosh out of her at the sight of the two dark blond heads bent together, but then she straightened her back and walked over to join them for a moment.

The toast popped up and she opened the fridge, buttered and halved all four slices and the handed two to him and one to Brontë. She nibbled on the final piece herself. Arthur accepted his gratefully and devoured it in a few bites, before jumping up and joining her in the kitchen.

Daisy looked up at him. 'How about I save you some leftovers now and then so that I know you're eating, and then in return you can help me with a bit of heavy lifting this weekend?'

When he didn't look convinced, she tried again. 'You did mention that you needed to go to the gym, or become a couch potato.' He groaned and she knew she had him. 'Contractors will cost a fortune and I haven't heard back from the companies I asked to quote for labour to help with Penny's Riverside café design. I was going to have to ask my dad, or start chatting up the Bowen brothers.' Arthur growled at that.

'Sorry,' she sighed. 'I've no idea why I told you that, but I've been panicking a bit. You don't have to help me, but I wasn't expecting to land a job like this soon as I moved home.' She batted her eyelashes at him and his shoulders sagged in defeat. 'Pretty please?'

Arthur thought for a moment, then his eyes glinted with interest. 'It actually sounds like a good deal. I don't get out much, and I do need to start exercising. I was thinking of running along the river at the weekend, but this works.' He paused. 'Plus, I get fed.'

Daisy looked at his firm muscles and frowned, as it didn't look like he needed to work out more. She hated asking for help, but in this instance, it seemed like the only way to get Arthur to eat properly. She packed away any thoughts about why that was important and then remembered how close they used to be as friends. It must be because of that, she reasoned.

'Maya mentioned that you're travelling a lot for work?'

Arthur stared out at the river and paused before answering. 'I'm going to be at home more, but I will still need to travel. I've landed a contract that finally means that most of my customers have to fly in to see me if they want a meeting,' he shrugged.

'That must feel good!' she said, wide-eyed.

'It does. I enjoyed seeing the world, but it becomes tiring when every day is about work and you hardly ever see your family.' He rubbed his temples and then turned and grinned at her, which made her heart sigh. This man was just too damn handsome for his own good. 'I stopped over in France a couple of times to see you, but Harrison said you were out, or busy.'

Daisy stumbled back slightly and grabbed the kitchen counter for support. He literally couldn't have said anything that would have surprised her more. For him to have come when Harrison was still staying there meant this must have been soon after they left.

'I had my doubts about him and wanted to see how you were with my own eyes.' He held his hands up in apology but didn't look that sorry. 'I guess you didn't feel like responding to the messages I left, or my texts, after Brontë was born?'

'What?' Daisy could feel the colour draining from her face. How dare Harrison interfere with her friendships this way? 'He didn't tell me you'd been, and I didn't see any texts,' she protested, her cheeks burning in humiliation. 'He must have deleted your messages or blocked your number. He used to keep my phone near him most of the time and I didn't go out much while he was living there. After the first few months with Brontë, he complained about the noise and lack of sleep and pretty much moved out. I got a new phone then because he took mine.' Daisy begun pacing the kitchen and Arthur looked as perplexed as she did, before he bunched his fists and started pacing too.

'He left you alone in a foreign country with a baby and no phone?' he asked, scandalised.

'It was okay,' she placated, even though she wanted to scream and rant at Harrison. 'I was happy there for a while.' She went and stood by the window and glanced at Brontë, who was happily colouring in her drawing.

Arthur came and took her hands. She felt their warmth seep into her own cold fingers and she leaned into him for a moment, before pulling away again. 'I can keep you going now,' he said. 'I'm your new neighbour and we are friends, aren't we?' he asked, a naughty light sparking in his eyes. 'Friends keep each other happy and relaxed,' he winked cheekily, and she snorted a laugh.

'I'm not sure my thoughts on relaxation are the same as yours, Arthur Lopez,' she said pertly.

'We can compromise,' he hedged. 'I can massage your shoulders after a hard day in the garden and you can massage...'

'Arthur!' she admonished.

'I was going to say my feet...' he said innocently, with a wicked grin on his face that made her flush. 'What were you thinking of?' he asked, his eyes shining.

'Nothing,' she said as she walked out onto the balcony to cool herself down.

'Daisy, you really are so forward,' he joked and she slapped his backside playfully, which he seemed to quite enjoy. 'I haven't seen that side to you in a while,' he teased gently. She ignored him, instead grabbing a pen and notepad from the table outside and drawing a quick plan of his balcony, to keep her hands from sliding towards his backside again.

'Your balcony is an oasis while mine's like the dessert,' he said, changing the subject. His eyes had darkened and he was looking at her lips as if he wanted to kiss her, which made her heartbeat ramp up. This man was such a flirt! 'Although yours even has sandcastles now,' he joked. 'I keep wanting to climb over whenever I see you outside,' he admitted. He frowned at his own admission. 'It's much more fun than my dreary outside space, although I can't knock the view.' She assumed that he meant the river, but when she looked up he was staring directly at her and she felt her skin grow warm. She looked at her feet before meeting his eyes again.

'Really? Are you sure it isn't your stomach telling you that there's sustenance with coffee and croissants on my side of the balcony and it's that which draws you?' she laughed.

Something dark and predatory crossed his face and a frisson of heat shot through her body. He took her hand in his again and they both looked at it, but then Brontë rushed out onto the balcony, her artwork held aloft, excitement shining in her face. She showed them her drawing of the three of them holding hands as they walked home from school. Something cracked and broke in Daisy's heart, and she quickly stepped back, so that Arthur had to drop her hand.

Chapter Fifteen

Arthur should be working, but all he could think about was the delicious breakfast that Daisy and Brontë had brought round. Brontë had knocked on his door about an hour after he'd begun work and hand-delivered a parcel of childishly wrapped crispy bacon rolls with an extra drawing balanced on top. Daisy had been standing outside her own flat door waiting for her, and he'd solemnly thanked the child and taken the meal inside. He'd thought he would have been irritated by the interruption, but he was glowing, as if someone had lit a tiny fire in his heart and it was warming his whole body from the inside. This time, Brontë's drawings were of a blonde mother and child with big smiles and huge yellow sunflowers towering behind them.

He recalled the number of mud pies his sisters had made in the tiny garden at his parents' house in central London, and the sunflowers they'd planted along the back fence. They'd had a competition to see whose would grow the tallest, and they had ended up much bigger than the children. Arthur hadn't won. He was sure that Romy was adding pigeon droppings to her plants' soil, because suddenly they sprouted and left his behind. Moving to their grandparents' huge rambling house, and the beautiful garden beside the river lined with willow trees, had been a revelation. They'd often visited before, but living there had meant discovering all the secrets the house and garden had to offer.

His grandmother had far too many sewing rooms and cats. His grandad had too many sheds and glasshouses in the garden. Each child had been given their own creative space outside. Maya loved to draw in the big greenhouse at the end of the garden that was partially hidden by the boughs of a willow, and Romy had a small outbuilding that she filled with any injured animals that needed nursing back to health. Their grandparents were friends with the local vet, who showed Romy how to feed and look after the menagerie she collected. Arthur knew that had influenced her career choice, even though she was now running a coffee boat for walkers. She had always taken animal welfare very seriously and often brought snails, birds and lizards into the house, only to be shooed out again by their grandmother. Arthur had named his tech shed the Chip Shop, because it housed his computer chips, screens and games, but also because he used to take his fish and chips in there and scoff them away from his sisters who would try and steal his dinner.

He'd been fascinated by tech from a young age, and it also gave him respite from two bossy and nosey sisters. Maya and Romy had seemed to adapt well when their parents had gone to work abroad. Arthur had been twelve at the time and it had hit him hard. It had fallen to him to step up to protect his sisters and he had got in numerous scraps as a result. He'd never told them, but it had made him build a protective shell of faux confidence around his heart and mind. Computers helped him to slip into other worlds, and he became fascinated about offering the same for others out there who might be like him. This drive had produced a multi-million-pound company, but it hadn't necessarily brought him happiness. He wasn't unhappy, exactly, but lately he'd become more and more restless. At first, he'd blamed the lack of travel, but soon he realised that he'd felt the same for years.

He looked outside and saw Daisy with her hair pulled into a high ponytail. He could see the curve of her neck and he gulped, his mouth suddenly bone dry. She'd always had this effect on him, but he'd buried it deep down with other things in his life that he hadn't wanted to think about. She clearly didn't see him as more than a friend anymore, and he should understand why. He'd tried gentle flirting, but she'd shut that down pretty quickly.

After their disastrous break-up as young adults, he'd tried to make her jealous over the years by dating some beautiful women, but she'd just come home from her job in central London, gushing about bloody Harrison. When she'd told him she was pregnant, it had been like a knife to the heart that had almost brought him to his knees. He had thought he'd got over her long ago, but that was the nail in the coffin.

Finding out that Harrison had alienated her from everyone who might have supported her made his blood boil – but that was in the past now. Her family and friends were around her again and he was determined that life would be easy for her from now on. If that meant digging up the grass at Penny's café, to make her business shine, then he'd do it. He'd been so focused on the inside of the flat and the views, that he hadn't thought much about the exterior spaces.

When he'd seen Daisy's paradise of a balcony garden, it had made him want to spend more time there than his own home.

Daisy had landed back into his life with a bang and his slightly grey days were now filled with a kaleidoscope of colour, and sticky fingerprints on his hallowed granite desk that had taken months to source and was very expensive. He grinned as he recalled wiping the desk down after one of Brontë's drawing sessions and not caring a jot about it. He knew he wasn't as tidy as he could be, but his desk space had always been sacred before. He'd never even let his sisters invade his work area, but somehow he didn't have a problem with Brontë and her coloured pens. Instead of feeling annoyed he felt re-energised and focused. He'd probably got through more work in the past few days than he had in weeks. He'd even noticed the frequency of his headaches easing.

Suddenly everything felt exciting, and catching a glimpse of Daisy as he entered, or left, the flat, gave him a thrill that he was beginning to rely on, which also scared the hell out of him. He knew his sisters would have kicked him to the curb for thinking about Daisy again. They were the only people besides his grandparents who knew how long it had taken him to heal. Daisy had always held a special place in his heart and now Brontë filled a gap that he hadn't realised was even there.

He understood he had set in motion a chain of events that had previously caused him so much pain. He'd thought he'd got over Daisy years ago. Apparently not... He'd also been adamant that he didn't want children of his own because he needed to travel, but he was slowly realising that coming home to a house filled with Daisy and Brontë would make all the travelling worthwhile.

Chapter Sixteen

Splat! Both Daisy and Brontë were doubled up laughing as Arthur brushed wet mud off his arm. Brontë had just thrown it his way. She clearly needed a break, as they had been digging up the garden behind Penny's café for hours, but Daisy looked so cute in her jeans and mud-covered T-shirt that Arthur couldn't help but laugh. He took up the challenge and roared around the garden chasing a squealing child for ten minutes, then came back with her under his arm. Brontë had a bit more mud on her face and she had let go of her favourite orange trowel, but they were both giggling so much that Daisy only shook her head at their antics and went to get them all some ice cream from inside.

After much nibbling of the chocolate-covered ice creams and even more mess on their faces and clothes as the ice cream rapidly melted, the three of them looked a right sight by the end of the day. Arthur had felt extremely athletic whilst helping Daisy clear most of the long thin garden that ran around the back of the café. She had shown him her detailed plan to have a new patio laid around the whole area, then she would fill the garden with a plethora of plants and erect a clear-roofed gazebo she'd pre-ordered to complement her design.

There was room for lots of cushioned bench seating and tables and chairs along the back and sides of her carefully drawn-out plans, and she'd made sure her design was child and dog friendly. Dog cafés and communal spaces were a growing trend locally. The popularity of Romy's tea boat and dog stop confirmed this.

It sounded incredible to him and his heart swelled with pride. He'd always known Daisy was supremely creative and talented, just like his own sisters, but hearing her enthusiasm, and the ideas behind the things they were digging up and levelling in the garden, had actually been fun even though his muscles had protested by the end of the day.

After her bath, Brontë had fallen into a dreamless sleep tucked up in her little bed. Daisy had already had Arthur's dinner delivered to his door by one of Penny's staff. Penny offered a takeout service, and her longest serving staff member and stalwart of the community (plus the biggest gossip), Marion, had offered to drop it in on her way home. She'd given Arthur an enquiring look as to why they were bringing him leftover food up from the café. Daisy had called with the order because they were both too exhausted to cook and his culinary skills left a lot to be desired. Brontë had candidly told him this after tasting some spaghetti Bolognese that he'd toiled over for hours, even though it was packet spaghetti and a jar of sauce over some browned mince and vegetables. He'd managed to burn the lot, and Brontë had scrunched up her nose when she'd tasted it. Daisy had promptly got up to make some plain pasta and cheese.

Penny's staff knew Arthur well as he'd popped in with

Maya and Romy over the years. Now he rolled his eyes at Marion's smirk and knowing looks.

'It's not like that,' he protested.

'Hmm...' she responded. 'You behave with Daisy, young man. She's been through enough. Young Fred has his eye on her, I believe.'

Wow, the town grapevine worked quickly. Plus, was that what they thought of him? He'd had no idea. He frowned and looked at Marion, who cooked and served the breakfasts at the café and helped out generally. 'Fred?'

'Our new pastry chef,' said Marion with a smirk. 'I've seen them chatting and she's the only one he gives free cake to. Penny has noticed it as well,' she grinned as Arthur's eyes darkened and he frowned. 'Penny's a sucker for love, so she doesn't mind. We all care about young Daisy. She's already part of the community again with her precious child. It must be hard bringing her up on her own,' she added and gave him a wink.

'Oh, *that* Fred... Anyway, I always behave!' he said defensively and she laughed.

'Half the population of this town spend their days mooning over you and you don't seem to even notice,' chided Marion. 'Now that our resident movie star is off the market, you and those Bowen boys are the talk of the place.'

'You've got to be kidding me,' he said, genuinely shocked. He'd never had a problem attracting attention and the gossip columns seemed weirdly fascinated with his love life, but why would the locals care?

She smiled and bit her lip to hold back her laughter. Marion had seen lots of the local teenagers grow up and she loved a good gossip with his grandmother, which hadn't bothered him until now. Ettie was a force to be reckoned with and she kept her ear to the ground where her grand-children were concerned.

He groaned again and wondered how long it would take for Marion to tell his gran that he'd been up to his knees in mud helping with the café renovation, eating ice cream with Brontë and getting food delivered thanks to Daisy? He tried to call Marion back to explain further, but she was already walking away and chuckling to herself as she waved to him over her shoulder.

Chapter Seventeen

Daisy finally closed her computer and leaned back in her chair, her body aching. She was glad that it was a warm evening. She had enjoyed watching everyone stroll along the riverbank in the sunshine as she worked. She could even smell a few barbeques, and it was making her tummy rumble. She got up and stretched her arms over her head. Making a decision, she brushed her hair. She didn't need a coat, it was still warm out as spring had finally arrived. She grabbed her keys from the kitchen countertop. Brontë was at a sleepover with Daisy's parents, so rather than work all day and then sit and watch a movie on her own, she would go for a brisk walk, get the ingredients to cook a healthy dinner and then watch the sun set on her own balcony with a glass of wine. She was single and without her child for a night, and she needed time out to recharge her batteries. She was also kind of hoping that she might bump into Fred, if he'd finished his shift for the day at the café. She grinned at her own deviousness.

It was about time she went out on a date or two, now that her life was starting to rebuild. Old friendships were healing and she had a routine in place for Brontë. She could find time for another person if she wanted to. She was wary of introducing anyone to her child, but Brontë already knew and liked Fred. He often sat with them on his breaks from baking, and he chatted to Brontë with the ease of someone who'd had many brothers and sisters growing up. He had several nieces and nephews as well, and he'd shown Daisy photos of their smiling faces on his phone.

It had felt weird at first to be working there without Arthur, but she'd got into her stride. Penny didn't mind Brontë sitting at a table and doing her homework while Daisy toiled at rebuilding the space to match her design. The garden was shaping up nicely and the patio had been laid by a team of contractors. It completely opened up and transformed the space, and Daisy had gradually added planting in big dark blue urns that could easily be moved around. The fence would be replaced with glass balustrading the following week. The bespoke furniture was arriving the week after, which was exciting to think about. The whole plan was coming together.

As she reached the river and was about to turn along the path to the café, she almost walked face first into Arthur, who was carrying two coffees. He held the coffees up high to save them and she apologised profusely for daydreaming and stepped back.

He smiled down at her and she couldn't help but return his grin. She didn't often see Arthur on his own these days, as they were both so busy and he'd had to travel occasionally.

'What are you doing?' he asked, looking at her smart new trainers and dark blue leggings, teamed with a sky-blue slouchy hoodie. Most of her clothes were covered in clay stains from digging up the earth by the café, so she'd finally bought some new clothes, including a beautiful flowy wrap dress and some lacy underwear that made her feel like a million dollars, even though it was just for her.

'I've been working on my new website all day and I needed to stretch my legs,' she said. His eyes took in her new leggings and he gave her a wolfish smile that made her heart flutter.

'I can help with both!' he winked and she felt her cheeks grow warm.

'Arthur!'

'I can walk with you, if you'd like company?' he clarified, laughing. 'I've just got back from France and was desperate for a coffee and some fresh air after the flight.'

Daisy took in his suit trousers and crumpled pale blue shirt, his jacket slung over his arm. Arthur would look good in just about anything, she decided.

'I can see that from the two cups,' she grinned, trying not to look into his big brown eyes to see if he was teasing her or not, but she couldn't help herself. Arthur's eyes drew you in and held you there for ages while they filled you with carnal lust.

'One of them is for you,' he said, and she frowned. 'I feel bad for always stealing your coffee so I was going to drop one in. Plus, I missed you,' he added quickly and she wondered if she'd misheard. 'Where's Brontë?' he asked. 'I brought her back some French chocolate, as I know how much she adores it.'

Daisy's mouth dropped open. Arthur Lopez had thought about her daughter while he was working abroad, and brought her back sweets? Harrison had never arrived home with a gift for Brontë in her life. Daisy reeled back on her heels before taking the coffee, sipping it and watching him steadily over the rim. What was he playing at?

147

'Brontë is staying at my parents' place tonight. They'd have her every night if I let them,' she hung her head for a moment. 'I shouldn't have kept them apart for so long. It feels as if they are making up for years of absence as quickly as they can.' Her eyes stung a bit and she sniffed and looked away, brushing her hair out of her eyes and composing herself.

Arthur tucked the chocolate back in his pocket and steered her towards the river path, as she was at a loss for words. They walked amiably for a while and then he sat down on a bench that looked out over the river and she joined him. Confusion was rolling around her mind, and she'd completely forgotten that she'd been hoping to see Fred.

'I really did miss you,' Arthur said, staring into her eyes and making her own fill with tears for some reason. He blinked and looked away, so she did the same and sipped her coffee, not knowing what to say. She'd let Arthur in before and it had ended in crushing heartbreak. Could he have changed that much? 'I can help you with your website if you'll let me?' he added when she clearly wasn't going to say she had missed him too. 'You remember what I said about friends the other day,' he nudged her shoulder gently and she finally smiled. 'Not the bit about the massage,' he clarified, laughing heartily. 'Although I wouldn't say no if you insisted.'

'Arthur!' she chastised again, but she was grinning now.

'Let me help you. How about you bring your computer round and I cook dinner while we sort out your website?'

'I've been working on it all day, but it's pretty basic,' she sighed. 'We used to be good friends,' she conceded. 'Before we spoilt it all by getting too close.' She gazed at the floor and he lifted her chin with his fingers, so she couldn't look away.

'I made one of the biggest mistakes of my life and I've regretted it every day since,' Arthur said honestly.

Daisy sat back in shock and before she knew it her hands had slipped into his hair and she was pulling his face towards her own with a little moan of pent-up longing, all restraint snapping. His lips touched hers and a fire that had been smouldering for years suddenly sparked back into a torrent of flames. He dropped his empty coffee cup and groaned as he pulled her closer and she ended up half sitting on his lap as they deepened the kiss and his hands slipped around her back and urged her closer. A sound came from further along the river and they sprang apart as an elderly couple meandered along. They were in a leafy clearing that was sheltered from both the river and prying eyes, but now more people were on the path they just sat side by side, their breath coming fast and their hands still touching.

Daisy stood up for something to do and began walking back along the path to their flats. Arthur grabbed their cups, throwing them into a nearby bin and jogging to catch her up. She itched to take his hand again, but they were walking too near the town now and she felt muddled inside.

'Come to dinner,' he said again, not touching her, but matching her fast pace. She stopped and turned to him, her eyes roaming over his face to see if what she was feeling was mirrored in his eyes, but she could just see his usual cheeky smile and that he really did want her to join him for dinner. She had a feeling that this might end up as a disaster – but she was finally ready to open herself up and try.

'Can you cook?' she asked, softening her face and tilting her head his way. 'I seem to recall you almost burning our beautiful new flats down last time you tried to make that Bolognese,' she smirked, her eyes twinkling with humour.

'You know full well that I can't,' he admitted with a smile, nudging hips with her. 'But I'm willing to take a chance.' She hoped that wasn't also an omen for what had just happened between them.

'Have you had a moment to shop since you got back?' she asked, shaking her head in exasperation.

'Nope,' he laughed. 'I literally dumped my bags and then went out for the coffees. I know I should be good at looking after myself, but cooking fills my brain with dread. I can make a jumble of coding fall into place and make sense, but it just doesn't work for me with food. I love eating it, but whatever I try to cook ends up tasting like mud.'

'That's reassuring, but I agree,' she joked and he grinned, his eyes twinkling as the sun set and the skies begun to darken. 'The pasta you made for Brontë tasted like burnt straw...' she was in her stride now and he pretended to look affronted, 'That had been dragged through a sludge-filled pond,' she added helpfully and he poked her in the ribs, making her laugh and jump away.

They walked back to their flats, sexual tension sizzling around them. They decided she would order a takeaway while he took a look at her new website. As the sky began to darken, they both settled side by side at her work desk. He stopped every so often to nibble her neck and make her squirm, but she batted him away. She sat in wonder as he finished her site in what seemed like minutes, but must have been around an hour because the food arrived and filled the room with the delicious scent of noodles and lemon chicken. They took a break to eat and chat about their days and then he kissed her soundly before he went back to finish her site. Tidying seemed a good way to distract her frazzled and lust-filled brain and then she sat on her couch and pretended to read a book while she watched him out of the corner of her eye.

She refilled his wine glass and sat next to him again as he talked her through her new website, which blew her mind. She now had an up-to-date portfolio that customers could roam around and see in 3D. She had customer reviews, a shop site that she could sell products on later if she decided to, integrated newsletter sign-up forms and 'welcome' and 'thank you' messages for clients. It boggled her mind that he could create such beauty from her pretty basic computer.

'I've uploaded you some design programmes that I have for my staff, so you can change the theme if you don't like it,' he scrolled across the screen and clicked a few links to show her. She nearly had a heart attack because she had been worried that he'd destroy or change her beautiful new site. She actually wanted to sit on his lap and kiss him in thanks, but felt that was probably the wine talking. She was pretty grateful, though!

As if he'd read her mind, his hands slid around her waist and he pulled her closer. He looked deeply into her eyes and before she knew it, she was leaning in and kissing him. It seemed to open the floodgates as his hands moved into her hair and he cupped the back of her head and groaned as he deepened the kiss.

He picked her up and carried her to the couch where they wound their arms around each other, kissing until they were both breathless. He tugged her core towards his and she thought she might pass out in pleasure as she sat astride him. She put her hand on his chest to try and create a little bit of space between them as they were both panting hard.

'What is this?' she asked, not sure she wanted to know the answer.

'It's what it's always been,' he said happily, his eyes shining. He tried to ease her back into his arms, but she froze. He seemed to realise his mistake immediately, but she was already backing away. 'I meant that you've always meant the world to me,' he fumbled, and she tried not to pout, or punch him, because he'd hurt her regardless. 'You're one of the most important people in my life,' he admitted, and she softened a little at his words. He wound his arms around her and gently kissed her lips again. 'I'm not sure I'll be able to keep my hands off you, or you out of my mind, now,' he admitted with a frown.

'You'll have to try,' she answered, quite liking the feeling of being in Arthur's thoughts all the time. 'Let's attempt to cool this down a notch first and see what happens,' she said to protect her heart. She kissed his nose and he growled and pulled her underneath him so that they were both lying on the couch as his lips plundered hers, leaving her breathless. 'I think we've had enough years of tepid feelings,' said Arthur as his hands slid into the back of her waistband. 'I'm about to bring the fire!'

Chapter Eighteen

S unlight filtered under the edge of her bedroom curtains and Daisy stretched out like a contented cat and then pushed herself to sit up. She smiled a secret smile. She'd fallen asleep thinking about those kisses with her red-hot neighbour, and the fact that he wanted more sent blood fizzing around her veins. Arthur made her feel womanly and powerful and seriously sexy, but being near him had a dangerous edge that made her nervous. He'd taken his time reacquainting himself with every single inch of her body until it hummed with bliss.

Harrison had never made her feel that way and, although she didn't need a man to validate her, it felt good to know that a man as delicious as Arthur still wanted her. He had whispered into her ear what he was going to do to her, which had made the hairs on the back of her neck stand up and her mind remember what he looked like, hot and naked. It had almost blown her mind!

She was wary of falling for him again, but knew that wouldn't happen this time. She was too worldly and had a child to think about now. She knew that Arthur wasn't looking for commitment, so a mutual understanding from the start that this was just temporary would be good, unlike the last time where feelings got confused. She'd already closed off part of her heart to protect herself and had decided it was time for this single mum to have some fun. Especially if it involved a deliciously naked Arthur.

There would be times when Brontë was with other members of the family, and those times would now be full of play for Daisy too. The idea of a fling with someone as exciting and dangerous as Arthur actually didn't fill her with trepidation anymore. She'd got over that the moment he'd touched her, because the excitement was worth the uncertainty. She wasn't scared of having adventures, after years of solitary evenings. Knowing it wasn't going anywhere meant she was free of any shackles of responsibility of nurturing it. They could have passionate clinches together and then walk away and still be friends... she hoped. Arthur had candidly spoken about a recent ex-girlfriend called Lillian during their meal the night before, and she'd told him about her dalliance with Nico.

Picking up her phone after hearing it ding with a notification, she smiled when she saw a morning text from Arthur saying he'd been dreaming about her! She quickly replied saying she'd been too worn out from running her hands all over her hot neighbour to have time for dreams and he'd replied almost instantly asking if she was thinking of bringing coffee and morning kisses out onto the balcony. She took a moment to fan her face and wondered if many businesses started their day this way. She was certainly open to trying it, she grinned as she quickly showered with her favourite lemon-scented body wash and shampooed her hair. Leaving her hair wet and slicking it up into a high ponytail, she felt mean at keeping Arthur waiting, but when she finally dressed and walked out onto the balcony, he was sitting with his head bent over his computer and tapping on the keys in rapid succession while he worked. He was wearing jeans and a soft grey T-shirt and his feet were bare. She sighed and wondered if she'd ever not feel winded at the sight of him.

He looked up and gave her a sweet smile before saving his work and coming to take the second coffee cup from her. He leaned in and kissed her. Fireworks exploded in her brain as their lips met, so that she couldn't string a coherent sentence together. He stepped back and grinned with a 'my work is done' look on his face and she grabbed the front of his T-shirt and pulled him in for another kiss that left them both breathless. Having the metal balustrading between them seemed to add to the excitement and he put his coffee down and grinned at her.

'That is definitely the best way I have ever received my first cup of coffee. Shall I join you?' Daisy gulped because they'd just agreed they would take things slow, but she was picking up Brontë later that day and only had so many opportunities to be alone with this man. Just as she was about to speak, her doorbell pealed.

'Um... I'd better go and get that. Hold that thought,' she winked and went back inside. She was smiling to herself and wondering how quickly she could get rid of whoever was at the door, when she opened it and came face to face with her old neighbour and recent ex, Nico!

She gawped in shock. She'd often spoke to Nico via text since she'd relocated and their flirty banter was a lot of fun, but he was the last person she'd expected to open her door to. 'Nico,' said Daisy. 'What are you doing here?' He stepped forward and grabbed her into a hug and then stepped over the threshold and swung her around as she squealed in delight at seeing him. They'd become close in their time as neighbours, and even closer when they'd deepened their bond as lovers, but with Arthur still standing outside on the balcony, this had suddenly got a whole lot more complicated.

'I missed you, so I packed my bags and came for a visit,' he said simply, kissing her on the lips and then looking around with interest. 'You know I was going travelling? Well, I decided that I wanted to see you and Brontë, so this is my first stop,' he said in his sexy French accent that made her stomach flip.

'Oh... Um... that's great. Where are you staying?' she stuttered, glancing back over her shoulder to the open balcony doors. The doorbell went again and Daisy had a sinking feeling that she knew exactly who it was this time. She opened the door to Arthur and then stepped back for him to join them.

'I heard you scream,' he said, looking at Nico with a question in his eyes.

'That was excitement,' said Nico, walking over to shake Arthur's hand to introduce himself. 'I've just told Daisy that I'm staying with her for a while,' he grinned happily and then wandered out onto the balcony, exclaiming about the gorgeous view of the water.

'He's staying with you?' hissed Arthur under his breath. 'Why?'

'I have no idea! He's just turned up.'

'Tell him no,' said Arthur, watching Nico's every move. 'You have a small child living with you.' Daisy's head snapped up and she felt her cheeks flame.

'I am very well aware of that, Arthur. Nico is a good friend and he's welcome to stay.'

'Your ex, Nico?' he asked pointedly, turning to face her

as her cheeks flamed even hotter. When she didn't answer he sighed and watched Nico lean over the balcony for a better view of the old town. 'You didn't mention he looked like that,' he grumbled, sounding jealous.

'He's a model,' she said, trying not to laugh at Arthur's obvious discontent. She'd never seen him this het up before, but certainly wasn't going to chuck Nico out because of it. She was happy to see him, even if his timing couldn't have been worse. Not only did she have an ex next door, now she had another one in her house!

Nico came back in, his eyes shining. 'What a beautiful place to live. Obviously, I'd seen the place on our video calls, but it's even more *magnifique* than I thought,' he said, admiring the gorgeous setting.

'He's a model *and* French?' Arthur asked after properly listening to Nico's beautiful accent, which had always made Daisy go weak at the knees. She bit her lip to stop herself from laughing at Arthur's appalled face and nodded. 'Bloody hell. You split up with the young French demi-god, who is now in your house – why?' he asked them both, serious now. Nico eyed Arthur and then looked at Daisy who shrugged at the question.

'We decided to remain friends because I am going to be travelling, but I realised that I missed her too much and stopped here first,' hammed up Nico, watching them both carefully. He came and put his arm around her and pulled her in for a cuddle, which made Arthur fold his arms over his chest, plant his feet and look like he was about to announce he was moving in too.

'There's only two bedrooms here,' stated Arthur, as Daisy untangled herself from Nico and gave him a warning look, which made his eyes fire up with mischief.

'Nico, Arthur is my old school friend. He owns the flat next door.'

'Arthur. Arthur?' questioned Nico, his eyebrows rising as he watched Arthur frown.

'Um...' Daisy had forgotten that she'd told Nico about her 'old school friend', and she'd also admitted that she'd loved him once but he'd broken her heart. 'Yes. We dated when we were younger,' she added. 'I told Nico about it,' she flushed as she explained this to Arthur and his eyes narrowed.

'We were literally just discussing the potential of us dating again,' stated Arthur and Daisy jumped and decided now was the time to usher him out.

'It seems my timing is perfect then,' said Nico, straightening his shoulders. 'We wouldn't want Daisy to have another broken heart.' Daisy winced as Arthur digested this new information and he let himself be led out of the front door.

'He's staying?' he turned in the hall to ask incredulously.

'Yes,' she stated firmly. 'But he can sleep on the couch,' she relented and she saw his shoulders relax.

'I meant it when I mentioned us dating,' he said, leaning in and capturing her mouth for a quick kiss that made her want more.

'I'm so confused, I don't know if that's a good idea,' she said, pressing her back into the corridor wall for support.

'Because he's here?' he asked, but he didn't wait for an answer – in case it wasn't one he wanted to hear, she guessed. 'I'm happy to persuade you,' he said in a determined voice, dipping in for one more searing kiss. He put his arms either side of her, not caring, it seemed, who might walk by, or if Nico should come outside looking for her. He deepened the kiss without touching her with anything but his lips, and she groaned and wound her hands around his neck and moulded her body into his, her skin scorching even though he was barely touching her.

Breaking the kiss with regret, she stepped towards her own door, as if this would give her safety from dragging this man to her bed. She had another handsome man standing waiting for her in her lounge and she regretfully told Arthur that she needed to go. He nodded and went back to his own flat, leaving her standing in the hallway, emotionally exhausted and confused.

Chapter Nineteen

The balcony was eerily quiet. Arthur put his feet up on his coffee table and gazed out at the darkening sky and watched a few stars begin to shine. Nico had been in situ at Daisy's flat for two weeks now. He'd also been helping her transform Penny's café into some kind of paradise. Arthur had been invited round for drinks and he grudgingly admitted that Nico was a really great guy, even if he was scuppering any chance of Arthur rekindling the romance between himself and Daisy.

Arthur felt like he was at boiling point and about to explode, his patience with the situation wearing thin. He'd managed to grab Daisy for one quick kissing session when Nico had popped out for some milk, but he felt like a horny teenager. He was too old to be hiding behind corners and waiting for her 'flatmate' to go out.

Every time Arthur went to Daisy's flat, Nico was sprawled out on the couch or playing games with Brontë, which Arthur found himself resenting. He'd begun to build a bond with the child before 'Uncle' Nico had shown up and become her best friend again. Arthur didn't know why this upset him so much, because it wasn't as if he was in a relationship with Daisy, but more and more he felt like that was what he wanted... which almost sent him travelling again. But there was no way he'd give Nico the opportunity to sneak back into Daisy's affections. Arthur had been clear that there had to be boundaries – Nico was sleeping on the couch, and Daisy had agreed for now, luckily. He knew his fear of commitment was irrational and Daisy and Brontë were enough to make any man want to stay at home, but he couldn't get the gnawing fear he'd felt while his own parents were abroad out of his mind. He didn't want that for his own family, even though neither Daisy nor Brontë were his.

Both of them were caught up in work during the week, but at weekends he turned up to help in the garden at Penny's café and worked alongside Nico. Daisy had seemed surprised to see him, but they'd agreed, and he hoped she might have popped round to his flat on her own with food as part of their deal, but Nico had knocked on the door and asked him to join them for dinner a few times instead. He'd gone, of course, but Daisy had ignored his signals to try to get her alone – and Nico seemed to be putting down roots.

He heard a noise and looked up as Daisy came out onto her balcony, dressed in simple grey joggers and a fitted white T-shirt that melted to her curves. He'd never seen her look so beautiful, and he wished she was his, which made him take a step back and pause for a second. He'd never been proprietorial over a woman before. She came over to the balcony and leaned towards him, quickly glancing over her shoulder to check that Nico hadn't followed her out, he presumed.

'We haven't had a chance to speak since last weekend,' she said as he got up to stand near her, but he didn't try to take her hand.

'I thought you were avoiding me on purpose?' he asked candidly.

Daisy hung her head. 'I guess I just wasn't expecting us to happen again, and I value your friendship so much that I don't want to lose it.'

Arthur turned to face her, his heart tight with pain, but he refused to show any weakness. He'd have loved to pull her into his arms, but it seemed like she just wanted friendship and she'd hurt him before. He clearly didn't mean that much to her now that Nico the model was here. Maybe he never had. All the years spent mooning over memories of her needed to be packed away, he decided, gritting his teeth and looking out at the river, not taking in any of its beauty as the lights from nearby houses and restaurants reflected on the rippling surface.

'I'm okay with being friends, if that's what you want,' he made himself say.

'Friends with benefits?' she asked, but looked stung, and he whipped his head back round to face her in exasperation.

'Seriously?' he asked, then threw his hands up in the air. 'Isn't that what you have with Nico?' Daisy flinched and then gazed out at the stars in the evening sky. Boats were bobbing up and down in the breeze and a few people were walking along the riverside with their dogs, the wind whipping their hair across their faces.

'Nico and I are just friends now. You know that,' she said quietly, as if worried Nico might hear. She wrapped her arms around herself and he dipped his head.

Could he have a casual relationship with Daisy? He didn't think so. He might be afraid of marriage and babies, but he was more worried about losing her, which froze the blood in his veins.

'You know what, Daisy. Maybe that would work?

Neither of us gets out much and it's not as if we'd have to travel far for a booty call,' he said caustically, and she stepped back in shock.

'I didn't mean it with disrespect, and this probably isn't the place to talk about it,' she said hurriedly. 'I was just trying to think of a way to keep this light and make it work, without either of us getting hurt.'

'You think that's possible?' he ground out and she flinched, maybe finally understanding that for him it was already too late. She frowned and turned as Nico came out to join them, holding the stems of three wine glasses in one hand and a bottle of red wine in the other.

'I heard you two whispering out here and decided you'd had enough time to sort out your differences,' he joked, and then paused when neither of them laughed. Arthur waited for Nico to pour the wine and then took a hefty slug which made Daisy grimace.

'How long are you staying here for?' Arthur asked Nico, his eyes watching Daisy for her response.

'I'm working my way around the world, and I've decided to stay for another month,' announced Nico, his head darting back and forth between them. He pulled up two chairs on their side of the balcony and Arthur did the same with one from his.

'Do you want to stay with me while you're here, so that you have an actual room to sleep in?' asked Arthur casually and Daisy paused mid-sip, her eyes bugging out of her head. Arthur grinned, and her mouth dropped open at his tactics to get Nico away from her. Nico turned to Daisy and she shrugged, still gawping.

'It would make sense I suppose,' she frowned again. 'It is a bit squashed here.'

'Plus it gets a sexy French model out of your *amour*'s

flat,' joked Nico with good humour and it was Arthur's turn to shrug. 'I'm happy to sleep anywhere, but the couch is getting a bit lumpy.'

'Are you sure?' she asked Arthur and he nodded immediately, even though he hated the idea of someone in his space. He'd only ever lived by himself after moving out of his grandparents' home, but it was the only way he could think of to finally get Daisy on her own and make her see sense about this terrible friends with benefits lark that she'd mentioned. He couldn't have been more shaken by that comment than if she'd told him she was still in love with him.

Dastardly plan after dastardly plan flittered through his mind. He was going to accept her challenge to make this work. He'd show her that he was the man for her, he decided, and then she'd never want to think about living with another man, or let the opportunity to rekindle things with him slip through her fingers again. She was his and he was hers and it was about time that she found that out. Well, he was going to convince her...

Chapter Twenty

Nico snaffled one of the croissants on Daisy's kitchen counter and she shook her head and turned back to her computer. She'd just dropped Brontë off at school for the day and really needed to revise the plans for Arthur's balcony, and visit his offices to be able to visualise the green spaces he wanted her to create. She'd also been in contact with the company that owned the ticket office next to *Bertha* and the land beside it, and had pitched the idea of a playground area for children and adults alike, to relieve the boredom of queueing. It was weird to think that she'd be wrapping up her job at the café soon and moving on to her next client... Arthur.

The flat was usually quieter with Nico now living next door, but it seemed that some sort of weird bromance was happening. She often heard the two men laughing. The three of them went out together when Brontë was staying with family. They'd all been to visit Maya and Noah in his huge mansion by the water recently, and it had been 'interesting' to see Arthur in his swimsuit and little else.

They still hadn't managed to find much alone time with

Nico around, but Arthur had pulled her onto his lap for a few scorching kisses and he'd even pushed her up against the cool back wall of the flat lift once. By the time the doors had slid open, she'd been breathless and her hair and clothes had been all over the place. She'd quickly smoothed her ponytail and straightened her top, but Nico had given them a knowing look when they'd walked into Arthur's flat straight afterwards and handed him the takeaway they'd just bought. Arthur seemed to be taking any opportunity he could to refresh her memory about their chemistry. She didn't need any reminders, though. The air sizzled between them and she was surprised that neither of them had been struck down in shock.

It was as if Arthur was trying to make her into a nervous wreck of sexual tension to prove a point. If she couldn't run her hands over his backside, or touch his firm shoulders, she craved him like a drug. She was beginning to need his touch badly and it was literally blowing her mind. Her skin was super sensitive, and all the holding back was making her toss and turn in bed each night and groan into her pillow to hide her frustration.

'How's things working out with staying next door?' she asked Nico, biting into a crumbly, golden croissant and sighing in bliss as the buttery flavour and tart raspberry jam hit her taste buds. Her kitchen smelt heavenly and she was surprised that Arthur hadn't come round to steal some too. The radio was playing *Single Ladies* by Beyoncé, reminding her of the first sight she'd had of Arthur after returning home. He'd been singing along to the music, and she let her hips jiggle along to the tune.

She knew Arthur was working on another huge project, so they hadn't seen as much of him lately, but he'd taken

Brontë for a boat ride across the river to see his grandparents and he'd also taken her to meet the birds on Romy's boat, so that Daisy had been able to do some extra planting at the café. Both Arthur and Brontë had returned with stories of their adventures, and Brontë had a face smeared with chocolate both times. By the excited babbling about their visits, Daisy couldn't be too cross about the quantity of sweets her daughter had clearly consumed. Brontë had drawn picture after picture of the water, the boat and its swans since then, so Daisy had been able to get even more designs completed, while her daughter happily scribbled away.

'Arthur keeps leaving travel brochures and printouts of exciting experiences abroad in my room,' laughed Nico between mouthfuls. 'I told him the other night that I might stay longer because his flat is beautiful and spacious,' he grinned. 'He's so easy to wind up.'

'You've already brought your ticket to Portugal!' she chided.

'He doesn't need to know that,' chuckled Nico and she couldn't help but laugh too.

'He knows we are just friends now, right? You two seem to get on surprisingly well,' she said.

'He does – we do! I'm surprised as well, because I was helping you avoid any more entanglements with Arthur at first, plus I was a bit jealous,' he admitted bashfully, and she flushed.

'I'm sorry,' she bowed her head, but he came over and hugged her.

'We'd agreed to stay friends ages ago and I'm not surprised that you were drawn back together with your history,' he nudged her shoulder and she smiled.

'If the timings were different, who knows what might

have happened when you arrived,' she said. 'Arthur and I aren't together, though,' Daisy added.

'But he clearly wants you to be, *ma chérie*,' said Nico seriously. Daisy smiled at being called his darling and snuggled into his arms, just as Arthur walked in and huffed.

'Nico left the door ajar when he came in. Anyone could have walked in and murdered you both,' he said, in annoyance.

'I left the door open for you,' Nico grinned. 'It's why I left a shoe propping it open. It's a fire door! And if anyone is going to be killed, it would be me from the way you are looking at me with my arm around your girl,' he laughed and Arthur muttered under his breath and went to get some butter out of the fridge for his croissants, which made both Daisy and Nico stifle a giggle. 'Are you coming to the opening of the café garden later? Penny was very appreciative when she saw the finished design,' Nico grinned.

'So appreciative that she threw her arms around you and planted a kiss on your lips!' teased Daisy, nudging his hips with her own and grabbing a croissant before Arthur ate them all. Arthur's head whipped round with interest and suddenly he was all smiles.

'You and Penny?' he asked in astonishment. Coming over and slapping Nico on the back, his earlier mood was suddenly nowhere to be seen.

'I have been known to attract a beautiful woman before, *mon ami*,' Nico winked at Daisy and just like that Arthur was scowling again.

Daisy shook her head in exasperation. 'Look. I have too much to do to be standing around while you two annoy each other. The café garden is opening at lunchtime, and I've got a whole lot of detailing to set up.' She looked at Nico. 'Are you free to help me?'

'Of course!' said Nico with a flourish and a bow.

'Arthur?' she asked, whipping the plate away from him and shoving it in the dishwasher for later.

'I've got to finish the piece of coding I'm working on, but I'll definitely be there for the grand opening. I think Maya and Romy are coming here first. We'll walk over together.'

'Okay,' said Daisy, not having time to stand between these two any longer and needing to get the boxes by the door to the café as soon as she could. Four more boxes had been delivered to the site and she was itching to sort out the final settings. She had ordered beautifully textured little brushed metal plant pots, with fairy lights entwined in the foliage, to sit on each table, and the deep blue leaf pattern cushions for the seating that she'd had custom made had arrived the day before.

'Brontë is being picked up and brought down by my mum and dad after school and Grandad has been advertising the café garden on board *Bertha*, so we are hoping for a full house.'

She bent into one of the boxes and pulled out two dark blue branded aprons for the café, with scrolled lettering saying 'Riverside' on the front. She handed one to each of them. 'The bar is being staffed but we might need extra pairs of hands, so these are for you.'

Both men took their apron without a word and before they could comment, she'd waved goodbye, picked up two boxes and tilted her head towards the others and then looked at Nico, who quickly rushed to follow suit. Then she walked out of her own front door and left Arthur standing there, holding an apron and shaking his head at her cheek.

Chapter Twenty-One

Cursing and tying the apron around his waist, Arthur tried to hurry his sisters up to Riverside. Could they amble along any more slowly? He couldn't wait to see how the finished garden design looked after hours and hours of lugging rockery rocks around and digging up pathways. He'd had his own workload to contend with, so he hadn't been to the café for the past week and the old fences had still been in place a few days ago. Daisy had insisted they stayed until the last minute to build up excitement about what was going to be revealed inside.

The café garden was long and ran around the whole building, but Daisy had cleverly maximised the space with bench seating with hidden storage and a new outdoor coffee bar that could be used for parties. The whole place was dog friendly, with dog bowls, a doggie menu of chicken pieces and sausages, and Fred had even made organic dog chews. Daisy had thought of everything – all the bowls and accessories were deep blue and had gold scrolled lettering saying 'Riverside'. She'd even ordered some dog beds, so that dogs could snuggle up while their families ate dinner or enjoyed some drinks.

The dog community locally was huge, with people walking their dogs wherever you went, so this was a smart business decision by Penny, who hadn't had space for dogs before.

Arthur swore loudly. He'd wanted to get to the café early, but Romy had had a disaster with another injured duck being delivered to her door earlier that morning, and apparently a stray cat had tried to eat it for breakfast before Romy had dived in. She'd probably saved the cat rather than the duck. Arthur wouldn't have fancied the cat's chances against a spirited mallard. Arthur had tried not to laugh, but there was a never-ending history of drama with his younger sister. Maya had been just as bad for a while, but her eyes shone with happiness now and she also seemed more relaxed, even with the press interest in her business and boyfriend. It hadn't stopped her sticking her nose into his love life, though, as he'd barely opened the door before they'd asked who he was dating.

'We're late,' he'd grumbled good-naturedly to his siblings when they finally arrived.

'I can't help my timing, when people keep leaving sick animals at my door and then running off!' said Romy in exasperation. 'I've barely had time to brush my hair today.' Both Maya and Arthur eyed a stray twig that was sticking out of it, and Romy sighed and pulled it out before throwing it at Arthur's head. He ducked and laughed, but she poked him in the ribs. 'What's with the apron? Are you working for Penny on the side?' she gave him a lewd wink and he rolled his eyes and ignored her.

'Where is your gorgeous new flatmate?' asked Maya in jest, watching her brother carefully for his response. Arthur guessed that the girls had talked, and that Maya would know Daisy and Nico's history.

'He's overstayed his welcome,' he said in a jokey tone – but he was deadly serious. Maya looked pleased by this response for some reason, but he didn't have time to figure that one out now.

As they approached the café, he was glad to finally be there as the place was swarming with people already and it had only opened five minutes before. They all stopped in awe when they worked their way through the crowd and saw the garden. Daisy was at the centre with Penny. Both were handing out free coffees and teas. They wore branded aprons, like the one Arthur was wearing. The bench seating was covered by a wooden awning with a clear roof, so customers could watch the stars and the space could be used at any time and in any weather. Daisy had installed modern slatted trellises wound with ivy, interspersed with hanging outdoor heaters. It gave each table a feeling of privacy, but meant everything could still be moved to accommodate larger parties of people.

The old fence had finally come down and the clear glass balustrading meant that from most of the garden, you could see further down the river and the boats, or up towards the pretty town. Each table had real plants in beautiful little pots. There were loads of dogs and their owners, sitting and chatting happily, fetching water from the dog station, or ordering snacks and a doggie menu for their canine family and friends. There was an interactive code set into each table so customers could scan it and order directly from their phones, which would keep foot-flow to a minimum between tables. The outdoor bar was strung with lights that zig-zagged across the space to make its own twinkly canopy. It really was breathtaking.

'Wow,' said Maya, gazing around and taking it all in. Romy accepted an Irish coffee laced with whiskey, sugar and whipped cream from a passing waiter and then grinned when she realised it was Nico. 'Stunning as always, ladies!' he greeted them all, kissing the women on both cheeks whilst complimenting their beauty, making them blush.

Arthur shook his head in despair, before poking Maya and making her jump to snap out of it. They made their way to Daisy, whose cheeks were red from all the excitement. After hugs and kisses all round, she asked Arthur if he could help out behind the bar. He'd much rather have stood by her side and fought off all the interested glances coming her way from the locals, not to mention the sudden interest in her from the school mums who were all ooing and ahhing over the success of the garden. He gave Daisy an extra hug of support and whispered how proud he was of her, and that he'd like to celebrate properly with her later. She went bright red and he noticed both his sisters standing to one side with a 'what the hell?' look on their faces. He cursed under his breath and headed in the opposite direction towards the bar.

Arthur didn't have time to think for the next few hours, but suddenly there was a small hand grabbing onto his leg and he grinned and swung Brontë up into his arms. He gave her a hug and then safely settled her onto one side of the bar where she could see everything and not get trampled on. Daisy's parents came and said hello, as they were looking after Brontë, and he began to sweat. Obviously, they knew his old history with Daisy, but he hadn't seen them in a while. Brontë was chatting happily to him about her day and then Maya and Romy joined them. Maya raised an eyebrow about how comfortable Brontë seemed with him and he shrugged and then smiled as Daisy's parents retrieved their granddaughter and went to chat to some friends. Arthur let out a breath he didn't know he'd been holding as the sun dipped below the horizon. Evening lighting sparkled in the inky black sky, reflecting off the shiny surfaces of the balustrading. People were still walking down from the town and could now see into the garden, so they kept adding to the throng of people. Eventually it spilled out over the promenade, and a party vibe filled the air. More drinks were served and clean glasses searched for as the evening ramped up.

Arthur felt fit to drop with exhaustion, but Daisy's eyes were still shining and she was talking animatedly to everyone. Nico approached her and swung her up into his arms and kissed her on the lips in congratulation, as everyone watched on and cheered – and just like that, Arthur's black mood was back.

Maya and Romy exchanged glances as people started to say their goodbyes and wander home. Arthur began stacking glasses to go into the industrial dishwasher and packing away supplies. His sisters moved behind the bar and began clearing plates that had been used to circulate food samples and temptingly stacked mini burgers. The delicate pastries that Fred had made had all been eaten within the first two hours. Arthur had managed to snaffle one and, credit where it was due, it had literally melted in his mouth. He hadn't been quick enough to grab a burger, and his stomach was rumbling now. He'd noticed Fred's eyes following Daisy here and there, and he couldn't fault his taste. Daisy's skin was glowing and she'd removed the apron and was wearing a sage green dress that crossed over at her chest and tied at her waist that he'd love to tug open. The dress skimmed her curves and stopped just above her knees, giving a glimpse of well-toned leg.

Arthur wondered why he hadn't pushed the status of whatever was happening between them, but he did know that he craved more time alone with her. He missed their longing glances over the balcony while they shared a glass of wine, and their mind-bending kisses when they were finally alone. Bloody Nico had put paid to anything else happening and Arthur was ready to pay for him to literally travel wherever the hell he wanted, if it finally meant time alone with Daisy. Supposing she'd changed her mind and liked Nico again? Arthur couldn't help fretting. She certainly hadn't made any real moves to show she was still interested in him, however much she enjoyed his kisses. His ego had taken a hit, but he'd been busy at work and the only thing he'd been able to do was move Nico in, which in turn scuppered any chance of alone time.

'What's going on?' demanded Romy, as she placed the last dry plate on the built-in outdoor shelves. They all watched Daisy bend down and hug Brontë and pull her into her arms. The little girl's head drooped onto her mother's shoulder and she linked her arms around her neck, her eyelids fluttering closed. Arthur winced at his sister's interrogation, but he couldn't take his eyes off Daisy and Brontë. He had a funny feeling in his tummy that he would lay down his life to protect them both, but he guessed he'd do that for most of his friends and family and firmly shoved that feeling away.

'Daisy's got history with Nico,' he grumbled.

'So?' asked Romy, waspishly. 'I wish I had. Lucky Daisy!' When Arthur finally turned back to his sisters and bit back an angry retort, Romy carried on regardless. 'What's that got to do with you?' She waited for an answer and then slapped the palm of her hand on her forehead and Maya groaned.

175

'Arthur!' they said in unison, and he wished he could run to his Chip Shop shed and hide, as he had as a teenager. His sisters were definitely about to show their wrath.

'Not Daisy!' said Romy, her fists bunching like they had when they were kids. They didn't often get into scuffles as adults but still relished winding each other up for fun. Romy looked like she'd enjoy blacking his eye right now.

'Not again, unless you're serious about her!' warned Maya, her eyes spitting fire. Arthur shrunk away and put his hands up in his own defence.

'Suck it up, or commit,' demanded Romy, brandishing a spoon his way and waving it about. He shuddered to think what the hell she planned to do with it. Maya took the spoon from Romy and put it back down. She placed her hand on Arthur's arm to gain his attention. He loved his sisters and always listened to their advice, but that didn't mean he always heeded it.

'Arthur,' said Maya, as if she was also controlling her temper and with great effort. 'There is a child involved now. You've always blamed Mum and Dad being away as an excuse not to get involved with anything serious, but we all felt you'd made a mistake with Daisy.'

His cheeks flushed, but luckily it was fairly dark now and they probably couldn't see. He knew Maya was right. 'Mum and Dad *always* let us know they loved us,' she went on. 'We knew they were coming home from time to time and although the situation wasn't ideal, we were safe and loved.'

Romy shook her head at his stupidity and he winced. 'Just because you work away a lot, it doesn't mean you can't have a family, you numb nuts,' she picked up the spoon again and then seemed to think better of it and gave him a hug instead, which he sank into. His sisters were mostly annoying, but they meant more to him than anything else in the world and he knew they were always on his side, even if they thought he was wrong.

'But they'll feel abandoned... like we did,' he said lamely.

'Mum and Dad didn't abandon us, little brother,' said Maya kindly, smoothing his hair out of his eyes like she'd done when they were children. 'They gave us a magical childhood with the people who loved us most, after them. They have skills that save lives and yes, maybe they should have thought more about having kids – but if they had, we wouldn't be here!'

'You are not them,' said Romy, clipping the top of his head with her hand to make him listen. 'Daisy and Brontë are not us. If you travel it's just for a few days, and maybe they'd want to travel with you. Have you spoken to Daisy about how you feel?'

'She wanted friends with benefits, but then Nico showed up,' he said glumly.

Maya and Romy howled with laughter suddenly and Arthur's face got even hotter. His sisters were holding their stomachs, tears springing to their eyes as they wiped them away with the back of their hands.

'Oh, how the tables have turned,' howled Romy, until Arthur nudged her and she had to grab the bar for support. 'You're an idiot. Why the hell haven't you made your intentions clear if that's not what you want? It isn't like you to stand back and let another guy win.'

'I'm not even sure she's interested in me,' he sighed, running his fingers through his hair and then stopping as the place Romy had swiped stung.

'Have you told her that you like her – that you've always liked her?' asked Romy.

'What?' he frowned.

'You followed her to Paris even though she was pregnant with another man's child...' she added.

'I was just checking up on her,' he protested to raised eyebrows and silence.

'I think we all need a proper drink,' said Maya, and Arthur and Romy nodded. 'Let's offer to walk home with Daisy and Brontë and then she can join us for a drink on your balconies when Brontë's sound asleep. I'll carry her for Daisy as she must be exhausted, and you grab a couple of bottles of fizz. We need to celebrate Daisy's success.'

'Did you know that Maya purposely asked her developer friend not to add a partition between yours and Daisy's balconies?' asked Romy jovially and Arthur gawped, speechless for once. 'Now we need to hatch another plan to make Daisy realise that you are husband material,' winked Romy and Arthur almost spat out the beer he'd just begun to sip.

Chapter Twenty-Two

A rthur was still like a bear with a sore head when they all got back to his flat. They'd completely forgotten about Nico, but he'd jogged up and joined them as they'd walked back up the hill. Arthur had carried Brontë who immediately fell asleep in his arms, her head resting on his shoulder, her blonde hair fanning across his back and her little arms linked around his neck. His heart had squeezed with love for her and he'd hugged her close to his chest. The problem was that Daisy was exhausted too, so Nico had given her a piggyback home. Arthur promptly felt all his earlier certainty, that his incredibly annoying and interfering sisters were going to help him win the girl of his dreams, fizzle away.

He'd ignored the husband comment, but so much for their plan for him to show Daisy he was indispensable when they got back to the flat. They hadn't banked on the dashing Frenchman wooing Daisy with his lilting accent and confusing chats in French. Arthur found it incredibly sexy to hear Daisy speak French, but the fact that it was always Nico she spoke to poured cold water on any good vibes. The man just wouldn't go away! Arthur actually liked him a lot and if they hadn't been interested in the same woman, they'd probably be great friends, but Arthur always felt proprietorial when Daisy was near now. Not because he wanted to dominate her, although he'd happily roleplay in bed if that made her pant his name – he tucked that thought away for later – but because his heart beat differently when she was near, which he guessed was why he'd never really got over her.

Their friendship was something he'd always treasured, but he'd messed things up bigtime before. Now he'd begun to dream about what little brothers or sisters for Brontë might look like, and this shook him to his core. His own warm skin tone, dark brown eyes and hair that curled at his neck reflected his dad's Mexican heritage more that his mum's British descent. He often thought that Romy got her expressive gestures and passionate nature from their mum, but he guessed that they were all like that. Their dad was driven and loving and they had learned that from him too. Even though his parents had been abroad a lot when they were growing up, they'd managed to instil their core values in their children. Arthur had always known he was loved, however much he'd missed them.

Daisy, unlike him, had a fair complexion, with cute freckles dotted all over her nose. Brontë had those too. If he and Daisy had a child... he stopped suddenly and his hands began to sweat. He looked at Romy who was smirking at his discomfort, and then she saw something was genuinely wrong and she steered him inside to the kitchen.

'I think... I know... that I really like her,' he admitted in a panic-stricken voice. 'What am I going to do?' Romy pulled him in for a big squeeze and he sank gratefully into her arms, glad that Nico was outside on the balcony with Maya, waiting for Daisy to put Brontë to bed. He could feel the warm evening breeze filter into the room from the open sliding doors and the chatter from the nearby bars and restaurants that were dotted along the road further along from the flats. They were a mecca for tourists, with outdoor tables overflowing with small urns of trailing plants and lanterns that glowed gently in the moonlit night, while tempting scents of sizzling barbeque-basted meat and vegetables wafted as you walked past.

'Firstly... breathe. It's okay to have strong feelings for someone. I know I got hurt, Maya too, but we both turned out okay, didn't we?' When he frowned she poked him in the ribs and he grinned. His sisters always knew how to pull him out of the doldrums.

'You're still single,' he pointed out and got another sharper poke in the ribs from his sister that made him jump.

'Yes, well. I choose to be that way. Men annoy me, present company included,' she winked and he laughed, kissing the top of her head. 'Daisy will be wary of you, because you let her down.' That stung. 'Prove to her what a stand-up guy you are now. You've always been one, you just got scared,' she soothed, and he went to the fridge to hide his own blushes. 'Plus Nico's just told us that he's off to Portugal in the next few days,' she grinned and he swung round in shock.

'What? Finally!' he punched the air just as Maya walked inside, looking for a bottle of wine. She picked one up from the sideboard in the lounge and read the label, even though Arthur knew she couldn't care one jot about which brand, or how pricey, it was.

'Happy?' she asked, her eyes twinkling, clearly already knowing what they would be talking about. 'Come on, we should all celebrate with a glass of wine.' Arthur couldn't move fast enough after that and Romy and Maya shook their heads in exasperation.

'I guess the girls have told you the good news?' asked Nico when Arthur handed him a full glass of rich red wine. He sniffed it and then sipped it appreciatively. 'I'll miss your fancy wine collection,' he teased.

Arthur grinned and clinked glasses with him. Daisy stood behind him and although Arthur could see how tired she was, she was clearly buzzing from the success of her design at the café and she held out her glass for him to fill. Arthur itched to go round and pull her into his arms, but he had renewed hope that they would find some alone time soon and then he'd finally see where her head was at. The thought didn't scare him anymore. In fact, he was excited.

'I won't miss the pile of travel brochures that appeared in my room most days,' Nico teased. They all burst out laughing, Arthur taking the jibe on the chin. He glanced at Daisy who flushed and lowered her eyes, but she was smiling.

Chapter Twenty-Three

Nico left in a whirlwind of kisses and goodbyes, leaving a void in Daisy's life. She was determined not to slide back into the isolation she'd lived in before. She wasn't quite sure why she hadn't made more of an effort to make friends. Waking up excited about the day ahead was new to her, and spending time working on making Arthur's balcony as beautiful as her own was keeping her busy. Getting the green light to rejuvenate the area by the boats and ticket office at the start of the following year was exhilarating too.

Arthur had given her a healthy budget for his balcony redesign and she'd enjoyed filling the space with lush green foliage. She'd built a living herb wall with wild sage, thyme and chives which smelt heavenly. It completely closed off the far side of his balcony from the flat next door. She had added a slim reclaimed wood outdoor desk and seating, so that he could work outside. She'd placed concrete planters in the spaces between the doors and added big leafy plants and smaller, colourful coleus plants, which were orna-mental members of the mint family. She tucked those underneath the bigger plants and their velvety foliage, in combinations of burgundy, yellows and bronze, lifted the whole display to new heights. Subtle outdoor lighting had been added to illuminate the plants at night, to bring a gentle and warm ambience. There was another concrete and brushed metal planter with a raised back that she'd turned into a waterfall feature, so that the calming sound of water could be turned on when the river was quiet.

She'd often had to shoo Arthur out of the space because he'd kept trying to sit her down for chats that looked serious. Seeing Nico go had made her feel a bit maudlin, as she'd got used to having him around and was actually afraid for her heart if she let Arthur into her life again. She was barely coping with being near him every day and sharing sizzling kisses and some pretty heavy fondling sessions that made her wander around in a daze afterwards. The thought of even deeper feelings terrified her, so she'd shut them down. Nico had been a useful barrier to the sheer force and magnetism of Arthur Lopez. She'd joked about them being friends with benefits, but he hadn't seemed as keen on her genius idea as she'd expected. Now she felt a bit on edge whenever he was near. He hadn't kissed her for a couple of days, making her wonder if she'd pushed him too far by letting Nico stay for so long. Maybe he'd lost interest now there was no one to fight off. Or perhaps he'd met someone else?

Her skin felt like it was on fire whenever he brushed past her and she was having to stop herself from jumping on him. The day before, he'd placed his hands on either side of her body, almost pinning her to the wall by the door, and leaned in, his breath touching her face, to brush her hair out of her eyes. Her heart had almost stopped and she hadn't been able to take her eyes off his, but he'd just smiled and moved away because Brontë had come dancing into the room. She feared that she'd drag him to his bedroom and never let him go if he made a move on her again.

She had got the impression that he might want something a bit more serious now, but she could be mistaken. She hadn't seen any women coming and going from his flat, and he hadn't been in the gossip pages for months. There had been a few articles speculating that perhaps the panther had been tamed, but she didn't know how that could have happened, unless he was back with an old flame. The thought made her want to vomit. Maybe he was just too busy with work and helping her, she thought, ever hopeful.

Brontë arrived home from school hand-in-hand with Arthur on some days, and they'd eaten dinner together quite often, but he hadn't touched her when they were at home because they were never alone. It was driving her wild with lust and making her forgetful. She wondered if Brontë was missing Nico, or had formed a bond with Arthur, which was why she spent most of her time with them instead of playing with her toys like she usually did. That could be an issue too, worried Daisy. Brontë's best friend, Flo, did visit often now, but that just meant an even busier home and less opportunity to grab Arthur for a chat.

Daisy stood up and watered the last of the plants and then plugged in the new watering system she'd purchased. She knew that Arthur would forget to look after the plants the same way he sometimes forgot to eat, so this had been her solution. The plants would thrive with or without him. She just wondered if she could do the same now.

She quickly finished what she was doing and then closed up the flat and wandered outside and up towards the town. The sun was beating down and she wished she'd put a summer dress on now that the days were warm and dry.

She let the rays heat her skin for a moment and tried to re-centre herself. She tended to stick to jeans when she was working because everything ended up covered in mud, but she did like to wear lightweight smart black fitted linen trousers and a short-sleeved shirt when she visited her new clients in town. She now serviced ten shops with plant displays, which brought in a steady income. She'd delivered their new planters and popped in each week to check the watering systems she'd set up and prune any stray edges. The plants really added something to the shop fronts and interiors, and she enjoyed hearing compliments from customers about the hanging baskets outside and the indoor arrangements.

She was dithering about whether to walk up and meet Arthur and Brontë when they returned from the school run, but then groaned as a group of school mums headed her way. They clearly had their sights set on her, though they'd not wanted to mix with her when she'd first arrived after the initial flurry of invites. Daisy drew in a deep breath of courage and decided to stop and chat.

'Hello!' said Imogen, waving at her and rushing over as if they were best friends. Daisy had begun to build real bridges with many of her old friends and had made some brilliant new ones like Fred and Penny. She was still unsure of this cliquey crowd, but was willing to give them the benefit of the doubt. 'Are you walking up to the school?'

Daisy cringed inside. 'Umm... a friend is doing the school run for me, but I've just finished work. I was thinking about meeting them halfway.'

'Join us, then,' said Flo's mum, Anne, who had just walked over to meet them all. Daisy was relieved to see a friendly face and fell into step beside her.

'So,' said Imogen. 'You've been busy since you moved in

around here,' she gave a tinkly little laugh but there was an undertone of something else.

'Daisy's family have always lived round here,' said Anne helpfully, giving Imogen a reproving look.

'Oh yes, I forgot! Didn't you run off to France to get married or something? I've never seen Brontë's dad around,' she said with a side glance to her friends, 'But I have seen Arthur Lopez walking Brontë home a lot lately.'

A few of the other mums looked at their feet uncomfortably and Daisy bunched her hands and tried to remain calm, her heart racing. Anne gave her a look of sympathy and then turned to face Imogen, making the group stop. Daisy took hold of Anne's arm and gave it a squeeze of thanks as she stepped in. She didn't want Anne to be ostracised because of her.

'I'm a widow,' she said carefully and Imogen's cheeks flamed. 'Arthur and his sisters have been my best friends since we were at school, but I don't think whoever collects my child for me while I'm at work is really anyone else's concern,' she said levelly, and she began walking again. The others had no choice but to follow suit. Anne was beaming proudly and Imogen was looking flushed and a bit ruffled, but the other mums seemed to want to drop it and began talking about the latest class project and the costumes that had to be made for the end of the summer term.

As they reached the gates she saw Arthur leaning against the school wall, with lots of mums surreptitiously glancing his way. He was too handsome for his own good and Daisy felt her own heart beating faster at the sight of him. He broke into a smile when he saw her and she couldn't help but smile too. Bloody hell, she could already feel the eyes burning into her back, and the rumour mill jumping back into full force again.

'Hey!' said Arthur, when he reached her, guiding her to a quieter spot. 'How come you're here?' Daisy felt her skin grow warm where his hand was touching her back and she let her hair fall over her face to cover her eyes a little bit as she suddenly felt cripplingly shy. He brushed her hair aside with his fingers and tucked a strand behind her ear. She wanted to lean into his touch but she was too aware of prying eyes.

'I was going to meet you both halfway along, with ice cream, but I bumped into the other mums and they are a bit like a tidal wave,' she sighed. 'I couldn't get away.'

'You ok?' he asked, looking over her shoulder protectively and then back at her face.

'Daisy!' called Imogen, beckoning them both over.

'Shall we grab Brontë and make a run for it?' he teased, and she smiled as the school bell finally pealed and the children began to filter out. 'She's light and I can throw her over my shoulder,' he grinned. Daisy saw the top of Brontë's head and had to move towards Imogen so that her daughter would see her.

'I wanted to book you to come round to my house and see if you could do something with the garden,' said Imogen in a tone that suggested she was doing Daisy an incredible favour.

'Um...' said Daisy, playing for time and frantically trying to think of a way out. The last thing she wanted was to be holed up with Imogen all day for weeks.

'Daisy's booked out solidly for the next year,' said Arthur helpfully and Imogen's mouth hung open in shock before she snapped it closed again and began primping her hair with her fingers. 'She's just finished designing my balcony, but she's got a corporate job in the city starting next week,' he added.

'Oh! My goodness! You're giving up your little garden business already?' tittered Imogen. 'Well, I can't say I'm surprised, although what you did with the Riverside café was inspired. Nicholas and I love going there after school, don't we, Nicholas?' she asked her son who was standing beside her looking bored.

'Um. No,' said Daisy with a wide grin. 'I've got my first corporate client. I'm building interior garden spaces for a creative business and its two thousand employees,' she smiled sweetly, trying not to laugh as Arthur snorted and turned round to take Brontë's hand as she finished chatting to her friends and joined them, looking slightly alarmed that her mother was chatting to Nicholas' mum. 'Have a great evening, guys,' Daisy said to Imogen and Nicholas. 'We might bump into you at Penny's, as I'm treating Arthur and Brontë to ice cream today!'

'Yay!' said Brontë, jumping in the air in excitement and nearly taking Arthur's arm off, so he jumped too. 'Let's go!' she said, pulling Arthur along so Daisy had to hurriedly say goodbye and rush to join them too.

'What are we celebrating?' Arthur asked with a wide grin, and she wished he could simply take her hand, too, and they could all walk home as a family. The problem was that she knew this would make Arthur run for the hills, however much he'd protested that he wouldn't. She'd already experienced that and she certainly didn't want to make the same mistake twice.

As they reached the café, Daisy grinned when she saw the outside space being used just as she'd planned. People stood chatting happily, drinking tall glasses of frothy coffee while enjoying the river view, their dogs sleeping contentedly by their feet.

Arthur nudged her shoulder and smiled when she

stopped to take it in. 'You did that,' he said with pride in his voice. She flushed and they all went inside, Arthur grabbing a table while she went to place their order at the till.

Penny finished serving the customer before her, but her eyes lit up at the sight of Daisy. She grabbed some ice creams and iced coffees for Daisy and refused to let her pay, putting a hand up to stop any protests. 'We are jammed full, the outside space is a godsend! Customers love it. Thank you, Daisy,' she said, pushing the loaded tray her way. 'How's Arthur?' she added, inclining her head towards the table where he was sitting with Brontë. Arthur was watching her and he smiled as their eyes met.

'I don't really know,' said Daisy honestly.

'He looks like he wants to eat you alive, you lucky woman,' joked Penny with a sigh.

'I've noticed recently that Fred does the same for you...' said Daisy in a hushed tone, winking at her friend. Penny flushed, but didn't correct her.

'He is kind of cute,' said Penny under her breath, as Fred replenished the cake counter and then turned to give them both a wide grin.

'He's gorgeous,' added Daisy with a pert look.

'I'm his boss, though,' said Penny with a longing glance over her shoulder to where Fred was still filling the chilling cabinets with fresh cream cakes.

'Penny! It's not forbidden. Loads of people meet their partners at work.' Daisy thought of how she'd bumped into Arthur on the balcony. She'd yet to show him the revamped space. She was really proud of it. She wanted him to walk out there and breathe a sigh of relief. The plants would heal after a long day at work, the scent of lavender and mint soothing his tired mind and reviving his creativity – not that he seemed to need much help in that department as his ideas were in such high demand.

Penny was nibbling her lip and staring at Fred with longing, and when he turned round and smiled at her, a matching smile slid straight onto her face. 'Go for it,' Daisy said as she took the tray and added a lemon muffin, as Maya was coming round later to look at the balcony and Daisy knew they were her favourite. She blew Penny a kiss and wished that love and happiness didn't have to be so complicated.

Brontë was swinging her legs back and forth in excitement when Daisy arrived back with her tray. Arthur practically demolished his ice cream in two bites. 'Hungry?' she asked and Brontë giggled, her own face now covered in smears that Daisy wiped off with a napkin.

'Ravenous,' he said and she laughed.

'Did you forget lunch again? I even brought some extra rolls and left them on the side for you, for after your meeting.' Arthur had been ensconced in his spare room all day and had barely come out for a drink. Then, when she'd refused to let him see the balcony yet, he'd offered to get Brontë while she'd finished up and the rest was history.

'I didn't see them,' Arthur apologised. 'It was a tricky meeting. Their requirements for the application they want us to design are a bit far-fetched. We often have to curb their expectations a bit, but this one is crazy!' he laughed. 'It should be a lot of fun in the long run though, so I didn't want to squash their dreams too early on in the process. I think they forget we are only human at times, and expect things that haven't been invented yet.'

He licked ice cream off his fingers and then helped Brontë up so she could go and say hello to a friendly Labradoodle who was just outside the main door and who lived a few houses down from her grandparents' place. Daisy waved to the owners and they bent down to chat to Brontë, who was already petting the dog and enjoying it licking her sticky face.

'How long are you going to make me wait until I can see what you've done with the balcony?' he asked.

'You're so impatient,' she laughed, rubbing a dot of ice cream from his nose with the napkin. He took her hand and kissed the inside of her wrist and she nearly jumped sky high as anyone could have seen them. Luckily everyone seemed preoccupied with their own families, but suddenly her heart was racing as if she'd just sprinted a few miles.

'Let's get going,' he said and soon he was running up the stairs to the flat with Brontë hot on his heels, both giggling like mad, while Daisy tried to keep up. When they got to the door, they were all out of breath and laughing, so she handed Arthur back his key and he opened the door and stepped inside. Daisy held Brontë back, so that Arthur could get a feel of the place, but he just stood there in awe as the girls joined him and then whooped and swung Daisy into his arms, bowing her low over his arm and kissing her very briefly. Brontë giggled and then he picked her up and swung her around before dropping a kiss on her cheek too, but suddenly everything had shifted. Kissing Daisy in private was one thing, but in front of her child was another.

Daisy could see that Arthur immediately understood his mistake and tried to apologise, but she quickly mumbled something about it being time for dinner. Although Brontë didn't appear to be at all worried by the kiss and was grinning from ear to ear, Arthur didn't have time to find that out, as Daisy swept out of his flat and left him with a wall of silence.

Chapter Twenty-Four

Daisy watched her fingers tap-tapping on her legs and tried to make herself calm down. She knew she'd overreacted the night before, but bringing someone romantically into her own life was one thing – but when it involved her child, it was a whole different ballgame.

She hadn't considered how attached Brontë had already become to Arthur, or how much he seemed to care for her too. Nico had been a kind of buffer for a while, but now he was gone she'd have to face whatever it was that was going on with the guy next door. She shifted in her seat as the train sped along the tracks, taking her further away from her comfort zone and into the panther's lair. She'd briskly walked her daughter to school and then jumped on the train to central London to visit Arthur's main office site.

Her nerves were starting to get the better of her and she stretched out her fingers and then rummaged around in her handbag for a packet of mints for something to do. She picked up her phone instead and began scrolling through some content ideas for her website, but even that couldn't hold her attention.

She didn't know if she was meeting Arthur today, or one of his team. Although she'd already done a lot of research on the building and visited his interactive website, nothing would compare to a site visit. She had drawn up her plans and she hadn't let Arthur, or his staff, see them yet, so they might want to make changes. She expected that, as she had utilised every penny of his generous budget, but the benefits to his staff would be immense if he went ahead with her proposal. It was well documented that creative minds needed stimulating environments, while nature also worked well for relaxation, so she hoped they would see her ideas were sound. She'd also integrated lighting and sound that could be used for inspiration. The rainforest soundtrack she had planned for the quiet area had even sent her to sleep the night before, after hours of tossing and turning.

She tried to settle herself while the train rattled along. There was an elderly woman opposite her, with a small child who was asking to play on her phone. The woman sighed and handed it over and then shared a smile and a shrug with Daisy. As the train pulled into the station everyone jumped up to disembark, but Daisy needed a moment to breathe, so she let everyone rush past and then helped the lady with the small child, collecting the woman's pull-along trolley for her. They walked amiably up to the ticket gates and then parted ways as Daisy headed for the escalators and the woman went towards the food court, the child hopping around in excitement about the prospect of a hamburger in a fast-food restaurant.

Daisy wondered if she had time to grab a coffee, and glanced at the huge digital clock on the station wall. No, she needed to hurry to get to Arthur's offices. They were a few streets away from the station, so she picked up her pace, then tried to slow down again just before she got there, so that she didn't arrive looking dishevelled, hot and sweaty.

The foyer was huge and breathtaking, with several flat screen TVs showcasing Arthur's tech prowess. The central desk seemed to float above the floor. There were banks of funky blue seating for guests and a refreshment station that gleamed as the sun shone through the plate glass frontage. The wall behind the reception desk was a muted mural of the inside of a computer, which looked hip and modern. There were four people sitting at the reception desk. Three were on calls, so she walked up to a dark-haired man with trendy black-framed glasses. He looked up as she arrived and welcomed her, asking her name and whom she was meeting.

After being directed to wait in one of the seating areas, she took a moment to glance around again. There were several potted kentia palms and a fiddle-leaf fig tree in the foyer, but there was definitely room for improvement. She could add some screening to one of the seating areas for private conversations and a living wall would bring softness to the space. If she added sage and thyme, like the one she'd planted at Arthur's flat, then the foyer would smell heavenly as clients and staff walked by.

She was so busy planning extras for her design that she didn't notice Arthur was standing right in front of her. She jumped up and shook his hand. He looked into her eyes and frowned, but followed her lead and didn't hug her. He introduced her to his staff as they walked through a beautifully light and airy space with streamlined glass desks.

As they passed, Arthur's staff were busily working, or chatting about projects, from the snippets Daisy heard. It all sounded a bit like gobbledygook to her, but she liked the hum of chatter anyway. She immediately began taking notes on the very cleverly designed interiors to see if she could add to them in any way.

There was an industrial feel to the place, with brushed metals, glass and wood and private co-working spaces and areas where groups could discuss ideas around tables. It all looked like very high tech, judging by the quantity of computers and laptops dotted around, but with comfortable seating. She hated it when companies forgot how important seating was. In a restaurant it was important, but in offices where staff spent most of their time at their desks, it was really vital.

Then Arthur led her into his office, which had huge floor-to-ceiling glass windows and views across the street. She could almost curl up and sleep in the huge padded bucket chair in the corner, as she'd spent most of the previous evening fretting about what to say to him today.

Next he showed her into a big boardroom where they had play areas arranged and lots of drawing and games scattered around. When she'd turned to him in confusion, he'd grinned and explained, 'We're having one of our four annual family days. Staff can bring their kids to work and we hire in staff and entertainment for them. You should bring Brontë up when she has an inset day, if you have time,' he said innocently, and her eyes narrowed until he held up his hands in surrender. She bet her bottom dollar that he knew full well the dates of Brontë's school calendar and had scheduled the next one to fit in. She shook her head in exasperation, but had to give him kudos for trying.

He carried on with the tour of the building, while she worried that he should be doing something else and leaving this to his staff. He didn't seem in a rush to leave her, though, and showed her exactly where he wanted green spaces.

Finally they returned to his office, which was huge, private and masculine, with lots of rich dark colours. It seemed to be the only room on this side of the building. 'I like my staff,' commented Arthur, noticing her confusion, 'but I've become a bit of a recluse, it seems... or I had before you moved in next door. I spent most of my time living out of hotel rooms. Now I can't wait to be at home.'

'Umm...' she didn't quite know how to take that. 'Wouldn't you rather be with people, in the other offices?' she asked, trying not to look in his eyes, or pass out, because he was saying things that she'd always wanted to hear, but her heart felt like it was beating out of her chest and she only had a certain amount of time to present her ideas and leave.

'I have a smaller light-filled office out there too. This is for my private thinking time, or meetings that I don't want overheard.'

'I see...' she gulped and he led her to sit opposite him at a little coffee table that had views of people rushing along the street outside.

'The windows are tinted so that I can see out, but no one can see in,' he said, taking her hand. Her skin felt like it was on fire. She stared at their interlinked hands but was at a loss for words. 'I'm sorry about last night. I got carried away and didn't think about the consequences for you.' He hung his head and she finally smiled.

'Arthur, it's okay,' she reassured him. 'I overreacted. You were just happy in the moment.'

She let go of his hand and he got up to make them both a coffee from the fancy machine on the cabinet behind his huge desk, but he seemed nervous for some reason.

'I'm excited about the project and can't wait to start, but perhaps it would be good to put space between us for a bit?' she ventured.

'That's the last thing I want,' said Arthur as he placed a steaming cup of coffee in front of her, filing the room with a delicious aroma.

'Are we back to my friends with benefits idea?' she joked feebly, her work forgotten for now, as it seemed that this needed to be sorted out first.

'It's not what I want anymore. I want commitment,' he said, his leg touching hers, which made her gasp in shock. What was it with her hormones and being near this man?

'I want you – to only want me,' Arthur added clearly, taking her hand and kissing her wrist like he had before.

'But I want something more serious than you could ever want,' Daisy said shakily. 'And after last night, I've been thinking that perhaps I do want to introduce someone to Brontë – but that someone has to want to stay around.'

'How about if we become serious?' he asked.

Daisy spluttered, but he didn't let her hand go and his face was earnest. 'You've made it crystal clear from the start that you're not interested in commitment,' she said. 'We agreed not to spoil our friendship and we haven't – so far. If feelings come into it, that might change.'

'My feelings have always been in it,' said Arthur gravely, clearly stung by the words that were said to protect her heart. 'I made one mistake, and I've paid for it by losing you. I don't want to risk that ever again.'

'But what about Brontë?'

'Brontë already loves me, and I love her. Maybe the future could bring a little brother or sister for her?'

Daisy's mouth dropped open and she stood up, then began pacing the room. Arthur got up and caught her hand gently, pulling her into his arms and resting his forehead on hers, their heartbeats thumping in unison. He lifted her chin with his fingers and touched her lips with his own, which lit a fire of longing within her and she groaned and deepened the kiss, winding her fingers into his hair and pushing her body into his until they were both wide-eyed and panting. His hand was splayed at the base of her back, urging their cores together, and she had to step back or completely come undone.

'I'm supposed to be at work!' she joked feebly, licking her lips, her eyes watching his mouth.

'Me too,' he grinned, pulling her in and wrapping her in his arms again. 'We are going to be working together, so let's look over the plans that you've spent ages detailing. I know how hard you work. Then I will give you a few days to get used to the idea of us as a couple before I start really persuading you that I'm the guy for you. How does that sound?'

'You haven't started yet?' she squeaked and stumbled back, pressing the back of her legs into his desk. He stood so close in front of her that their chests were just touching and smiled down at her, his eyes predatory and full of lust. He bent in and gently touched his lips to hers and she barely dared to breathe. The he went and sat at his desk as if nothing had happened, and asked to see her plans.

She gulped in some air and sat opposite him, not able to look him in the eye at first, but as soon as she set out her plans and began to speak, her confidence in her own work began to flow through her body. He asked question after question about how it could all fit together and suggested a few minor changes that she could instantly see working. At the end of the conversation she looked at her phone, and two hours had sped by. He grinned and stood up, rolling his neck and then placing both hands on his desk while he looked at her, his black shirt moulding to his muscled chest.

'I love it. The plans are incredible, Daisy. I can't wait for you to start work. I've told my team to be as accommodating as they can. You're welcome to wander round and chat to anyone who seems to have a free moment, if you want to show them your designs, or ask if there is anything they'd like added.'

'You'd let your staff decide?' she asked in surprise.

His eyes crinkled at the corners and he tilted his head for a moment in thought. 'They don't have the final say, but I wouldn't employ them if their ideas weren't brilliant. They might think of something they need that has passed me by. Only small adjustments though,' he laughed. 'The plan is perfect just the way it is. I can't see how they'd improve it, but they might have an inspired suggestion that you like too.'

'I love that idea,' said Daisy. She was always open to learning new things. It felt exciting to be working in a whole building of creative minds, making a green space for them in the city. Her skin was still on fire from where he'd touched her, but now he was all business, and that kind of excited her too. She glanced at her watch and then jumped as he walked round behind her, but he was just opening his office door.

'I need to get back to pick up Brontë,' she said in what she hoped sounded like a normal voice. How she could speak calmly after Arthur's declarations earlier she didn't know, but for now she was pretending that they'd only talked about work.

'I've got to work late tonight, but if you're still awake when I get in, then maybe we can rendezvous on the balconies and share a bottle of wine to celebrate us officially becoming a couple?'

Daisy froze for a moment and stared at him to see if he was joking, but he looked supremely confident and annoyingly smug.

'Take a step back there, lover boy,' she said with false joviality. *Lover boy?* she never said things like that, she cringed. 'Nothing's been decided. And what happened to all the wooing and 'convincing me that you've changed' dinners that you promised me,' she added quickly and then back-tracked. 'Actually, I've tasted your cooking and that's not going to work,' she shrugged and he laughed and turned to take her in his arms.

She didn't pull away, and when she looked up at him his lips captured hers, making blood fizz in her veins. She pushed him into the door this time and pressed her body into his, which he seemed to enjoy by the way his hand reached down and cupped her backside and pulled her in closer. When they finally pulled apart his hair looked ruffled and his eyes were glazed. He rocked back on his feet and she laughed, finally feeling some tension dissipate.

'I'll buy you all the iced coffees and hamburgers that your heart desires,' he said in a gravelly voice, referring to the food they sometimes grabbed at Penny's café. 'Or diamonds and caviar.'

He caught hold of her hand before they both left the room and turned her back to face him. 'But what I do want, Daisy, is for me to be yours and for you to be mine.'

Daisy gulped and nodded but couldn't quite meet his eyes. She left him standing by the door and quickly placed her drawings back in her bag as she walked towards the lifts without a backward glance.

201

Chapter Twenty-Five

Daisy wiped some sweat off her brow and rubbed her aching back. She'd spent the past two weeks taking delivery of all the plants and planters that she was placing around Arthur's offices. She had huge Swiss cheese plants with their bold character and enormous leaves that reminded her of rainforests. Weeping fig trees with their graceful foliage and small pale leaves had been placed by the windows in the foyer, and tall butterfly ferns gave a sophisticated feel and offered natural screening for the smaller desks and chairs that she'd rearranged in reception for impromptu meetings.

She had chatted to lots of the staff and they often popped by to see what she was doing now. She had two young women working for her who she'd found by asking around amongst the other school mums. They were both working really hard. Kitty was the daughter of Mrs Hawley in the school office, and Trudy was Anne's niece. They seemed to love the environment and travelled up and down with her most days. They giggled a lot when Arthur joined them and often fanned their faces when he walked by, which made Daisy shake her head in mock disgust.

The first time Arthur had turned up and offered to travel home with her, she had been mortified, but he had acted as if it was the most natural thing in the world for her to be on a train home with her client. In the end, she'd given up protesting because he ignored her anyway. He sat opposite and shared a secret smile with her, which made her skin grow warm, and thrilled and annoyed her in equal measure. The girls were often on their phones for the whole journey, so luckily they didn't seem to notice a thing.

She felt a sense of satisfaction in seeing her ideas coming together. Her parents had been a great help with school runs and giving Brontë her tea here and there, if Daisy had to be late. Her team had set up a huge living wall and watering system in the foyer, which made people stop and stare. She'd noticed customers immediately heading for the seating area she'd arranged there rather than other meeting places. She'd built a tall herb wall of sage, mint and rosemary in the café, which smelt delicious. The staff loved it.

There were now three hanging rattan egg chairs, as well as trailing plants dangling from the ceiling with discreet lighting angled to warm the area up. The contractors she'd employed to set up the chairs, move desks and incorporate lighting systems had only been there for six days due to her detailed plans. She could be quite bossy too, she'd discovered.

In one office area she'd created an oasis like her balcony, with pure white desks interspersed with lush almost tropical greenery, like kenita palms and money trees with their interwoven and twisted trunks, so it almost felt as if you were working in paradise. One room had tall two-tiered wooden and slate metal troughs designating different areas, with trailing plants on top and leafy botanical monstera, with their waxy wide, deep green leaves below. It made quite a squat room suddenly appear much taller and offered privacy for the single workstations. It also allowed workers to glance at their colleagues through the greenery, without them invading each other's creative space.

She'd even built a low sloping hill area in one unused room with high quality fake grass and potted miniature flowering trees. People had crowded round to see what she was doing, and they were already using the space as if it were a park. A few of the spaces she'd made would be darker and more intimate. A project this size would have made her baulk before the café garden refurbishment job, but that experience and her careful planning made it seamless.

She smiled as a few of the staff stopped by for a chat. She loved the feeling of camaraderie at the office and she could see why they all enjoyed working for Arthur – he was a great boss. 'We're going to the pub across the street later if you want to join us?' asked Jerry, one of Arthur's tech guys, who was regarding her with interest. He was tall, slim and had a very cheeky smile and a mop of dark curls that he was always brushing out of his eyes.

Daisy wiped her muddy hands on her summer trousers, thankful they were a dark colour, so they didn't really show the dirt. She quite liked the sound of going for a drink with her city colleagues, so she said she'd meet them out front later and they all said their goodbyes and moved on. Kitty gave her a wink and Daisy rolled her eyes, but grinned anyway. It felt good to be in demand, even if it was just with a friendly group of co-workers.

'You're both welcome to join us,' said Daisy, as she

pushed the earth firmly around the base of a tropical-looking imperial red philodendron. The plant had a subtle bronze flush to its cluster of large leaves and Daisy settled the huge urn it was in beside the wall, where it would get sunlight to keep it warm.

'He didn't invite all of us, though, did he?' giggled Trudy. Daisy stood up and let the warm sun wash over her skin through the windows. It was a glorious summer's day with bright blue cloudless skies. Although the offices were cool and air conditioned, she enjoyed watching the sunbeams dance across the rooms when they hit the windows.

'Have you got a minute?' asked Arthur as he walked by. Daisy almost jumped out of her skin. She'd been caught daydreaming, when she'd just done hours of hard slog.

'Me?' she asked and he nodded.

'You're all doing a great job,' he said, turning to Kitty and Trudy, who both almost swooned.

'Thanks, Arthur,' said Kitty brazenly. 'Are you coming to the pub tonight? Jerry just invited Daisy, and we might all come along if the boss is going,' she joked.

Arthur raised an eyebrow at Daisy who felt her skin warm up and her cheeks flush red. 'Kitty!' she said, her voice sounding very squeaky. 'I'm sure Mr Lopez is too busy to go to the pub with his staff and contractors.' Kitty just gave her a secret wink and then turned back to her work.

Arthur frowned and then put on an amiable smile, but Daisy could see he wasn't happy from the sudden rigidity in his shoulders. 'I'd love to. Thanks for inviting me, Kitty. The first round of drinks are on me.'

'Yes!' said Kitty, punching the air and high-fiving Trudy, who was grinning from ear to ear.

'Do you have time to come to my office?' he asked Daisy

again, very politely, but there was now a clear undercurrent of tension.

'Of course,' she said brightly and followed him to the lift, where he didn't speak for the whole journey. When they walked into his office there was a beautiful lunch laid out, with frothy tall glasses of her favourite coffee on the table. The plump fresh strawberries in a glass bowl smelt delicious and her stomach immediately grumbled. Arthur turned to her and finally cracked a smile.

'You've been working so hard, I haven't seen you take any lunch breaks. So I thought you might be hungry,' he said gruffly and her heart melted a little.

'You planned all this for me?' she asked, a wide smile appearing on her face and butterflies taking flight. He'd already been true to his word, sending her beautiful brightly-coloured bouquets of flowers from Maya's best friend Leah's flower shop, and a painting for her bedroom like the one she'd treated herself to from the artists showcased aboard *Bertha*. She had wondered what her grandad Joe and Roman would think of Arthur buying her that gift, but she was too tired to care right now.

'Of course,' he said, pulling out a chair for her and settling her at the table, laid with crisp white linen which looked like it had been brought in just for this meal. 'I know I can't take you out to dinner on your own, because Brontë would be asleep, so I was thinking outside the box, and thought I'd create our own little piece of paradise here.' He gestured towards the black planters that ran along one wall and brought fresh oxygen into the room. 'Now I have my own mini oasis, it's nicer than most restaurants, and we have a great view of the city.'

Daisy's stomach fizzed with excitement that he wanted to take her on a date and that he'd also thought about her not wanting to leave Brontë at night. They had spent a few nights snuggled up on the sofa together watching movies, but he'd always been respectful of Brontë's presence in the flat, and had regretfully gone home at a reasonable hour. They both had a heavy workload right now, so they were exhausted. Being in each other's company had seemed to be enough, but this was stepping things up another level. Suddenly she couldn't meet his eye and kept fiddling with her fork.

'Thank you,' she said and he leaned down and touched his lips briefly to hers. She could have easily swooned, but she just about held on to her sanity. This man pretty much held her heart in the palm of his hands, and it scared the hell out of her. She'd let down her guard once before with him and never really recovered.

'Are you really going to the pub? Or was that just Kitty vying for free drinks?' he asked, sitting opposite her and watching her closely.

'Brontë is staying with my parents for the next week,' she shrugged. 'I was going to tell you, but to be honest I was a bit nervous about what that might mean for us,' she nibbled on her lower lip and Arthur drew in a deep breath and finally sat back in his seat, his hands in his lap.

'I make you nervous?' he asked, his lip quirking and his eyes sparkling suddenly.

'Don't get a big head about it,' she grumbled, and he moved the plate of perfectly quartered sandwiches closer to her so that she could take one. She bit into the corner of one. It was delicious – cream cheese and cucumber. 'You're right, though. This is a huge job for me, so I keep forgetting lunch. Thank you.'

Arthur grinned and helped himself to a couple of ham and salad sandwiches but left them on his plate.

'Mum and Dad are taking Brontë to a pretty little holiday cottage in the Cotswolds straight from school, as it's the holidays next week. I was worried about how to juggle finishing this job, so Mum made the suggestion and Brontë literally couldn't have jumped around the room more in excitement and begged me to let her go,' she shrugged.

'That must have been hard for you. I know you love being together.'

Daisy felt warmth spread through her body. Arthur hadn't just assumed she'd be happy to spend a week without the love of her life, her daughter.

'I am a bit nervous, I can't lie,' she finally met his eyes and they both grinned. 'We've never really been apart for long before, but she will have an amazing time and she can tell me all about it each day on a video call.'

Arthur reached out for her hand and when she took his, he moved his chair next to hers and then gave her a gentle tug to pull her onto his lap. She squeaked in surprise, but didn't protest too much because she always missed him, from the moment he left her to the moment she saw him again. She was just confused about how to act around him at work.

'I've missed you,' he said, his eyes darkening as he looked at her lips and licked his own. She gulped and her hands wound around his neck of their own volition. 'I didn't like the idea of you going to the pub on a date,' he ground out, visibly restraining himself from kissing her, which made her want him even more.

'It isn't a date. Jerry said loads of the tech team are going to be there,' she protested feebly, quite enjoying Arthur's protective streak. 'Plus you've promised the girls that you'll be there now, so you can see for yourself.'

'I trust you,' he sighed, linking his arms around her waist

and pulling her closer. 'But each time I try and talk about what this is, you dodge the question. It's making me feel insecure,' he admitted sheepishly, before kissing her gently.

Any resolve she'd had snapped and broke away with his vulnerability. He'd been patient, understanding and romantic – and she'd been deliberately obtuse. It was time to take a chance on love, if that was what this was. She deepened the kiss and felt his resolve crumble as he pulled her hips closer and groaned her name. His hands cupped the back of her head and they rested their foreheads together, their breath coming thick and fast. They moved apart and grinned at each other.

'I'm sorry I've been evasive,' said Daisy. 'I've been protecting my heart. You've got the power to hurt me,' she admitted finally.

'I won't hurt you,' he promised, his smile wide as he put one arm round her and handed her some food with the other. 'Now eat. If we have to go to the pub tonight, then you'll definitely need lots of energy for afterwards,' he joked and she quite liked that idea suddenly.

'So... what is this?' she asked, shy suddenly. He lifted her chin so that she had to look at him.

'I don't know about you, but I'm in love,' he said gruffly and her mouth dropped open in shock, before she snapped her lips back together, her pulse racing. Arthur loved her! 'You're all I can think about,' he added, kissing her softly once again. She wished they didn't have so many clothes as a barrier between then, so she slid a hand into the back of his trousers and she smiled as he froze for a second and then deepened the kiss.

'I love you too,' she admitted, trailing her fingers along his cheekbone and then remembering where they were as the phone on his desk rang.

'Finally.' A smile lit up his face and he gently pulled her to her feet, kissing her nose first and then going to answer the call.

'You were waiting for the call?' she asked in confusion.

'No, for you to admit that you love me too,' he said, and then grabbed the phone as she flushed again. He quickly answered the call and ended it as soon as he could. 'Come home with me tonight?' he asked.

'I live next door!' she laughed. 'Plus you've promised Kitty and Trudy a free drink at the pub.'

'One quick drink and then I want you to myself,' he said sternly.

'One quick drink,' she agreed, taking his hand and making him sit down and finally eat some of the beautiful lunch he'd gone to all the trouble arranging for her. The air sizzled with anticipation and they both ate up quickly and then went back to work with the promise of meeting later for that quick drink – and then an evening alone together at last!

Chapter Twenty-Six

Anticipation filled the air as they all walked amiably to the pub. If Jerry was surprised to see Arthur with them, he didn't show it. When Arthur slipped his hand into Daisy's she flushed, but didn't pull away.

'Finally!' joked Kitty, parroting Arthur's earlier sentiment. 'We guessed that would happen by the way you can't keep your eyes off her,' she said with a hand on her hip as she stopped outside the pub.

'Kitty!' flushed Daisy in horror, dropping Arthur's hand, but he just grinned and then put his arm around her.

'Daisy's my girlfriend... finally,' he grinned to Kitty who burst out laughing as the rest of the staff cheered and nudged them both with affection. 'It's taken me a long time to persuade her that I'm not all bad.'

Daisy flushed again, but she was smiling now. The thought that she was Arthur's girlfriend made her skin fizz with excitement. She didn't really care what anyone else thought about her choices, but she was a bit hot under the collar about the prospect of a night alone with Arthur.

Things had been building up between them for months and she didn't know how much longer she could go without touching his face or body. His natural magnetism had always drawn her to him. She quite liked the feeling of having such a compelling man in love with her, as he'd given her the power to break his heart. It was a responsibility she took seriously and she never wanted to hurt him. He'd always been the love of her life, if she was completely honest. In fact, she was tired of denying it. She didn't care if he was also currently her client. She was self-employed anyway and she knew she was doing a great job. His staff would benefit hugely from the changes she'd made to his offices. Hopefully it would make everyone feel more creative and productive, which meant more business for Arthur.

'I thought we were only staying for one drink?' Arthur whispered into her ear a while later. Her eyes twinkled with mischief and she snugged into the crook of his arm. More people had joined them from the office, as the grapevine had clearly told them that Arthur was buying the drinks, and it had been a lively and entertaining evening. Daisy was starting to flag now, though, as her team had such a physical job every day. She had noticed arm and leg muscles forming, and her stomach was becoming more toned, but she still had her curves and she liked the combination. She knew she'd never be model perfect, but that had never seemed to bother any of her boyfriends, and Arthur could barely keep his hands off her most of the time. He was looking at her with such longing that she had to give the man a break.

She might be tired, but the thought of a night alone with Arthur suddenly made her heart beat ramp up and her eyes glitter with promise and lust, which he noticed. He sat up straighter and rapidly began to say their goodbyes. He checked to see if Kitty and Trudy wanted to join them on the journey home, which made her like him even more, if that were possible. The four of them wandered towards the station and they had to grab Kitty just before the train doors closed because she was dawdling. The girls fell asleep pretty much as soon as they sat down, so Daisy eased them into each other so that they didn't slide off their seats and then looked up at Arthur who was watching her with laughter in his eyes.

'I think that last round of drinks Trudy ordered might have been one too many,' she grinned, shaking her head at Kitty's soft snores.

'You look just about all in too,' he said, noting her trying to hide a yawn. 'How about we just snuggle up and get some sleep tonight, and we can see how you feel tomorrow?' he said, kissing her nose and putting his arm around her. She settled into his warm body gratefully, kind of disappointed, but also really exhausted from a long and emotional day. She leaned up and kissed his lips gently, not caring who saw.

As the train slid into their station, they roused the girls and shared a cab home. When they got to their front doors, Arthur took her hand and led her to his flat. Once inside he pulled her into his arms and kissed her with all the pent-up longing of the day, and then handed her one of his T-shirts and started to strip off his own clothes. Daisy's eyes were out on stalks and she suddenly wasn't a jot tired, but he grinned mischievously and ushered her into the huge black and white bathroom.

'We need to get some sleep and then we'll have lots of energy for tomorrow,' he said with promise in his tone, but she ran her fingers along his muscled abdomen and around his hips before he grabbed her hand to stop her teasing and groaned, trailing kisses up the side of her neck as she arched her body into his. Arthur's chest was sculpted, and the trail of dark hair that dipped lower as he loosened his trousers filled her mind with lustful images of ripping his clothes off his body.

She eased his trousers away from his hips and let them fall to the floor. Then she ran her fingers along the edge of his boxer shorts. He grabbed her hands and held them against the wall above her head, while he plundered her mouth and then let her go as he began to unbutton her shirt and pushed the fabric back to expose her breasts as he slid her trousers to the floor and they both stood, panting and looking at each other with glazed eyes. His glinted with promise and he hitched his finger under her bra strap to ease it from her shoulder, trailing hot kisses along the same path. Then he picked her up so that her legs straddled his hips, walked them both into the shower and turned it on.

She gasped as the water streamed over them and Arthur eased her down his body and kissed the sensitive part of her neck as her own hands explored his taut backside. When his hands cupped her breasts and then slid between their bodies as his mouth followed suit, she closed her eyes in ecstasy and willingly succumbed to his knowing touch.

* * *

'Don't you ever buy any food?' Daisy asked the next day, every single one of her muscles aching, but in a good way.

'It's an excuse to come to your place, if I don't,' he admitted cheekily and she burst out laughing.

They had been touching and smiling secret smiles all morning and to be honest she wasn't that bothered about food and would happily spend all day in bed. Harrison had never really been interested in what made her satisfied or happy, but Arthur had got to know every part of her body intimately and had wanted to know if it felt good and what she liked, so he could bring her to the edge of reason. It was empowering and she could easily get used to him kissing his way up her inner thigh and his hands gliding along her hip and dipping lower.

Even Nico, who had been blessed with a clear under-standing of what made women tick, hadn't made her feel like Arthur did. She guessed it was the addition of recip-rocal love, but it also made her a bit nervous about how long it would last. She didn't think her heart could withstand another battering, but she had a feeling that Arthur wouldn't let her down...

Chapter Twenty-Seven

They both looked up as the doorbell pealed. Daisy was buttering croissants that she'd bought from the bakers the day before and Arthur was pressing buttons to try and get his coffee machine to work, cursing under his breath at the same time, which made Daisy smile. Daisy gave him a questioning look and he shrugged and filched a croissant before she could add any jam, munching on it as he walked to the door.

Daisy took the rest of their breakfast pastries out onto the balcony to give him some privacy, unable to hide her smile. She put the plate on the table and was about to go back for the coffees when she heard a high-pitched woman's voice. She could see Arthur was trying to block the doorway and his shoulders were tense, but he then hung his head and stepped back as a very glamorous-looking blonde woman with immaculately highlighted hair and perfect make-up strutted into the room and looked about, her hair swishing around her shoulders.

'Lilian,' said Arthur in exasperation. 'You can't just barge in.'

'We were together for months, Arthur,' she said tightly as Daisy shrank back behind a piece of ivy-clad trellis, her heart feeling as if it had just jumped out of her chest. She tried to make herself as invisible as possible and felt tears sting her eyes as the woman turned sideways and Daisy saw she was definitely pregnant.

'The least you can do is help me when I need it. I know I didn't tell you about this, but I'm on my own and I didn't know who else to turn to. This child needs a father.'

Daisy saw Arthur note her stomach and blanch, but he led the woman to his couch and then glanced in panic at the balcony. He quickly settled Lilian and rushed out to speak to Daisy, but when he stepped onto the balcony, she was gone.

Daisy put a hand on either side of her bathroom sink and retched, but nothing would come out as she hadn't eaten anything yet. Arthur was about to be a dad! So much for him saying how cute their own children might be, when he'd already fathered one with another woman while they were figuring things out. She knew Nico had been in situ and in the way for some time, but Arthur had clearly been seeing that woman all along, so once again the whole thing was a joke. He hadn't changed after all. One woman would never be enough for Arthur Lopez.

Arthur had told her that he'd dated Lilian on and off over the years and that they'd been seeing each other before Daisy had come back, adding they'd parted amicably and they were now friends. She'd been stupid to assume a virile man like him hadn't been dating anyone while Nico stayed with her. Knowing Arthur's track history, he'd probably done it to get back at her.

All the past recriminations about why they hadn't worked flooded back and she'd just climbed over the balcony to get back into her flat. She'd left the double doors open when she'd come back for food earlier and it had meant she could make herself scarce without being seen. She could imagine the look on Lilian's face if she'd found another woman in Arthur's flat when she'd just announced he was about to become a dad. Daisy retched again and then slumped onto the cold tiled floor of the bathroom. This should have been one of the happiest days of her life, but once again Arthur had let her down. He might not have known about the baby, that was clear from his shocked face, but Daisy knew the kind of man he was. He might be a player, but he wouldn't shirk his responsibilities.

Her phone shrilled on the floor next to her, where she'd shoved it as she'd sat down. Out of instinct she checked that it wasn't her parents about Brontë, and then slid the tab to silence it when she saw it was Arthur. She heard him knock on her door and call her name, but there was no way she could face him right now. He'd have excuses and she just didn't want to hear them.

There was no way she'd stand in the way of the mother of Arthur's child. Daisy knew how lonely that journey could be, and however much it tore her heart through her chest and left a gaping hole, she wouldn't wish that on her worst enemy. Fresh tears sprang to her eyes and she angrily dashed them away. Arthur Lopez didn't deserve a single drop.

Chapter Twenty-Eight

Arthur tried to calm his frazzled nerves and his temper, but Lilian always managed to rile him... and so did Daisy. He guessed she'd listened to his conversation with Lilian and then jumped over the balcony. He was fuming with her. It had been a reckless and dangerous move, however close their properties were and he was furious. Supposing she'd fallen? Not only that, but she was ignoring his calls. He groaned and held his head in his hands.

'Bad timing?' asked Lilian, as she rubbed her belly and sipped the glass of water he'd handed her, after she'd looked through his cupboards and raised her eyebrows over the fact that they were pretty much bare. They'd only ever met in hotels before, so she wasn't aware of his lack of shopping skills. He put down his phone with a sigh and turned to face his ex.

'You could say that.' His head had started pounding. He realised he hadn't had a migraine for quite a while, but now a headache was back with full force. He sipped his coffee. It was cold. He'd woken up to the best day of his life, with the girl of his dreams in his bed – and now it had all been ruined by a misunderstanding.

'Oops!' laughed Lilian. 'Sorry about that. It's the hormones. One minute I'm sobbing my heart out, and the next I find anything anyone says hysterical. It's making me look slightly unhinged,' she smiled, but her eyes started to water so he moved up the couch next to her and put an arm around her shoulders. She leaned her head on him gratefully and sniffed, wiping her eyes. 'I was very much living the single life, as you well know, but then this happened by chance. Stupid food poisoning,' she sighed.

'Food poisoning got you pregnant?' he smiled, staring out at the water for a moment. He could see the queues forming for the boat rides and hear Joe's voice calling for everyone to get on board *Bertha*. Hearing Joe's voice in the distance usually made Arthur smile, but now it just reminded him of Daisy and he flinched.

Lilian rolled her eyes and then turned to face him. 'I forgot that with the contraceptive pill you can get pregnant if you've been vomiting for a few days. It can stop being as effective, apparently.'

'Was it a shock?'

'Not really,' she admitted, hanging her head, before looking back up at him. 'I think I kind of wanted to get pregnant, if I'm honest.' She put her hands on her stomach protectively. 'I remembered that you told me you were moving in here and I've just had a huge argument with my family about my decision to be a single parent. They said I had to tell the dad, or they'd cut me off, as it's half his responsibility. I'm sorry, Arthur, but I didn't know what else to do. Can I stay here tonight? I can't go back to their penthouse when they spoke to me like that.'

'Umm...' said Arthur, rubbing his chin and wondering if

he'd gone grey in the past twenty minutes with stress. He glanced at his phone again but Daisy wasn't even opening his messages. 'Ok.'

He pictured his amazing weekend alone with Daisy going up in smoke. Not that she was currently talking to him anyway, and he couldn't blame her. He was in shock at seeing party animal Lilian's very pregnant tummy. She'd loved going out every night and had zero tolerance towards children whenever they'd been together. They'd had fun, because neither of them had wanted anything else. Now here they were, sitting side by side on his couch, while he sweated about how to reconnect Lilian with her usually very patient and supportive family. She'd pushed them away over years of partying and excess spending, but they usually came round.

He cared a lot about her happiness, because she was a friend, even if she was a lot to handle at times, so if it meant he was sitting here with her instead of Daisy right now, then Lilian probably needed him a bit more. Gloom descended on him because this looked really, really, bad, but as he sent an emergency text to his sisters to explain his predicament, he tried not to let Lilian know that she might have destroyed his own chance of happiness by turning up.

He opened the door to Maya and Romy exactly twenty minutes later. His heart melted a little because he'd never sent an SOS call before and they'd clearly dropped everything and run to his side. He looked behind them and groaned, because his grandad and grandmother were both patiently waiting to be let in as well. His grandmother was wearing a beautiful outfit of flared grey trousers and a matching tunic top with purple lavender stems sewn all around the hemline. His grandad was last in line, carrying an exotic plant that had tall stems and scary-looking red buds with what seemed like tiny teeth along the edges. Arthur dreaded to think what they were for. Pops was fast becoming a bit of an icon as a plant specialist. His television show growing in popularity by the day, it seemed. He got fan mail by the truckload from people of all ages, which his grandmother found most amusing. His grandad found it bewildering, as he would be eighty-two in a few months. He was never one to overthink anything, though, and just left the letters for his wife to sort out.

'Um, come in,' Arthur said, stepping back to let the posse through. He sent a questioning glance to his sisters and Maya pulled a face and shrugged helplessly.

'We were in their kitchen when you sent the message,' she hissed under her breath. 'Gran picked up the phone and read the text. Sorry!' Then she looked at Lilian with a frown.

Romy had got as far as the lounge, then stopped dead when she saw Lilian and her full baby belly. 'Where's Daisy?'

'Hi Romy,' said Lilian, her face breaking into a smile as she eased herself out of her seat and went to greet them all. 'Who is Daisy?' she asked, turning to Arthur as they all followed suit. He quickly greeted his grandparents and went to make them a coffee after ushering them all forward without an explanation. They had met Lilian quite a few times over the years and knew they'd dated, but seeing her predicament had stunned each and every one of them to silence – except for Romy, who started stomping around the room in a huff. No surprises there, he sighed. They were supposed to be helping him, not bombarding him with more dramas.

They huddled and began murmuring quietly, apart from Maya, who was looking at Lilian with a worried frown and asking her how she was. After a few pleasantries, Arthur couldn't wait any longer.

'Daisy was here but now she won't answer my calls,' he said lamely.

'I'm not surprised,' said Romy, her words scorching his brain. 'So, Lilian, we can see that congratulations are in order. Who is the lucky guy?' she gave Arthur a pointed stare and he held up his hands in surrender.

'Romy!' said Maya, aghast, but Lilian just laughed her tinkling laugh and sat back in her chair. She was used to Romy's blunt conversational style and often ignored it. She'd spent the past evening telling Arthur what had been happening in her life and this morning she had said she might be ready to go and talk things through with her parents. Meanwhile, Daisy still wasn't opening Arthur's messages, answering his calls, or coming to the door when he knocked.

Arthur checked that Lilian was okay with him telling his family her current dilemma. When she nodded her consent, he spoke. 'It's Connor.'

All their mouths dropped open at this. Connor was one of the guys Arthur hung around with when he went on London nights out in Soho, or Mayfair. Gregarious and full of fun, Connor was the life and soul of any gathering. He was also married with a small child. He'd visited Arthur's grandparents' house many times over the years for parties, which was probably where he'd met Lilian, now that Arthur thought about it with a sigh of regret.

He didn't know whether to be fuming about the fact that that a close friend had dated his ex-girlfriend and got her pregnant while he was 'happily' married, or angry at Lilian for going there in the first place. The baby would most certainly bring the world crashing down for Connor's wife, and now Arthur had been dragged into the whole mess. Lilian had wanted him to approach Connor as a friend, but in reality, Arthur was too mad at them both to want to interfere. He wasn't judging anyone – it was their life – he just needed advice from his sisters on how to handle the situation. For all he knew, Connor and his wife, Sade, were living separate lives... but he didn't think so.

Sade was also a good friend of Arthur's. Connor and Lilian had put him in an impossible situation. He'd actually known Sade before Connor. Daisy had bruised his heart him by assuming the worst and ignoring him, and now half his family were involved.

'I'll kill him!' said Romy, as she began pacing the room, her fists bunched.

'He doesn't know,' said Arthur, gently taking her arm and leading her to sit next to Lilian, but she was still growling. Romy's last relationship broke up because her boyfriend hadn't been truthful about still sleeping with his not so ex ex-wife, so maybe she hadn't been a sensible choice for unbiased advice. Lilian pretended not to know what he was talking about, but then sighed and put her drink on the side table and her hands into her lap, where she fiddled with a huge diamond ring on her middle finger.

'It was brief fling,' she said ruefully. 'He was having a rough time in his marriage and I consoled him, I guess. I thought they would separate, but it didn't happen. There was no way I could tell him about the baby after that.'

'Lilian's parents are refusing to help her unless she tells him, but she's scared of the fallout,' Arthur explained to the room.

'Connor should have thought of that before he got himself into this mess,' said Romy cattily.

Maya jumped up to soothe things over. 'Romy!' she said, giving her sister a warning look.

'Sorry, Lilian,' Romy mumbled, after seeing Lilian's flushed cheeks. She hung her head, the anger dissipating as quickly as it had arrived.

'None of us know the circumstances of someone else's relationship, so let's not make this situation worse. A baby is in the mix now. We should try and work out what to do,' said Maya, rubbing her temples and taking the plant from her grandad who was still using it to hide behind. She led him out to look at the planting on the balcony and he gave her a grateful kiss on the cheek and bent down to examine the lush green oasis Daisy had created.

'Have you decided to tell Connor?' Maya asked Lilian when she returned to the lounge. Everyone was sitting in silence, which was unheard of in her family. 'Do you need an intermediary when you do?' she added and Lilian nodded. 'Oh, I guess that's where Arthur comes in,' Maya said, understanding clearly dawning.

'Well yes, I was kind of hoping that Arthur might be able to speak to Connor first.' Lilian puffed out her cheeks and then batted her eyelashes at Arthur, and he groaned and put his head in his hands.

Arthur's grandmother Ettie cleared her throat and stepped in. She had been unusually quiet for such an opinionated woman, but she clearly had something to say now. 'I'm not sure that's Arthur's role,' she said, going to sit on Lilian's other side and taking her hand. 'It looks to me like this needs sorting quickly,' she glanced at Lilian's belly and made Lilian smile finally. 'Whatever the outcome, Connor deserves to know. It might be difficult at first, but hopefully you can come to an arrangement that is best for your child.' She patted Lilian's hand and then rummaged in her handbag that she'd just placed by her feet. It was beautifully crafted from contrasting layers of woven ribbons and was her latest hobby.

She drew out a packet of chocolate biscuits and handed a couple to Lilian. 'You must keep your strength up. I know Arthur never has any food in the place. I have to bring my own snacks,' she chided, and he grinned too.

Arthur decided it felt good to have his family's support. Even though they had arrived en masse and taken over, he was kind of glad they had. He could command rooms full of people, talking about the latest technology, but when it came to matters of the heart he was sadly lacking, he knew. He'd thought he'd finally cracked the code for love, but then Daisy had run off at the first sign of trouble and he'd not heard from her again. He'd even thought that she might have been able to help Lilian, as she'd coped with a baby on her own herself, but as usual, she'd assumed the worst of him, and now it was his turn to have his heart broken.

Chapter Twenty-Nine

Daisy had just reached the lift when she heard Arthur's front door open. She dived behind a tall pot plant and peeked, only to see the woman who had arrived the day before lean in and hug him, her pregnant stomach between them. Then she turned and walked towards Daisy, who hot-footed it down the stairs.

Lilian had clearly stayed the night. Daisy's stomach turned over and she felt bile in the back of her throat. She certainly wasn't going to put another woman through what she'd experienced, having to bring up a baby on her own. Arthur had seemed as shocked as Daisy was, so she guessed he hadn't known. She wondered if it happened shortly after Daisy returned home, or perhaps when Nico had turned up on her doorstep. She knew she had no real right to be annoyed, but Arthur had acted like he'd missed her from the moment she'd arrived. Well, not that much, it seemed.

Daisy refused to be broken by that man again, even though her heart was currently shattered into a million pieces and she'd literally had to pull herself off the floor and drag herself into the shower to wash her tears away. Their night together had been all she'd hoped it would be, and now she didn't think she'd ever recover. She picked her feet up because she'd been dragging them along the street and headed to Penny's for some consolation cake.

Never would she put what Arthur wanted in front of her own needs again. She had the whole weekend and the next week to herself, but now she was at a loss about how to spend her leisure time. She might as well throw herself into her work and start planning her next big design job, which was the land adjacent to *Bertha*'s dock.

What she really wanted to do was to rip Arthur's head off and then curl up into a ball in her bedroom and cry. She still had to finish the project at his office and now he'd announced to his staff that they were together it would be horrendously embarrassing that they'd only lasted one night. She cringed and tried to smile at Penny as she breezily asked what she'd like to order. Penny took one look at her face and quickly guided her to a table and told her staff to bring them both a strong coffee and a huge slab of the toffee sponge cake that Fred had just placed under a dome on the counter. He gave them a worried frown, but Penny brushed him aside and pulled out a chair for Daisy, who sank into it gratefully.

'What's happened?' she asked.

'Arthur's happened,' said Daisy with a grimace. Penny paled and got up to bring the cake herself. She placed it and a fork in front of Daisy. Daisy took a bite gratefully and finally felt her muscles and manic smile easing.

'Tell me all about it,' soothed Penny as their steaming coffees arrived and the staff hastily retreated after one look from their boss. They all knew Daisy well now and it was clearly troubling them that her usual sunny disposition was missing.

'His ex-girlfriend turned up at his flat.'

'So?' frowned Penny, with confusion.

'She's pregnant,' added Daisy and the colour drained from Penny's face.

'What? But I thought something might happen with you two. I had such high hopes.' She glanced at Daisy's pained expression and pulled a face. 'Oh... okay. That's bad timing,' she winced.

They both jumped as their phones dinged at the same time. Penny grabbed hers from her pocket and tried to hide her smile. 'Your grandad is hosting a party for Ettie and Owen, on *Bertha*. Apparently it's their anniversary and they decided to throw a last-minute party at the best venue in town, after this place of course!' she grinned, her eyes full of mischief. Daisy frowned and read the party invitation on her own phone.

'I'm not going,' she grumbled. 'Ettie is always saying she can't remember how many years she's been married for... and Arthur will be there!'

'You are going,' said Penny with a firm tone. 'You will show him that you're strong and can stand without him. Brontë is with your parents this weekend, so it will give you a chance to relax and have a few glasses of wine for a bit of courage. Plus, you should wear a red-hot dress and show him what he's missing,' she added with a wink. Daisy hung her head. The last thing she wanted to do was stand on the deck of her grandad's steamboat chatting to Arthur's family. On the other hand, it might make Monday at Arthur's offices slightly less awful, breaking the tension if they'd already tried to be civil around one another. She shoved the cake around the plate, even though it was sacrilege to leave any. Her stomach just couldn't take food right now. She leaned in and gave Penny an almost desperate hug.

'Thanks Penny,' she said. 'You're right, but I need to go dress shopping now and I'm really not in the mood.'

'Call one of your school mum friends and make an afternoon of it. Pamper yourself a little,' advised Penny firmly. 'Get your hair and nails done, and Fred and I will pick you up at seven thirty,' said Penny, ushering her out of her chair. 'Make sure the dress is a killer!' she called out to her retreating back.

Daisy sent a quick text to Anne asking if she was free to go shopping, assuming she would be busy, but she got an immediate call back.

'I'd love to,' gushed Anne when Daisy answered. 'The kids are exhausting, and Darren was out playing golf all day yesterday, so I need some pampering. I can be there in fifteen minutes.'

Daisy finished the call and stood stunned for a moment. She hadn't been shopping with a friend for years and couldn't recall ever having her nails done at a salon. The thought was thrilling and a bit daunting, but she was determined to let people in and finally begin to live again, with or without Arthur. Her lip wobbled slightly, but by the time Anne arrived and rushed up to her, throwing an arm around her shoulders, Daisy couldn't help but grin at her enthusiasm.

'You saved me,' Anne joked. 'I was about to go food shopping, or do the laundry.' Her eyes were sparkling with mischief and Daisy felt hope rise in her chest. Penny had been right about keeping busy, and Anne was already leading them up into the high street towards the hair salon.

Chapter Thirty

Arthur could hear music coming from Daisy's flat. The double doors to her patio were open. He'd been tempted to climb over and make her listen to him, but she'd moved a very heavy plant pot to the meeting point between their balconies and it made jumping across almost impossible and the probability of death very high. He wondered if this was her plan. Then he tried to ignore the scent of her delicately floral perfume with its deep undertones of spice. It was hitting his nose as he sat on his own balcony, feeling glum. He'd been there for an hour so far, hoping she'd come outside, but she'd resolutely stayed indoors.

He was wearing a smart pair of dark trousers and a light blue cotton shirt that was rolled up to his elbows. He was already feeling hot and sweaty in the warm summer breeze and he really didn't think his grandmother's master plan of a sudden anniversary party (when it wasn't even her anniversary) would work. For a start Daisy might not turn up, so it would be a whole lot of hanging around for nothing – not that his family or their friends would ever waste a party.

Secondly, his body was craving Daisy after spending that special night with her, and it was making him even more grumpy. He'd huffed and puffed his way around his flat all afternoon and even kicked a few stray boxes he still hadn't unpacked. Daisy was supposed to be his girlfriend, and he was damned if he was going to let her strut away without a fight. It had taken months of wooing to get her to let her guard down and he wasn't about to give up now, however hurt his ego was that she'd jumped ship at the first chance she got.

He'd tried to focus on his work, but he couldn't concentrate when all he could visualise was waking up and seeing Daisy, naked and tangled in his sheets. She still had work to do at his offices and he knew she wouldn't let him down and not finish the project, so if today didn't work, then he could try again the following week. It was exhausting, trying to persuade someone you loved that you had their best intentions at heart and would never hurt them – especially when you knew you'd hurt them before. He cursed under his breath and went to pour himself a big glass of Pinot Noir. He savoured the rich flavour and fruity scent and then straightened his back and went to look out on his balcony.

Joe's boat *Bertha* was resplendent, even though the whole party had been pulled off in a matter of hours. Maya's best friend Leah had been roped in to decorate the boat with flowers and bunting, and he could already see that the steamboat looked magnificent. Garlands had been woven around fairy lights strung across the deck and were twinkling in the darkening early evening sky. Even from this distance he wanted to go down and see the spectacle.

The air was warm and dry and people were wandering up towards the dock. A few were in full eveningwear, the ladies in beautiful gowns and the men in smart trousers, shirts and jackets. As with all his family parties, there were also people in every kind of outfit possible. He could see a lady wearing what looked like purple silk pyjamas, and a man with an incredible tan, bare-chested and wearing the teeniest pair of orange shorts. No one cared a jot what others wore. His grandparents were always surrounded by their incredible group of friends. Arthur had never been to a dull party thrown by his family, but he didn't know if he was ready for this impromptu one.

He caught sight of his grandparents as they stepped on board. His grandmother was dressed in a flowing silk gown made from a breathtaking pattern of exotic blooms and his grandfather was dressed in a suit with a velvet jacket that matched the deep red of some of the flowers on Ettie's dress. Arthur closed his eyes for a moment and then gave one more longing look at Daisy's balcony, before he slid his doors closed, locked them and left the flat. He shoved the keys in his pocket, staring at Daisy's front door as he passed by. He set a determined stride and went to join the rest of his family and friends to celebrate his grandparents' half-anniversary.

His parents had asked after Daisy on a video call that morning, so he'd told them about the whole cock-up and the last-minute party. They were sympathetic but couldn't help laughing about the madcap party idea.

'Typical Mum,' his own mother had commented. She wasn't at all surprised by Ettie and Owen's plans, as she'd grown up with their flamboyant lifestyle. 'You must fight for Daisy if she means that much to you though, sweetheart,' she added gently. 'Don't let her slip through your fingers again.'

Arthur had felt his skin grow warm and he'd taken a moment to think on his mother's advice. Not having been open about his feelings for Daisy before made it a difficult conversation, and he'd seen his mother had a tear or two in her eyes before she'd brushed them away. He felt weirdly closer to them both afterwards and they promised to come back for a visit soon, which had buoyed his flagging energy.

As he reached the dock, he noticed the Bowen brothers loitering around. They owned the other boats docked there, so they were probably wondering what was going on, he guessed.

'Last minute party for my grandparents' half-anniversary,' he explained to their bemused faces. 'Come on. You should both join us.'

'Are you sure?' asked Luca, who seemed a little reticent, but Alex was already walking over, so Luca had to follow suit.

Arthur motioned for them to follow him. It felt good to have company after the day he'd had. He travelled so much that he didn't worry about going anywhere solo, but since Daisy had reappeared in his life, his emotions were all over the place. He enjoyed chatting to Alex and Luca as they strolled towards *Bertha*. The brothers were often the life and soul of a party and Arthur knew they'd looked out for Maya when she'd worked on Joe's boat.

He grinned as he saw Maya, dressed in a stunning golden gown, her hand in Noah's. Both were smiling and chatting to their grandparents' friends, who all seemed to have a glass of fizz in hand or *Bertha*'s special gin and strawberry lemonade. There was a buzz in the air and although most people knew it wasn't actually his grandparents' anniversary, they all seemed keen to celebrate anyway and had brought an assortment of gifts, including one that was shaped like a guitar – and one that was moving!

Roman came over to greet them. He was wearing black

jeans and an untucked blue shirt, and his dreadlocks were loose and flowing around his shoulders. 'What is that?' he asked, pointing to the wriggling gift.

'I've no idea, but if Romy finds an animal in there all hell will break loose,' said Arthur and both men quickly went to investigate while Alex and Luca stood guard to distract Romy if she appeared. Arthur handed the gift to Roman, who peered inside and they both jumped back when the Venus flytrap plant snapped shut on a fly that buzzed past, almost catching Roman's fingers. Both men stood there in shock and put the carnivorous plant safely behind the bar, just in case anyone decided to look at it later after a few drinks.

Romy was wearing a knockout fitted blue dress with tiny birds flying all over it. She wasn't as groomed as Maya, but to Arthur she always looked perfect. Romy's hair would never fall in sleek waves like Maya's, because she never bothered to condition it, and you wouldn't catch her in make-up, because she called it a waste of time. Arthur grinned to himself. Both of his sisters were absolute stunners and neither of them needed anything to make them more beautiful, in his opinion. Romy was currently scowling at him so he frowned, and turned to see she was actually looking at Luca and Alex. Oops! He'd forgotten Luca wasn't that keen on Romy's tea boat and was quite vocal about her small menagerie of birds living there. Arthur chuckled to himself. Luca was a brave man if he thought upsetting Romy was ever going to work out.

Maya stepped up beside him and kissed him on the cheek. 'Is she here yet?' he asked as Romy joined them. She completely ignored Alex and Luca and led Arthur further onto the boat. There were flowers everywhere, filling the air with a delicate fragrance of jasmine mixing with the sweet citrusy scent of the peonies Leah had dotted around in tall glass vases. More strings of fairy lights were tied back and forth across the bow. As the sun began to dip, the lights shone and the scene was kind of magical, he had to admit. If he wasn't so nervous he might even actually enjoy himself.

'You both look incredible,' he complimented his sisters. Maya smiled but Romy was watching Luca again.

'Why did you invite them?' she asked in disgust.

'They were on the dock, Romy. I could hardly walk past them and not ask them to come,' he laughed, trying to let go of some of the tension he felt. His muscles were wound up tight and his mind was buzzing as his gaze darted round to look for any sign of Daisy. His headache was back, so he pinched his nose with his fingers and tried to relax.

'Did you manage to make contact with Daisy?' asked Maya, in a soothing tone.

'No. She still won't answer my calls or texts,' he sighed, rubbing his tired eyes.

'You're so stupid,' said Romy and Maya nudged her to soften her words. 'You should have told her about Lilian,' Romy continued, regardless.

'I didn't know she was pregnant, having an affair with Connor, or going to turn up just after I'd asked Daisy to be exclusive and my girlfriend.'

'Your girlfriend!' chorused his sisters in unison.

'What the hell?' said Romy. 'That's a piece of information you left out. Right, I'm going to find her and make her listen. This is silly,' she raged. Arthur quite liked Romy being on his side for once and preened a little. 'You're still stupid, though,' she added, and his chest deflated and he hung his head. Maya took his chin and lifted his face.

'I'm glad you finally realised what we all already know. You two are made for each other.'

'Well, she doesn't know,' grumbled Arthur sulkily.

'Yes, she does, you idiot. She wouldn't have run off otherwise,' said Romy, shaking her head at his idiocy. Arthur frowned and then a flutter of hope filled him. They all turned as they heard more guests arrive and Arthur almost felt like he'd stopped breathing, or he was about to have a heart attack. There, talking to his grandparents, were Daisy, Penny and Fred.

Daisy was dressed in an off the shoulder long red dress that stole the air from his lungs. He could see a good expanse of leg as she moved, thanks to the deep slit in the side of the dress. The fabric clung to her curves and made his heart almost stop. He didn't have a coherent thought until Romy nudged him, a little too hard, in the ribs and almost shoved him over.

Daisy had tiny diamond clips in her softly curled hair and she was wearing beautifully applied make-up with a deep red lipstick colour that made him want to drag her away and kiss it off, as her lips looked so lush and tempting. He gulped and centred himself. 'Go and get your girl,' said Romy softly, before she turned and scowled at Luca again.

Chapter Thirty-One

The party was in full swing by the time Arthur had worked his way around the boat and said hello to his friends and family. He'd tried to get away, but couldn't be rude to his grandparents' crowd. There was a band playing on the bow and a few people were now dancing and swaying to the beat, with much hilarity. Plates of bruschetta with fresh tomato, drizzled with balsamic vinegar, were being carried around and he realised he'd forgotten to eat again. He grabbed a couple of the canapés as they went past on a tray held aloft by a waiter.

He applauded Ettie for pulling this off at such short notice. It was all about who you knew, he understood. Penny and Fred would have been contacted about the food and cake. The band were the nephews of his grandmother's neighbour, and Leah had been roped in for decoration and ambience. He'd said hello to Leah and her boyfriend Matt, who were now standing with Maya and Noah. Romy had moved on from Luca, who was actually trying to chat to her. He seemed quite amused by the fact that she was patently ignoring him. Alex had begun trying to speak to Daisy. Fire burned in his veins as he joined the conversation and politely asked to have a private word with her. She flushed but Penny answered on her behalf and she, Fred and Alex began chatting about boats.

Arthur gently took Daisy's arm and led her to a quieter area of the deck. The majority of people were listening to the band, so he made the most of this and drew her to the furthest area at the back of the boat. 'No pregnant ex-girl-friends with you today, then?' Daisy asked waspishly.

Arthur flinched but wasn't about to let this nonsense continue. 'I'm hurt that you ran out on me and didn't give me a chance to explain,' he said honestly. He didn't touch her, but he could see she was holding her temper by the flush on her cheeks. He brushed a few tendrils of hair out of her eyes, but she moved out of reach and went to sit on one of the tour benches that looked out across the river.

'I'm hurt that you were clearly sleeping with your ex when you said we were getting to know each other again,' Daisy fired at him, her fists clenched.

'You had Nico living with you!' he said incredulously.

'We weren't sleeping together,' she parried back. 'You made that impossible by inviting him to live with you!'

'I'm glad I did!' he retaliated without hesitation. 'Did you want to sleep with him?'

'No, but that's not my point,' she hissed.

Romy stomped over and interrupted them. Her arms were crossed over her chest and her cheeks were deep red. 'That man is impossible!' she said angrily, seemingly unaware of what she'd walked into.

'Um, Romy...' said Arthur in exasperation. Then he saw his sister's expression and followed her eyeline to Luca. 'What's the problem? Do you need me to have a word with him?'

Romy finally glanced between her brother and Daisy and then noted the tension in the air. 'No. I can handle it. He's just being annoying. He hates my boat, but that just makes me want to put down even bigger roots and paint it bright pink!' she seethed and Daisy snorted and finally laughed. 'Have you told her it's not your baby yet?' she threw that bomb into the ring.

'What?' gasped Daisy.

'You idiot!' said Romy, slapping her palm on her forehead. 'Honestly Arthur, for a smart man you can be incredibly dumb. That's the part you lead the conversation with!' she scolded and then leaned in for a hug, rolling her eyes at Daisy who was looking aghast and very upset.

Romy then hugged Daisy too, and then wandered off muttering about needing a huge glass of wine and a handsome man to engage in intelligent conversation after having to put up with ten minutes of listening to Luca blathering on. Arthur tried to calm his mind and grabbed two glasses of Sauvignon Blanc from a passing waiter.

'She's a lot,' he sighed, watching his sister stomp off towards the buffet table. It was bursting with tiny triangle sandwiches full of cheese, ham and homemade chilli jam, crumbly sausage rolls and huge slices of Fred's cakes that had just been laid out by Penny's staff, which smelt delicious.

'She's looking out for you,' huffed Daisy protectively. 'Also, she's dealing with her own heartbreak.' Daisy could barely look at him, so he lifted her face. 'So, the baby isn't yours?'

Arthur shook his head. 'Lilian has got herself in a bit of a pickle with a close friend of mine and she needed somewhere to stay for a night, and a shoulder to cry on.'

'And while you were being a knight in shining armour, I'd done a bunk over the balcony?'

'Please don't ever, *ever*, do that again,' he shuddered. 'You almost gave me a heart attack.'

'Sorry,' said Daisy, her bottom lip wobbling. 'I guess I have trust issues. I thought I'd got over that, but my first instinct was to run.'

'Whereas mine was to find my girlfriend and sort things out, but she wouldn't answer my calls. Then she then turns up at a party in a dress that makes her boyfriend want to throw her over his shoulder and jump overboard with her so that he can take her back to his cave,' he tried to lighten the mood, but his feelings were still tender and sore. Daisy had winced when he'd mentioned that she was his girlfriend and he hoped she wasn't regretting that too.

'I'm sorry, Arthur. It's not that I don't trust you. I think... I don't trust that this is real.'

'It's real for me.' He said, taking her hands in his own.

'Being vulnerable is scary,' said Daisy, her eyes misting over. She sniffed and wiped her eyes with the back of her hand.

'Loving is scary,' admitted Arthur. 'But being without the person you love is scarier.' Daisy's big watery eyes looked into his and her bottom lip wobbled, but she moved closer to him and he put his arms around her shoulders in comfort.

'I actually thought that you might be able to help Lilian,' he added hopefully.

'Me?' she squeaked in surprise, hiding her face behind her glass as she picked it up from the bench beside her.

'You pretty much brought up Brontë on your own and I thought it might not seem so daunting after speaking to you

– if she did choose that route. My friend Connor, the dad – he's married.'

Daisy flinched. 'Ouch,' she said. 'Poor Lilian. What a mess. How awful for Connor and his family too. One fleeting decision and a whole lifetime of pain for them. Having Bronte was a blessing, however much I'd messed up by choosing Harrison and losing you.' Harrison had done a complete number on her, but in the end she'd thrived, despite her husband.

Daisy gazed out over the water in thought and was silent for a moment before looking at Arthur again. 'I should have left Harrison after I found out he'd cheated the first time, but some families survive it. Excuses don't take away the heartbreak. There are no winners here.'

Arthur took her hand and they both leaned on the rails and looked out at the stars that were appearing in the inky night sky. 'I'm sorry Harrison did that to you,' he ground out, keeping a check on his emotions. 'I'm also sorry that I let you down when we first got together, but I never cheated. The way I felt about you scared me,' he admitted, and she turned to face him.

'You aren't your parents,' she soothed. 'We can still be a family and be apart occasionally. Your parents are together and they've brought up three great kids, even from another country.'

Arthur nodded and stared at the view again. The stars were twinkling now and the music was heating up with a few more upbeat songs with a female guest singer that led to cheers from the partygoers. They struck up the first few notes of Beyoncé's song, *Single Ladies,* and Daisy burst out laughing.

'This was one of the first songs I heard you sing when I moved in,' she grinned.

'I bet you thought you were living next to a pop legend,' he joked. 'I do have a penchant for a good lyric.'

'You were soooo out of tune,' she giggled and he poked her in the ribs, making her jump and giggle more.

'You'd never guess my grandparents are supposed to be retired and taking it easier,' he shook his head and laughed as his grandad twirled his grandmother past them and she blew them a kiss mid spin. 'They work more now than they ever did while we were growing up. There is never a dull moment in their lives.'

'Never!' Daisy laughed. 'I hope we're like them when we're older,' she chuckled, watching their retreating forms as they joined their friends. 'Your mum and dad came home for visits, they were a big part of your childhood and made sure you had a safe place to grow up. They didn't desert you. Harrison lived in the same country as us and we felt more alone than you probably did,' she added sadly. 'I'm not minimising how much it hurt, but you knew you were loved.'

'Why did you date Harrison?' he asked quietly.

'To get you to finally notice me after you ran away,' she replied sadly.

'I did notice you. I've always known when you're near.'

'Then why didn't you tell me?

'You had the power to hurt me. You still do,' he admitted, his eyes shining in the darkness.

'I'm looking for stability now,' Daisy said. 'Playing the field isn't for me. I don't want to bring a string of people home to meet Brontë,' she sighed, rubbing her temples and putting her wine on a nearby bench.

'So, it's just about finding a replacement dad?' he could see that his words stung, but he was still hurting and needed to know, as the thought had been niggling at him over the past few days.

'She has never really had a dad, so we manage perfectly well on our own.' Daisy fiddled with the fabric of her dress and then leant on the railing next to him again. 'I know we said we'd be girlfriend and boyfriend, but after our night together, my feelings terrified me. That's why I didn't hear you out and blocked your calls. I would have listened eventually, even if the child had been yours. We weren't dating then, so I had no claim on you.'

'You claimed me the first day we met,' he said seriously, and tears sprung to her eyes. He brushed them away with the pad of his thumb and then pulled her gently into the circle of his arms. 'I've missed you,' he said as he dipped his head and dropped kisses all over her face. She sniffed and then placed her hands on either side of his face to bring his lips towards her own for the softest kiss that made his heart soar. When they surfaced they both had stupid grins on their faces and also an audience who cheered and raised a glass to them.

Arthur felt adrenaline fire through his body and he put his arm around Daisy to hide her blushes, but she seemed quite happy to be seen in his arms and locking lips with him publicly.

'I only left your flat a day or so ago,' she teased, brushing her hair out of her eyes. He caught her hand and kissed her wrist.

'I've missed you from the moment we broke up all those years ago,' he said in a gravelly voice. She gasped, and then linked her hands behind his head and pulled him in for another scorching kiss.

'I guess those two have made up,' said Luca as Romy walked past.

'What do you know about it?' she asked frostily.

Luca gave her an easy smile and shrugged, which made her growl. 'Maya told me they'd fallen out and this was an emergency party to get them back together. I like the way your family works!' he joked and raised a glass to her.

She shuddered, as a woman had just walked past and very clearly looked Luca's (very fit) body up and down and given him a come-hither smile. He ignored her and kept his gaze focused on Romy, but she walked away seething and mumbling about local Lotharios, and finding ultra-violet paint to make her boat visible from space.

'Do you think those two will ever get on?' asked Arthur, watching his sister and noting her bunched fists with a chuckle.

'Arthur...' teased Daisy. 'I don't think Luca *not* liking Romy is the problem. It's that he likes her too much, and he'll do anything in his power to annoy her to get her attention. Mind you, nothing seems to work.'

Arthur gawped in shock and Daisy patted his arm in sympathy and then took his hand and led him towards his grandparents and Joe. Arthur laughed loudly then and swung Daisy back into his arms for a final scorching kiss before his family swarmed around them chattering about how their "dastardly" plan had worked, and Daisy was officially welcomed into the fold.

'I hope you realise that my family will never let you go again now,' Arthur sighed happily as he snuggled her protectively under his arm, as they tried to dodge questions about their relationship status. 'Neither will I,' he added. Daisy looked up into his eyes and grinned, wrapping her arms around her love.

'I'm exactly where I want to be. I'm home.'

Chapter Thirty-Two

Daisy padded out of her bedroom and into the kitchen, holding on to the island for support. She couldn't wipe the grin from her face and she'd stopped twice while she was pulling her pyjamas back on to stare at Arthur's sleeping form. He looked like he'd been sculpted by angels, and she'd felt her heartbeat ramp up again at the sight of him.

She switched the coffee machine on and wandered into the lounge, exhausted from the emotion of the past few days, but exhilarated by the fact that Arthur had given her a second chance, even though she'd not offered him the same courtesy all those years ago. She glanced at the fridge with Brontë's colourful paintings stuck to the front with magnets, and postcards that Nico sent them from across the world. The light wooden cabinet that sat under the flat screen television in the lounge was dotted with vintage photo frames that she'd found at the weekly market that had just begun in town. They were full of the smiling faces of Brontë, Flo and their school friends. There were a couple of Daisy with Maya and Romy, some with her family and of course, one of *Bertha*, with her grandparents standing proudly beside her.

Daisy picked up her phone and scrolled to the photo of her and Nico that she'd asked him to take at her apartment in France. She looked so wistful. She couldn't believe how much her life had changed. She jumped as strong arms wound around her and she was pulled into a solid chest. Arthur leaned over her shoulder to see what she was looking at and she relaxed against him, enjoying the feel of his naked chest.

'Do you miss him?' Arthur asked, as he began nibbling along her shoulder. She arched her neck to give him further access to her skin and she couldn't think straight for a moment. She turned round in his arms, throwing the phone onto the couch. She wound her arms around his neck and pulled him in closer while she kissed him good morning, which made him growl.

Daisy grinned when they parted and moved to make them both some coffee. 'I do miss him. He's a good friend to us both, and I bet you miss him too,' she teased, her eyes sparkling. Arthur was standing there in dark Calvin Klein pyjama bottoms and nothing else, so she fanned her flushed face as she looked at him. He still had a predatory air about him, but it was playful and it made her flustered!

'I don't miss him in my flat,' said Arthur with a laugh. 'Or yours. He was the biggest passion killer I've ever known. I'm sure he did it on purpose,' he added with a grin.

'He kind of liked you,' she coaxed.

'I kind of liked him too,' he admitted, taking the cup of coffee she offered him and opening the freezer to search out some frozen croissants to bake. Daisy knew Arthur loved them and always stocked them for him.

'You know you'll burn those,' she chuckled and he

whipped round and grabbed her by the waist. She shrieked as he picked her up and threw her over his shoulder, but she reached out and copped a quick feel of his backside while she was upside down, which made him laugh and throw her onto the unmade bed. He stood looking down at her with his hands on his hips, which made her insides quiver.

'Are you sorry for your comments about my cooking?' he asked with a raised brow, his lips quirking.

'No. They were all true!' she laughed as he jumped on her and they rolled around the bed as his hands ran all over her body and things quickly turned from play to an inferno of passion. He trailed kisses along her collarbone, making her squirm in pleasure, but then he pulled back and leaned his head on one arm as he watched her skin warm up and flush. He cupped her face with his hand and kissed her gently on the mouth, the temperature cooling slightly.

'What will Brontë think of this?' he asked, serious suddenly. Daisy frowned and he laughed and pulled her body into contact with his again, so that they were lying side by side, facing each other. He looked deeply into her eyes and she gulped at the intensity in his.

'This?'

'Us,' he clarified. 'Us being in love.' Daisy's heart melted and she captured his face in both of her hands and kissed him sweetly.

'She already loves you and we can work the rest out.'

'I've never lived with a child before.'

'You don't live with one now,' said Daisy in confusion.

'Isn't that what we're working towards?'

'You want us all to live together?' He couldn't have said anything to shock her more. Harrison had released himself from any parental expectations early on, but Arthur wanted to step up, for a child that wasn't even his?

'Isn't that what couples in love do?' he asked.

'I hadn't thought that far ahead,' she admitted, her heart beginning to race. 'My tenancy runs out on this place soon and I was thinking of renewing, or buying the flat,' she told him. Their situation worked fine right now, with flats next door to each other, but would Arthur run away if he had a messy and excitable five-year-old around him every day?

'I have thought about it,' he admitted sheepishly and her heart soared. 'I'm not saying we should make major changes right now, as it might be too much for Brontë, but we could knock an interconnecting door through the flats if you buy it, and then open up the wall at a later date?'

'What?' Daisy pulled herself up into a sitting position and stared at him. Her mouth was hanging open, so she snapped it shut. She frowned because that was actually a genius idea, and would mean less upheaval for her daughter – but it sounded pretty serious.

'I don't want to scare you away, but I see more little Brontës in our future, don't you?' Arthur said.

Daisy flushed and tried not to show that she'd thought about what any children she had with Arthur might look like. Could they all live there together? It was a perfect setting, and she was just getting used to being near her family again.

'I guess...' her bottom lip trembled and his eyes sparkled at her and then darkened as his hands slid up her leg.

'Don't you think we should start practicing, then?' he teased, kissing his way up her arm and she almost lost all coherent thought again. She tried to focus, but the man of her dreams had just pulled her underneath him and was staring into her eyes, waiting for her reply. She smiled and slid her hand around to capture his backside as he gave her a wolfish grin and swept her into his arms.

'We should definitely practice,' she said breathlessly as his fingers touched the base of her spine and he kissed her in triumph.

'I'm yours and you're mine,' he clarified and she nodded enthusiastically, wondering how much practice they could get in before breakfast...

Order book 3 today: The Windsor Love Match

Acknowledgments

A big thank you to my friends, family and readers - you mean the world to me. There are so many people to thank when writing and publishing a book, but I really wanted to use this space to remember one of my writing friends, Kate (Katie) Owen. Kate was one of the original members of a group I run with fellow author, Chris Penhall, called Writing Buddies, at Fête Cafe, in Chelmsford, Essex. Kate was an incredibly talented writer and a shining light in our community. She shared her wisdom and smiles and occasionally bought one of her children to our group, to join in with the writing sessions. It was an absolute honour to know Kate. Kate lives on in her family, friends and children and her stories will continue to enrich the lives of anyone who has the privilege to read one.

Thanks to my wonderful advance readers, supporters and street team. I appreciate everyone who is part of my writing journey and that especially includes those who read my books and shares news about them to others. This helps me find others who might also enjoy my writing. I always feel that finding a good book is like finding a friend and I have discovered so many incredible friends throughout my writing career. I continue to do so with new readers and fellow writers that I meet. Without you I wouldn't be able to keep writing. I appreciate you for picking up my books, for telling your friends and for the amazing reviews you write and share. From Lizzie. X

About the Author

International bestselling author and award-winning inventor, Lizzie Chantree has been featured on television and radio. She discovered her love of writing fiction when her children were little. She now writes books full of friendship and laughter, that are about women who are far stronger than they realise. She lives with her family on the coast in Essex. Visit her website at www.lizziechantree.com or follow her on X @Lizzie_Chantree

Sign up to Lizzie's newsletter for a FREE pdf book tracker where you can record your favourite reads, reviews, characters, wish list, swoon rating and more. Plus a monthly prize giveaway! www.lizziechantree.com

If you liked reading my novel, please consider leaving a review. Many readers look to the reviews first when deciding which book to choose, and seeing your review might help them discover this one. I appreciate your help and support. Make an author smile today. Leave a review! Thank you so much. From Lizzie :)

facebook.com/lizziechantree

x.com/Lizzie_Chantree

instagram.com/lizzie_chantree

Praise for Lizzie Chantree

'An absolute page turner, full of romance that will make you swoon. A 5 star read. I now want to visit Windsor.'

'The start of another enchanting series! I'm now getting impatient to read the next one!'

'I LOVE, LOVE, LOVE this!'

'Romance at its best!'

'I would recommend this book to anyone.'

'My recommendation: Get a copy!'

'This book has spice, lost love, new beginnings and a beautiful storyline. I can't wait for the next book!'

'Wow what a stunning story! A beautiful setting. It was perfectly described and it has made me long to visit wonderful Windsor. Can't wait to return for the next book in the series!'

'I absolutely loved this, fake dating, modern day fairytale with a strong female lead twist! Roll on for The Windsor Love Connection .....'

'Dive into this fun, romance filled with art, drama, design and diamonds, as well as devoted family and friends. The swamp girl made me laugh. Recommended summer must read for romance fans.'

'Lizzie Chantree writes lovely romance novels and her latest is no exception. Her strengths lie in creating wonderful characters, beguiling settings and simple but effective story lines.'

'Couldn't put it down.'

'A great bit of escapism!'

'I would happily devour a second sitting.'

'I was enthralled by this beautiful book.'

The Windsor Love Match

Romy and Luca's story. One bed, hate to love, riverside romance!

Chapter 1

'Argh!' Romy screamed as she sat on the edge of the bed. Something under the duvet was moving. She sprung up, her heart beating through her chest, as she floundered around for something to protect herself with.

'What the hell?' came a male voice as someone fumbled on the side table and then switched the lamp on, filling the room with stark brightness.

Romy leaned on the chest of drawers to stop herself keeling over, and blinked rapidly in case she was hallucinating.

A very sleepy and naked-looking man pushed himself out from under the duvet and stood up, making Romy's eyes go wide. It was Luca Bowen.

Thankfully, he was wearing black Calvin Klein boxers, because Romy already felt like she might have a coronary. She was clasping a small vase that she'd grabbed to protect herself with, but now she glanced down at it in disgust. It wouldn't make a dent in his impressive six-pack – but she was still tempted to throw it at his head.

'Romy?' he asked in a puzzled voice as he rubbed his eyes. Then he ran a hand through his short black hair, making it all mussed up and sexy. He squinted as if he couldn't quite believe what he was seeing. She faltered for a second and tried to work out why he'd been sleeping soundly – and very rudely – in her bed!

'What are you doing here?' he asked in a gravelly voice.

Her eyebrows rose in shock. 'What am *I* doing here?' she raged, her fists bunching once she'd placed the vase safely back on the set of drawers. Then she took a moment to rein in her anger. She didn't know if it was the adrenaline from the fright that was making her feel like she'd just run a marathon, or the sight of the very uninvited Luca in her bedroom. 'What the hell are you doing in my bed?'

She stomped over to stand straight in front of him, and then wished she hadn't because he was over six feet tall to her five eight, and her chin was now remarkably close to his naked chest.

'Your bed?' he asked in confusion, before his big brown eyes focused back on her and humour sparked in his eyes. 'Is this a joke to get me back for my comments about your ridiculous duck tea boat?' His eyes scanned down and noted her black silky pyjama shorts set and he frowned.

'Stop messing around,' snapped Romy. 'Get out of here!'

'I'm not going anywhere,' he retorted. 'This is my bed.'

'It isn't!' she bit back. 'I moved in yesterday. It's definitely mine.'

Luca frowned again and then turned to look in confusion at the simple sage green duvet set he'd just climbed out of.

'You can't have,' insisted Luca, making no move to put on any clothes, so she picked up a black T-shirt that had been discarded on the back of a chair and threw it at his head as she backed away.

It had been a long day and the last thing she needed was Luca messing about with her already exhausted mind. He did that most days anyway. She knew he hated her little business, a houseboat moored at the end of the garden belonging to her new landlady, Clara.

Romy had moved back to the pretty little village she'd grown up in over a year ago now. She'd bought a five-year lease on the tea boat by the river in Windsor on a whim. However she found living there uncomfortable because the bedrooms were all used for storage. Clara had persuaded her to move in with her as her lodger, after a few break-ins along the river. When Romy had first moored the boat, its position opposite the dock where Luca and his brother Alex Bowen ran their cruise liners hadn't seemed an issue. She'd felt lucky to have such an accommodating landlady. Unfortunately, Luca had taken umbrage at her 'eyesore' of a boat, and he enjoyed telling her about his issues most days. The man was insufferable!

A handful of ducks had taken up residence on the bow. Romy found them charming, but Luca thought they were a health hazard. Leaving as much mess as she could to wind him up was getting tiring, but she wouldn't let anyone tell her what to do again. She'd left docile Romy back in Essex with her broken heart and duplicitous ex. She'd adored living there, but now she felt she could never return.

'This is my grandmother's house,' said Luca, clearly exasperated at her, as usual. Romy felt as though all the air had been knocked out of her lungs, and glanced around in confusion. Was she in the wrong house?

'Wait a minute. Clara is your grandmother?' she snorted incredulously, then saw that he was serious. She thought back to the number of times she'd sat in deckchairs on the dock with Clara in the early morning, before she opened the tea boat up to dog walkers. Clara loved an early morning coffee and a teacake, or thick slices of buttery toast with marmalade, which was about the extent of Romy's culinary talents and her tea boat menu. Romy had often spent this time venting to her new friend about the 'bloody Bowen brothers and their stupid posh boats!' She cringed inside and bit her lip, wanting to run and hide under the duvet – but this was still her room, and Luca had just got out of her bed!

Luca and his older brother, Alex, ran modern cruise liners operating tours along this stretch of the river. They went from the castle nestling amongst the trees, up to a popular racecourse and back again. They also ran cruises sailing away from town, towards Romy's grandparents' house, which was also beside the river. Romy's grandad's best friend, Joe, ran *Bertha*, the only steamship on the river.

The rivalry between Joe and the Bowens had simmered for years. Alex and Luca wanted to scoop up *Bertha*, modernise her and run her themselves. But why would you modernise a steamboat? Half of the charm was the old-world glamour that *Bertha* had in buckets, from her crystal chandeliers to the Art Deco bar selling a *Bertha* classic, strawberry gin and lemonade. She was a floating master-piece that drew tourists from miles around. She often featured in travel magazines and social media images, too. *Bertha* had even had a plethora of famous visitors, like Dame Rosalie Alton, their local megastar.

Romy had been inside Clara's bungalow a few times before she moved in, but had never seen a photo of Luca. Maybe Clara despised him as much as Romy did? Romy would have run a mile if she'd realised they were related.

She frowned. Clara had never once mentioned she knew either of the brothers. This was so bizarre – although Romy would never acknowledge Luca if he was in her family, either. He was a constant pain in the backside. Maybe Clara felt the same. It didn't explain why he was in her bed, though. Romy felt the burn of humiliation, which made her anger flare as she glared at him mutinously. He still hadn't put his T-shirt on and she looked at it pointedly.

'Look. This is my bed now. I'm exhausted after a long day and I need sleep.'

'So do I,' he stated, rolling his eyes at her – like he did most days.

'Have you been busy fending off hordes of admirers all day on the boat, as usual?' she scoffed sarcastically. Alex and Luca's Italian good looks made women simper and drool around them, and it annoyed the hell out of Romy for some reason.

'I've been at the hospital all evening with *Nonna*,' Luca stated drily, his voice suddenly filling with emotion.

Romy gawped, her hand going to her mouth. 'You mean Clara? What happened? Is she ok?' She dropped all her angst and began rummaging around for the clothes that she'd been wearing earlier. She'd only moved in the day before, so most of her things were still on the boat. In her hurry she completely forgot Luca was there, and pulled her silky pyjama top off and threw her T-shirt back on. Then she froze. She turned back to him. His eyes were out on stalks. 'Stop staring!'

'Stop getting naked,' He retorted, mirroring her movements by pulling his own T-shirt over his head. 'Where are we going?'

'To see Clara, of course,' she said, as if he were a complete idiot.

'Romy... it's 2am.' Luca's shoulders sagged and she looked at the clock on the wall.

'Is the hospital closed for the night?'

'It is,' humour sparked in his eyes again. 'Visiting time finished hours ago.'

'I need to see her. What happened?' she asked.

'I didn't realise you were so close,' he said. She swung around to see if he was being sarcastic, but he just looked exhausted. 'She had a fall. They think she might have broken her hip. She needs an X-ray. My brother is with her. They sent me home in the end because I was pacing the corridors and annoying everyone.'

'I can't imagine that,' she snapped waspishly.

He groaned and sat on the edge of the bed, which made her feel like angry little ants were marching up her spine. However tired she'd been a minute ago, she was now wide awake.

'Can I see her in the morning? She visits me most days on the boat. She insisted I move in here after the recent break-in,' Romy said.

'There was another break-in?' Luca jumped up again and began pacing the room.

It had little in it, except a queen size bed, a chair, mirror and chest of drawers. That suited Romy, as she hated clutter. Her previous job as a vet had meant everything had to be scrupulously clean, but her standards had slipped a little since she'd been home. She thought back to the beautiful veterinary practice she'd run with her long-term partner, Aaron, before that had all gone horribly wrong, and she flinched.

'Why didn't she tell me about it?' Luca asked.

'She probably didn't want to worry you,' Romy soothed, catching his arm and feeling solid muscle, then hastily

263

letting go. She shook herself. Why was she being kind to a guy who complained about her business almost daily? She already knew it was a mess – that she was a mess. She didn't need him to constantly remind her that her decisions were bad and her boat was a blot on the landscape. It was her past choices that had got her into this predicament.

'I need sleep,' he growled, rubbing his eyes. She couldn't deny that he was a hard worker, always the first at the dock and the last to leave. Not that she'd noticed...

'So do I,' parried Romy. 'You'll have to go somewhere else.'

'I can't. I promised *Nonna* I'd stay in the bungalow tonight. Now I bet it was because of the break-in.'

'But she knew I'd be here,' said Romy in exasperation.

'I guess she forgot,' he shrugged. 'What with breaking her hip and everything,' he added, deadpan. Then the light of mischief came into his eyes. 'Although she probably knows you need looking after.'

Her eyes sparked with fire and she stomped her feet. 'Get out of my bed!'

'It's my bed, and I've stayed in it since I was about three years old! I have first dibs.'

'Sleep in Clara's bed.'

'No way! That's weird. Plus, she's the size of a sparrow and has a tiny single bed now. I always joke that she must have bought it from the children's section, but she said the marital bed felt lonely without *Nonno* – my grandad.' He rubbed his eyes in exhaustion for a moment and Romy's bottom lip wobbled. Clara often spoke about how much she missed her husband, who had passed away years previously. 'You sleep in it,' he added, and just like that the fire was back.

'No way! That's weird,' she parroted. 'She's my landlady. It wouldn't be right to take her bed... and besides, I'm almost as tall as you.' He looked at her sceptically and she huffed because she was five foot eight. 'We can't both sleep here.'

'We'll have to. Look. We're both clearly exhausted and I'm guessing you're too tired to try and jump my bones, so I can sleep safely,' he joked.

She scoffed in disgust. 'I wouldn't "jump your bones" if you were the last man on earth!' she retorted and he grabbed his heart and pretended to be wounded by her comments as he snuggled up under the duvet again and pulled the covers up to his chin. 'What are you doing?' she asked in horror as he stripped off under the duvet and threw his T-shirt on the floor.

'I need sleep, Romy! I've been in Accident and Emergency at the hospital for over twelve hours, and I intend to get at least a bit of sleep before I head back there. Our team will have to manage the boats without me tomorrow. Alex will want to see her again too. Our parents live in Italy, so she only has us.'

Romy knew how close Luca and Alex were, so she bet she wouldn't be getting much sleep either, if they were early risers. Tomorrow was Monday, the only day her tea boat was shut. She could already feel her eyelids drooping. She glanced at the cosy bed that she'd been dreaming of snuggling into for hours, after attending to a poorly duck that she'd just saved from a fox. Her profession in her past life seemed to be creeping into her new one lately, though she'd tried to leave it behind when things imploded thanks to her ex-boyfriend, Aaron, and his web of lies. She was determined never to rely on anyone again. That way, if life fell apart, she'd have no one to blame but herself.

With a big theatrical sigh, she grumpily sat on the opposite side of the bed to Luca and glared at him, but he was already snoring soundly. She gave him a shove and he gratifyingly moved over and shut up, his dark lashes brushing his cheek in sleep. How could someone so annoying go from argumentative to angelic in seconds, she wondered. He must be worn out, or he'd still be sparring with her like usually did.

She was too tired and worried about Clara to think deeply about why her landlady hadn't told her who her grandsons were. But then, if Romy were related to Luca, she would certainly have disowned him too.

Continue reading this riverside romance series with book 3, The Windsor Love Match.

Also by Lizzie Chantree

Romantic Fiction

www.ingramcontent.com/pod-product-compliance
Lightning Source LLC
Chambersburg PA
CBHW060904250626
47159CB00008B/2867